HEADWATERS

NANCY LEONARD

booktrope

Booktrope Editions
Seattle, WA 2015

Cover Design by Greg Simanson
Edited by Elizabeth Thorpe, Earl Blacklock, Anna Quinn

This is a work of fiction. Names, characters, places, brands, media, and incidents are either the product of the author's imagination or are used fictitiously. Any resemblance to similarly named places or to persons living or deceased is unintentional.

PRINT ISBN 978-1-5137-0556-9
EPUB ISBN 978-1-5137-0607-8
Library of Congress Control Number: 2015919752

ACKNOWLEDGMENTS

Thanks to my primary editor and friend, Elizabeth Thorpe, for endless levels of editing, support, laughter, and encouragement. Additionally, many thanks for fitting me into her busy university teaching schedule with (almost) no whining—and the willingness to take on an enormous project, of an entire series of eight books, already drafted.

Thanks to Anna Quinn, who did not laugh me out the door when I approached her with a first draft of a first novel and asked her how to get it published fast. She instead provided serious editing, and a bridge into the world of writing.

Thanks to Beth Jusino, editor, marketer, and former literary agent, who helped guide me into maze of publishing.

Thanks to my Blackfeet editor, Margie Yellow-Kidney, who has become increasingly vital as the full series developed, particularly for Native American authenticity, point-of-view, and friendship. And thanks to my other Blackfeet friends, Terry Yellow-Kidney, Kenny and Amanda Kennerly, Charlie Mountain Chief, Nolan Yellow-Kidney, and Russell Kennedy for their friendship, good suggestions, and a larger window into the Blackfeet world.

Thanks to my wonderful friends who have supported me with endless time, discussing my passion, plot lines, and characters' souls: Susan Jewell, who has to be considered an editor, Debbie Peterson, Gail and Willie Jackson, Linda and Steve Lockwood, Patsy Lamberton, Linda and Scott Graebel, Janet Richmond, Jan Hanson,

Dave Lambert (deceased), Sue Alexander, Cheryl Sack, Linda Frost, Chris Styan, Mary and Wiley Hall, Bev Malagon, Dave Ferrier, Vince and Lola Cedola—and the neighborhood.

Thanks to two singer-songwriters, Sam Bradley and Bobby Long, who inspired me into their world of music which, in turn, pushed me forward into the creative world of writing.

It's impossible to adequately thank Terry and Nicole Persun, both as mentors and educators. This series would not have seen the light of day without them. Thanks to Alan Rinsler, a true professional, who pushed me to do better.

Thanks to Booktrope Publishers and my team whose vision has increased the project's quality in ways that I could have never imagined.

And last, but not least....

Thanks to my family: my wonderful sons, Tristan and Noel; my daughter-in-law Amanda, who speaks the language of writers; David Varsos; and most of all my longsuffering husband Peter, who has borne the brunt of listening endlessly, with good humor and ceaseless 'creative' support.

Dedicated to the military air-ambulance services, and especially the 571st and 236th Dustoff Units. My husband served proudly in both. These soldiers introduced me to their world of loyalty, honor, humor, and most of all bravery—the characteristics that inspired the *HEADWATERS* family.

Who knew when my brother killed me that I would stay dead for so long? I realize now how close we are to death, to the loss of warmth and color and bright pictures, not yet faded by endless time—years of never being nurtured or giving to anyone. And always having enough, and nothing at all.

—SAM THOMAS

CHAPTER 1: SAM

I SPENT 15 OR 20 MINUTES horsing around with the other musicians, talking girls and music, before we went on stage. We were laughing about using the music, the emotion, and the rhythms to attract women. We knew what we were doing—and we used it.

The town was electric with the start of the fall semester at Linfield College. I was spending that Friday night being the opening performer at The Hairy Grape Tavern, a great venue in a classic old brick building, dating from the late 1800s. The bar had a beveled glass mirror, spanning the entire 25 foot back, renowned because it had survived bar fights down through the ages.

The joint was packed, standing room only, with people standing out on the street waiting to get in. I'd been trending toward folk-rock and blues, but these days, everything was blended. You got a feel for your audience and played what got them going; that particular night it was the wilder the better. The drummer and bass guitarist from the next group had been kind enough to back me up, so we were blasting.

We were doing covers that we all knew, starting with some Foo Fighters stuff, a Black Keys song from their new album, "Month of May" by Arcade Fire, a Jefferson Airplane song and one of my favorite Fleet Foxes songs, "Montezuma." But I took a chance and closed alone, with a moving Sam Bradley song, "Wide Open." That song called to me that night. The place went absolutely quiet, then broke into wild applause at the end.

I started coiling up my cables and mike and packed up my guitar. It had been a good night. The music was appreciated, and I planned to disappear back stage for a while, stow my gear, and decide what to do next. If I stuck around in front, I tended to be approached by women who wanted to get to know me better. It was a plus side of the music scene, especially if there was a good-looking girl in the audience showing interest, but I liked to meet girls on my own terms.

There was a blonde that night giving me one of those stares that I'd come to recognize as interested and available. She was definitely my type with long legs, tight jeans, and eyes smiling up over the rim of a plastic beer cup. That was the first decision. Did I want involvement? In so many ways, it was easier to have a couple of beers alone and go home.

I decided I'd do what I usually did, wait a bit and mingle with the crowd. If the blonde were still around, I'd probably have a beer with her and see if there was a connection. Of course, there were all kinds of connections. Sometimes, one progressed to a very long evening away from the bar at my place.

I walked in through the back of the room, looking for the blonde. She was still there with some friends so I got a beer and carried it over toward her. The next band had started and it was hard to hear anything over the music.

"Hello." I said loudly, leaning in toward her. "Enjoying the music?"

"Wonderful!" she yelled back. "You were really great!"

I smiled back. It was impossible to have an in-depth conversation 15 feet in front of the band. We listened 'til the end of the song and then another. Then I said, "Want to get some air?"

She nodded and followed me outside the front door.

"My name is Sam Thomas," I said as an opener. "Have you been in town long?"

"Katherine," she said. "I just transferred here for junior year. I'm in Economics and I'm hoping to get an MBA eventually. And you? Are you a professional musician or what?"

"No," I said. "I'm officially between careers. I'm a part-time computer geek, but I'm finding myself."

"Well," she said, "you should stick with music—for a while anyway. There was something special there. I could feel the emotion. That last song—it moved me. It was painful."

I gave her a closer look. She seemed serious, not delivering a line. And it was a painful song.

She gave me another interested smile and took a sip of beer as we listened to the music. She was a beautiful woman and I thought it over. I was tempted. She smiled fleetingly up at me, and then looked away with some embarrassment, which I found alluring. But I finally decided that this was the wrong kind of connection. She was too nice a girl to be persuaded easily into the kind of connection I had in mind for a long night. Or, if I were an ordinary guy, I'd pursue her—maybe ask her out for coffee or Chinese food in a few days. But I wasn't ordinary.

After a few more minutes, I suggested we go back inside and listen to the band. She sensed my disconnection. She was better off. After a few minutes, I made an excuse and left.

I remember thinking that my life was a mess. I felt alive playing my guitar, but so many songs were about loss. What was the old line about nothing left to lose? Never mind, I thought. I'd just keep moving on.

* * *

Possibly it's too easy to change locations. All I have is my laptop and iPhone, an ancient electrified acoustic guitar with a beaten-up top, and a duffle bag of clothes. I rent as small a place as I can find and keep it month-to-month, staying sane by playing my guitar weekends in local college dives.

I'll be 28 in December and have been moving-on in my beater Toyota for over 10 years. I keep my dark brown hair fairly short because it helps me fit in and get jobs; I guess you'd call it rumpled. I topped out at 6'2" and get along well with people—when I care to bother.

It's still warm and sunny, typical mid-September weather in this small western Oregon town of 25,000 people. Putting my legs up on the bench seat, I feel the late afternoon sun on my face and close my eyes. Against my will, I think about my current situation. My wall is down and I reflect once more, trying to understand what happened.

I know now that life doesn't begin at birth—that old lie. It starts when an event shapes you, makes you who you are. But that's a place I don't want to go to now, and forcibly push it safely under.

This is a nice place, McMinnville, Oregon. And I suppose I could live here if I could live anywhere. Two-story century-old brick and frame buildings dominate the downtown section, and classic bungalow-style houses in the older neighborhoods surround the college with tree-lined streets. It's been hot these past few months—good for grapes. There are vineyards popping up in every direction from town. I'll finish out the month and think about moving south as the weather changes. Western Oregon in the winter months can get very wet.

My usual employment is fixing computers. There's always someone who's screwed-up their hard drive or lost their files, and I make a good living. Plus it allows the transient lifestyle that suits me. Sometimes I do construction as an alternative, but that work has dried up with the recession. Still, I put away some money every month and have the $35,000 from the insurance settlement and the small amount from the estate, stuffed in a savings account drawing abysmal interest.

I don't worry about the stock market. I'd probably have lost my shirt like everyone else. I became a wanderer after I dropped out of high school. That's the way I like it and I know why. The last time I really cared about anyone, I almost killed him.

I hide behind my sunglasses and begin to watch people. I'm pleasantly relaxed after my run. I like watching kids the best, especially the ones that are screaming happily and out of control. A redheaded boy, who looks about five, runs by, followed by his father who's yelling and losing ground.

Go, kid, I say to myself.

I don't often allow myself to think about a future, but someday, I'd like to have a son to teach to play soccer. Then I grin to myself—I can almost hear my mother's voice. "If there's any justice," she used to say, "You'll only have out-of-control girls who have lots of boyfriends." I sigh, and feel the smile melting off my face. Thoughts of my mother always end badly.

The boy almost crashes into a young couple, holding hands and walking in my direction. The man and woman have their heads down so I can't see their faces clearly, but the guy is tall like me and well built, with dark, almost black hair, worn longish like a musician. The girl is medium height, slender, with dark brown hair tied back with a black ribbon. They look happy, in high spirits, and I feel an unusual stab of loneliness.

There's something about the man that draws my interest— something familiar about him, something vaguely unpleasant. As I watch, the man glances around and laughingly pulls the girl off the trail. He puts his arms around her, pulls her against him, and kisses her deeply. Her arms reach up and around his neck and they stand that way, fused together. Their connection annoys me and I look away, trying to ignore it.

Finally they separate and the girl looks up, more in my direction, and I can see her face. She is intriguing, although not overtly sexy, with a relaxed attractiveness. He's studying her, trying to see something in her face, but when he too raises his head, I gasp out loud. I recognize him now—it's Paul. My older brother. I haven't seen him since he last tried to repair things three years ago. The disaster in Reno.

Abhorrence wells up in me. My past overwhelms me so quickly it destroys my equilibrium. I squeeze my elbows into my sides in an effort to control the urge to attack him. I breathe in and out deeply until I feel more under control.

I'm usually able to handle my anger well. I've had a decade to practice. My retreat into numbness is so automatic that I usually don't have to think about it. The pain and loss of control makes me grip onto the bench seat. I'm holding on so tightly my fingernails are digging into the wood.

I thought I'd beaten back the image that I'd imagined of my mother's face when her car became a ball of fire, the image that occasionally destroys my sleep and causes me to wake up screaming from time to time.

I observe my brother now with stony eyes through my shades, and I begin to calm down. A slow-moving coldness descends.

As I study him, although I'm furious, I no longer want to beat him to a pulp. I have become subtler in the intervening years. *Mental torment is what I want for him. That's what I've suffered. I want him to be the walking wounded; an eye for an eye.*

I take a deep breath. It's astonishing that my hatred remains so intense, undiminished by time. I thought I had been making progress, not thinking about the past as much, starting to think about creating a life for myself.

The relaxed feeling from my exercise is gone. The door that I constantly strain to keep closed has been thrown open. I've been dead inside.

My focus is suddenly on movement.

Hidden behind my sunglasses, I watch as he and the girl pass within three feet of me. I wonder sardonically if he can feel the waves of hatred as he passes by.

When we last saw each other, three years ago, I was still thin, weighing 160 pounds or so. He was a 180-pound man. Now I'm his weight and build, plus wearing my mirror sunglasses and with different hair. He doesn't recognize me. I'm a man on the exterior. *Inside, maybe a monster*. I thought I was working past this obsessive hatred, but now I see it's been my constant companion.

I decide to follow them. As soon as they pass me, I wait a minute or so and keep a safe distance. They stop by the river and sit on a bench. I hunker down on the ground nearby with my back to them, partially hidden by the wide tree trunk I'm leaning against, hood pulled up and earphones dangling from my ears. But it's them I listen to. It becomes apparent that he's very involved with her.

It seems he was her college chemistry professor at Linfield College. They're joking, laughing, and making plans for when she graduates next spring. He says he wants to marry her. She wants to wait, and accuses him of cradle robbing.

It wells up unbidden. *I know how to hurt him, no, decimate him. Her*! I'm making a deliberate effort to slow my breathing and my racing mind. This is so deep, so rich, so energizing, to stumble onto Paul. He's the one who's always sought me out.

I need some time to think and plan how best to accomplish this.

All of a sudden it feels like stunning freedom. As I resume eavesdropping on their conversation, the contrast between Paul's life and mine devastates me. He's made a stable life for himself, found a serious relationship, and is making plans for the future. I on the other hand am floundering through life, closed off from humanity, a shell of a man. He's been able to move on in a way I never could.

My psyche screams. *Unfair! Unfair, unfair, unfair.* For the past 10 years or so, I've never been able to plan more than a month or two ahead, sometimes no more than day-to-day. I want to have a better life but, for all that's holy, I don't know why I can't move on. Paul is evil, not me. He caused all this pain, not me. What he did 10 years ago turned me into a 17-year-old orphan.

The rage transforms into a frigid calculation. I have no future that matters. Time extends endlessly. I have nothing to look forward to. No goals. No changes on the horizon. I'm putting one foot in front of the other. No one in the entire world will miss me, or even notice, if I disappear off the face of the earth. Maybe a landlord will miss me, looking for a rent check.

Fuck. *I will kidnap this girl to torture my asshole brother.* She's nothing to me, a means to an end.

I get more scraps of information; he's trying to get her to move in with him. He has a house; she's getting a degree in biology and is discussing job ideas. She has a flaky roommate who disappears for days at a time with her boyfriend's rock band, which is starting to take off. Her absence is becoming a problem; the rent is sometimes late, food spoils in the refrigerator, and she has erratic hours.

"All the more reason for you to move in with me," he points out.

Her dad lives a few hours away, apparently Seattle. She doesn't talk to him often, every few weeks or so. I sense there's tension there and she doesn't go into it. An old friend is coming to town and they'll get together. She needs to get the cable on her bicycle adjusted.

Her name is Cora, but I don't want to focus on that. I don't want her to become a person—not with what I have in mind. In contrast, I haven't learned much about Paul. He hasn't mentioned any friends or interests.

Paul's cellphone rings and he answers. He's meeting some co-workers and they want him to pick up some wine to facilitate a planning session. He'll see her later this evening. I stand up to follow them. They appear to head toward the same parking lot that I'm in so I jog past them toward my car. It starts immediately, something which I can't always count on.

Paul unloads her bicycle from a rack on the back of a newish, black BMW coupe. He kisses her, then gets into the car alone. I make a fast decision to follow her rather than him.

He watches with an appreciative smile as she gets on her bike and pedals off. He pulls out of his spot, temporarily blocking me from following her—I have to wait as she leaves the park and turns left. She's moving fast and it's starting to get dark.

When Paul finally gets out of my way and drives out of the park, I have lost her. *Damn!* I follow in her general direction hoping that she hasn't already turned off the main road. It forks right and left, and I catch a flash of her yellow windbreaker, a quarter mile away, as she disappears down the left-hand fork. I gun my engine, weaving through thin traffic, and manage to get close enough to follow her easily.

Five minutes later she pulls into a nondescript gray apartment complex and stops in front of a building with about eight units. She hauls her bicycle up a flight of stairs and disappears inside.

I circle the area and find I can move my car into a back parking area, close to a dumpster, which gives an unobstructed view of her doorway, allowing me time to think. *What do I want to do? Am I willing to kill or harm this girl?* Even if I don't kill her, I'm probably on the run forever if I pull this off.

And I'm not a killer; at least I don't think I am. Is that something you decide? I never thought about it, except involving Paul, and that doesn't count, does it?

I realize, now that I've calmed down, that I have no desire to hurt the girl. Keep this impersonal. I've never seriously harmed anyone, but I'll think about that later. I have no desire to protect her either. She's a piece to be moved around a game board. I don't know how this will play out. I'll keep my options open.

I want to hear Paul pleading for her life. I want to stretch this out—maybe video her and let him have excerpts.

I know hatred is doing as much harm to me as I intend to cause Paul. But I can't control it, nor do I want to. My life's been on hold forever. At least there's movement, no matter how this ends. I want to control the manic part of myself, to develop enough calm to step outside of myself and watch the drama play out.

I settle in to watch her door, and develop a kidnapping plan. I have decisions to make. Should I follow Cora for a few days, let an activity pattern develop, or just wing it and grab her at my first opportunity? And more specifically, what do I do with her once I have her? If I'm going to keep her for a while, I'll need a secure place out of the area. Am I thinking a few days or longer? It's possible that I've overestimated the depth of Paul's feelings. He's a very complicated person. Maybe she's not that important to him. I guess I'll find out soon. I know he'll take this personally, no matter what.

I don't expect him to give me much lead time. My most despicable, darkest self tells me to kill her anonymously, disappear, and let him wallow in the unknown. But I want Paul to understand I'm behind this. I want him to hate me as I've hated him, to feel the life-destroying obsession. And I can't let myself descend into that final black step. *Never. Never.* I shudder when I think about that.

One decision made. I'm really pushing for another showdown, something to get away from this stalemate. Paul will know it's me, and it will be as personal as it can get. The more I think about it, the longer I want to stretch this out.

I need a place out of the area—somewhere Paul can't track us easily. I know he'll be extremely motivated; he's smart and tech-savvy. When he knows it's me, he won't get authorities involved; he has too much history to be revealed. He's avoided retribution all these years. I won't let him stew in the unknown for long.

This is going to be a real dilemma for him. If he reports her missing, he'll automatically become a suspect. But if he doesn't report her disappearance, it will increase his appearance of guilt when it finally does come out.

I wonder how long before her friends or family will get worried and I start feeling the heat. I'll need to think about that, maybe set up a reason for her to be gone for a while. Or maybe I'll turn that little chore over to Paul.

I also know she's going to be traumatized by being kidnapped. She won't know if I'm going to kill her. I hate to think about that. I understand, on a barely conscious level, that things can get out of hand. Once I have her, all bets for the future are off. I don't care what my end will be and she may get caught up in it. I allow myself to think of what Paul did to me, all those years ago, and I get a red haze of rage. I let myself enjoy it for a while.

I'll need to get her out of the McMinnville area fast. Other decisions made: I'll drug her, load her in my car, and drive like hell – south, I think. In 13 hours or so, I can be somewhere in the desert of northern Nevada. That's about as isolated as it can get. I'll need Internet access and supplies, but I want to be far enough from civilization that I won't have to keep her tied up and gagged every minute.

I'll go on-line and find a remote vacation rental for a week or so. I decide to go home to start researching isolated houses in the Reno area. I'm familiar with the region, remembering my last encounter there with Paul, but I drag myself away from that memory and start the car.

I have work to do.

CHAPTER 2: CORA

MARCH 29TH, 2011

IT WAS TUESDAY AFTERNOON, and I was putting my final work hours in before spring break. I had my third final that morning, and a last one to go, the next afternoon. Then I was off for 11 days and headed home. I was lucky to have the same summer job arranged that I'd had last year, at the Winchester Grill in Wallingford, so I wouldn't have to worry about interviewing over the break. Last summer, I'd made a good chunk of tuition money and one more season would put me over the finish line, money-wise, for my degree in biology.

And then there was Mom, who was very ill. I adored my Mom. She was my favorite parent and my pragmatic, reasonable anchor. We all depended on Mom's calm attention to the details of our lives. Suddenly, she had to focus on her own illness. Dad knew he was going to be lost if something happened to Mom.

I'd signed up for spring quarter, but my faculty advisor knew some of the specifics of Mom's illness, and we had several contingency plans.

There were no men in my life. I didn't have the time, what with full-time school and a job at the administrative building, putting in four afternoons a week, organizing new student applications for review. I used Friday and Saturday nights to sleep 12 hours.

My chemistry final was two days ago, and Professor Thomas had just walked in to file the grades. That was fast work. I suspected he had major plans for the break. Many of us female students spent a lot of time fantasizing about him, wondering what his personal life was like.

Besides being gorgeous and approachable, he had an aura of the tortured men of the Brontë Sisters' novels. Tall, with an angular face, he had longish dark brown hair that tended to fall over his forehead and into his eyes. Every girl in the class wanted to race to the front of the room and brush it back for him.

I smiled to myself at the thought.

"What are you grinning at?"

I looked up and Professor Thomas was smiling down at me. My body tightened and I had to grin again at that. "Private joke," I said.

"I just turned in the grades. You got an A-. Not bad for a biology major."

"How do you know what I'm majoring in?"

"Don't you know? We intellectuals know everything. Ask me anything and I'll make up an answer."

"Hmm? Okay—what are you doing over break?" I couldn't believe I said that.

"Are you taking any more chemistry classes?"

"Nope. All I had to do was survive yours."

"In that case, I'm asking you out. What are you doing for dinner?"

"You're kidding."

"Dead serious."

"Um, when did you decide this?"

"It's been coming on all quarter. Ever since you almost destroyed the lab the first week by dumping water in the phosphorus container. I thought you handled it spectacularly well, much better than your lab partner."

"I did improve over time," I smiled, remembering Tara screaming and running out of the building.

"Yes. I've decided I can risk getting to know you better."

"You don't know my computer skills. I've been known to crash entire networks."

"So, are you going to go out with me or not?"

"Only if you let me brush the hair out of your eyes." I grinned mischievously up at him.

"Done," he smiled. "Shall I pick you up at seven? Same address as your file?"

I smiled and nodded, thinking it was a little weird that my address was so accessible. He walked off and I craned my neck to make sure he was gone before high-fiving the air.

* * *

The evening went remarkably well. The Italian restaurant was dark and intimate and I'd almost forgotten that he was my professor two days ago. He was older, almost 32, and was trying very hard to put me at ease. I got the feeling that he wasn't seeing anyone, maybe for quite a while. I probed gently about past relationships and got nowhere. Not that I cared. I was incredulous that he'd asked me out, and wasn't about to get too worked up over his vague history. I kept trying not to look at his lips and embarrass myself.

We'd been sitting and talking for hours and the restaurant was about to close.

"What time is your final tomorrow?" he asked.

"One o'clock. Genetics. I need an hour or so to review, but it was an easy class for me, just a basic requirement."

"Do you need to get back to study?"

I looked up into his gray eyes, "I could review it easily tomorrow morning."

"Would you like to have a drink at my house, just for a little while? Then I could run you home."

"Okay," I smiled. "That's fast work, though."

"I'm making up for lost time," he said ambiguously.

* * *

We pulled into a long curved driveway leading to a shadowy house, hidden by thick fir and cedar trees.

"It's a little scary in the dark," he said. "Stay here and let me turn some lights on." He left the car running, then ran to turn on more lights, on the porch and in the house. "There, that's better," he said as he returned. "I didn't want you to think I was Count Dracula."

I quickly found myself sitting on big pillows in front of a roaring fire with a good bottle of red wine. He'd taken off his sports coat and replaced it with a grey hoodie and jeans. It helped. I was trying to let go of the professor thing.

"Do you realize you haven't called me anything all evening?" he said. "You do know my name is Paul?"

I flushed a little. "Yes. It's just a little hard to get used to."

"Maybe if I kiss you," he said, taking me in his arms and lowering his lips to mine. His lips were warm and soft. "What's my name?" he murmured.

"Paul," I answered.

"Much better. And yours is Cora."

"You can call me anything you want. Just as long as you kiss me again."

He did.

"You really are an enigma, and a major topic of discussion among us ladies. Tell me something about yourself."

"I'm pretty boring. Got a Masters in chemical engineering and thought I'd try teaching for a few years. I decided I liked it."

"What about family?"

He paused an unusually long time before he answered, almost as if he were rehearsing a speech. "My parents are both dead and I have a brother somewhere. We're not close."

"When did you see him last?"

"Several years ago. We don't see eye-to-eye on a lot of things."

"I'm sorry," I said. "Especially since he's your only family."

He sighed, looking at the fire. He obviously didn't want to continue the topic.

After a while he said, "Are you going home after your last final?"

"Yes, I have to. I mentioned at the restaurant that my Mom is very sick."

"Seattle, right?" he asked. "What would you think about me driving you up?"

I turned to look at him. In spite of myself, I felt a little unease.

"Look," he said. "There are no strings. Don't take me up on the offer if it doesn't feel right. I don't want to make you uncomfortable. You barely know me. I'm sorry. It was wrong of me to put you on the spot like that."

"Paul," I said, "I'd love a ride to Seattle with you."

He gave me the biggest, unguarded smile. "That's nice. I guess what I'm really saying is, I don't want to wait to see you again."

"I'm not quite done seeing you tonight," I said, and got another of those beautiful smiles.

*   *   *

We had a wonderful drive up, but as soon as I walked in the front door, things fell apart in my life. Mom was trying not to say anything until I got through finals, but she was worse—much worse. I could tell as soon as Paul dropped me off. She'd lost a lot of weight and her beautiful, rosy complexion was grayish.

She was on a lot of pain meds, but was herself, and we were able to have the kind of direct talks we'd always had.

"So, tell me about this guy," she said.

"We're going out for dinner tonight before he drives back to Oregon tomorrow. I've only been out with him once before the drive up. But holy crap!"

"You've been on one date and he's already reached the 'holy crap' level. I can hardly wait to meet him."

"Tonight, if you feel up to it."

"I'll feel up to it. I'm not missing this. I'll take extra pain meds and if I act loopy you can explain it to him."

"You're a wonderful drunk. I'll tell him you had a bottle of gin right before he got there."

"Perfect. Now tell me about school."

"Mom, I'm not going back, not this quarter. I've already called my advisor. I'm putting it off a quarter or two."

She sighed heavily, "Honey, please, you don't have to do this."

"This is not something I feel pressured to do. I want this part of my life to be with you. The school will bend over backwards to help. That's the nice part of small colleges. They take an interest on a personal level. It's already arranged. I'll take spring quarter off and the summer, and work here at the restaurant."

"See? I was right all along. I never had more kids because I got perfection the first time. Now let me sleep. I want to save all my energy to meet Mr. Holy Crap."

*   *   *

"Mom and Dad really liked you," I told him later. Paul and I were finishing key lime pie after dinner at Ray's Boathouse, a classic seafood restaurant on the waterfront. The voices were subdued, the waiters inconspicuous but available, and the views of the dark water with the Olympic Mountains across Puget Sound were classic Seattle beauty. I was very emotional, torn between the happiness of being there with Paul and worry about my Mom.

"I really liked them, too," he said. "Especially your mother. I can see where you get your charm. Even as sick as she obviously is, she made me feel special and welcome."

I looked out over the water. "I'm going to be here, for the duration. I want to and it's been arranged with school. I—I'm sorry that I won't be able to see you for a while."

He reached across the table and took my hand in his. "McMinnville is only four hours away. I'll come up some weekends if you'll let me."

My eyes turned back to his. "I'll let you. It will give me something to look forward to. This is going to get pretty grim."

"If I can help in a small way, it would make me happy," he said.

"Paul. Let's go somewhere I can kiss you."

*   *   *

"He's an absolutely beautiful man, Cora," Mom said later. "Classic, tall, handsome, and brooding—a devastating combo."

"That's the problem. He's so perfect I can hardly breathe. I'm totally amazed that he's interested. I'm not bad looking, but I don't stand out in a crowd, that's for sure."

"You have a dramatic, understated side you haven't quite discovered yet, and that beautiful thick chestnut hair....

"He had a chance to get to know you in his class. I'm not a bit surprised he made the big grab."

I giggled, "He has grabbed, hasn't he? He's not letting his attentions be misunderstood. He wants to drive up on weekends."

"Those deep grey eyes. He looks like he should be in movies. What's particularly interesting is what he doesn't say. He certainly avoids talking about himself."

I sighed and changed the subject.

* * *

My mother died quickly. It meant everything to be there, but along with her, she took my center.

I'm still reeling from the news that Dad dropped on me last week. He's set on remarrying in two months. It seems he met this person only weeks after Mom's death, if that can be believed, when he took our dog to the vet. Sheila was the new receptionist. If it weren't for this development, I'd still be working at the Seattle restaurant, socking away money, but I couldn't stand to see her face or Dad's happiness. Each time she came over, I felt it was an invasion of Mom's house.

And of course, there was the pull to be with Paul. So I packed my critical belongings, put the things I didn't need in the basement, and moved back to McMinnville, driving down in Mom's car that she gave me. McMinnville seems to be more home to me now than Seattle.

Dad's finances were a mess, at least in the short run, and it became clear that I was pretty much on my own to finish school. I couldn't stomach taking out more student loans, so I immediately got a good job waitressing and a second one at Sears. I don't want to see Dad for a while. I'm hurting and I know I need time to mourn Mom. He calls and I'm polite.

I'm waiting for Paul to arrive. He's eight years older than me, and there's the professor thing. I have a glass of white wine in hand and smile to myself, remembering the day he changed from professor to more.

*   *   *

I hear Paul's car pull into a parking space below, pulling me out of my reverie. He always takes the stairs two at a time and I meet him at the door.

"Hi, beautiful," he says. "Kiss me, it's been six hours."

"You are so pushy," I say, then attack him.

"I'm so glad you're down here," he says. "I wish you didn't have to work so hard."

"It was the weekend. I make twice as much in tips as I do working all week. One guy tonight was especially appreciative and left a fifty on my table."

"Did he wait for you to get off?" he asks, a little too seriously.

"No. I did look around, but unfortunately...."

I find myself swept up in Paul's arms and delivered to the bedroom. This is fairly new for us—we waited until I got back to college.

I feel his hands wind in my hair and I mold against him, but then I can't help but laugh.

"What?" he asks, kissing my neck.

"It's just that if the girls in Basic Chemistry 101 saw me now, they'd be floored."

"We could videotape us and I could use it for an orientation session. You know, how to pull an A for the class. You did get an A-out of me, if I remember correctly."

"I always wondered if I got any advantage out of flirting with you all quarter. It did seem like it could turn out to be an investment. You know, sort of like dollar-cost averaging."

"Let's see if you got your money's worth," he murmurs, and starts unbuttoning his shirt.

I pull his shirt out of his jeans and kiss the hair on his belly. I hear a moan and feel the response of his hands caressing my breasts. He stops. "I'm feeling guilty," he says. "Knowing what I know now, I should have given you an A."

I'm roiled under him and writhe beneath him. I can feel him removing his jeans and I reach down for him. "Cora," he gasps, "you're insatiable. I may have to spank you for that."

CHAPTER 3: SAM

I PARK IN MY USUAL SPOT on a side street below my building. It's only four miles from Cora's apartment to mine, but a world away. She lives in a college environment and I live in an industrial area because the rent is cheaper.

It's nearly deserted now. After five or six o'clock, the area just closes down. The wind blows impersonally between buildings with a piece of discarded paper or an occasional plastic bag. The air smells of dust and old asphalt and there's an unnatural atmosphere of light from the streetlamps reflecting a harsh yellow glare on the buildings.

I'm disturbed. Already I know—there's no going back. I climb up the 14 steps to my apartment and unlock the door. As I glance around, I notice how empty and colorless it is, despite the fact that I've been living here for almost four months. There are no pictures on the walls except a faded print of an Indian, sitting on a paint horse, silhouetted against the sky. The picture has obviously been there for many decades. There aren't even any fucking throw pillows on the couch, no sports equipment, no magazines. Even junk mail hasn't been able to catch up with me. Usually it doesn't bother me, but now I sink into a deep funk. At times I fight serious depression, and even consider ending this monochromatic life.

I close my eyes, trying to escape the dullness, the threadbare blandness of my existence. Long ago I had a vivid world of warmth.

I take out my memories filled with vivid colors—but that inevitably takes me back to the day everything changed.

* * *

October 19th, 2001

It was one of those perfect fall evenings in Glendale, California. The sun was already going down, but the air was still warm and the horizontal light had turned the colors into such an intensity that I stopped to make a mental picture. Our high school team had crimson red uniforms and Capital Southern had bright yellow jerseys. The grass was the Kelly green color it gets after the fall rains begin. It was just goddamn beautiful.

I remember being in a great mood. We were going on to the State semi-finals. The game came down to the final seconds. Castro made a Hail Mary kick from way back and the damn thing went in, with a lucky tip from me, making the score 2 – 1. But where was my brother? I couldn't believe he didn't show.

I'd had satisfying adoration from Gloria and her friends and headed across the parking lot to wait by Castro's car. He was going to give me a lift home and we'd planned on pumping up each other's egos. I was in a hurry and yelled across the parking lot at him. Couldn't get him away from the girls. He grinned and gestured that he was helpless. I smiled indulgently at his orange colored hair. One of his girlfriends dyed it for him and he loved it because it stood out on the soccer field.

The nagging question about Paul continued. He'd been as excited as I was. It would have taken a major event for him to miss the game. He used to play, center forward, and earned it. Paul was raw power on the field—could have made a career of it, everyone said, but he lost interest when he went to college. I was relieved when Castro finally headed toward me.

As we pulled around the last corner, I saw seven or eight cars parked at our house and two of them were police cars. "Shit," I thought.

"Do you want me to come in, man?" Castro asked.

I grabbed my gear. "No, I'll call you," I said, and ran for the house.

"Sam's here," said a voice that I recognized as our favorite neighbor, Louise. I set my sports bag down in the entryway and looked for Paul. He was sitting on the couch in our living room with Louise's husband Rick. He had his arm around Paul's shoulders, who had his head in his hands.

My blood ran cold. I walked over to my brother.

"Paul?" I said, as firmly as I could.

He looked up and his eyes were terrible. He tried unsuccessfully to talk until Rick finally said, "There's been a horrible car accident, Sam."

I felt the color and noise in the room fade as I looked at Paul's torn face. "And?" I managed.

"It was Mom."

I sunk down on the couch beside him and we wrapped our arms around each other.

"We're all we have left," Paul said. "Just us, Sammy."

I was numb. I could only concentrate on one thing. Paul hadn't called me Sammy since Dad died, 10 years ago.

* * *

Two days later and Paul and I were barely able to listen to people. Louise had been wonderful. She practically moved in to care for us—making comfort food that we couldn't eat, listening to our confused ramblings. She handled all the calls from lawyers, police, insurance people, and family friends.

It seemed that Louise was going to drive Mom to the doctor, but had to cancel at the last minute. Rick had almost cut two fingers off with the lawnmower and she had to run him to the ER. Mom decided she could drive herself, even with her leg in a cast. Her car had been out of commission, but she knew Paul had recently charged the battery.

The police had given us a preliminary report. An old guy, who'd had his license revoked after a series of accidents, crashed into her. It appeared that Mom had started to drive through a yellow light, changed her mind at the last minute, and slammed on the brakes. The old farmer following her didn't even make an attempt to stop and rammed into her full speed.

Louise had been on the phone most of the day with our auto insurance company, which also insured the farmer. Mom shouldn't have been driving with her leg in a cast and since the police report implicated both parties, the insurance bozos didn't want to pay much of anything. They offered a small payment, $60,000, if we agreed to sign away our rights to contest the settlement. We did it just to make them all go away.

The police told us that there was residue of ammonium nitrate, the same fertilizer that was used by the Oklahoma City bomber, at the site. The old guy was using it to fertilize his fucking roses and under the right circumstances it can be extremely explosive. Were these the right circumstances? It was impossible to know. The horrific explosion and fire destroyed almost all the evidence.

They wanted us to know that no one would have suffered. I guess that was supposed to make us feel better. I didn't think I'd ever feel better.

The funeral was two days later. Louise agreed to handle it all, with a few requests from us. She even got out mom's address book and made phone calls to friends who then called other friends. Most had already heard. It had been on the TV news here, over and over.

Paul and I sat stunned in the living room after Louise left. I was always a momma's boy, but I thought Paul was in worse shape than I was. When I tried to talk to him he winced. "I'm sorry," he kept saying, over and over. "I'm so sorry."

*   *   *

Damn that memory. I'm having trouble getting my breath. I can't hide in the past, either. It's more disturbing than my current existence. My building looks abandoned even though I live here. I realize that I haven't eaten for many hours, but I don't want food. Dredging up the old memories makes me physically ill. This drab apartment is all I have to show for the past 10 years of my life.

I interact with the people at work to get basic things done, but after some initial attempts to engage me they give up. If it weren't for my music, I'd never go out in the evenings. Who was it who said, "If you have your guitar, you're never alone?" Music has kept me sane, at least until now.

I grab a glass of milk and an old bagel, and sit down at my kitchen table. With a little searching on the Internet I find the perfect place, an hour's drive southeast of Reno up in the desert. "Upscale retreat down a picturesque country road in a totally isolated area." I contact the owner and nothing is booked for a few weeks. I'll get a hold of him again when I've finalized my timing.

I search Linfield College on the Internet and there is Paul in all his glory. He's been teaching beginner chemistry for freshmen and a more advanced organic chemistry class for chemistry majors and pre-med students. I stare at his picture for a very long time. He looks different, too. Three years since our last encounter in Reno can change anybody a lot. I'm surprised that I recognized him in the park. In the picture, he's dressed in a suit with shorter hair than he has now. I'm struck by how much he looks like me. His eyes bother me. They're flat like mine, not a hint of humor; not at all like the relaxed guy in the park with the girl.

I'm probably the most changed since we were together last. If I quickly scanned his picture, I would probably have thought it was me. We're both grown men. I was closer to a skinny kid when he saw me last. I'm almost certain he wouldn't recognize me if he saw me on the street with sunglasses, unless he thought he was seeing himself. It's the eyes that gave him away—that and his distinctive gait. That's how I knew Paul.

Tomorrow I'm going to visit the campus to get a window into Paul's world. With shades and a hoodie, I'll be invisible. I'm looking forward to acting the spy. He has an organic chemistry lecture in the morning and a lab session after lunch.

I sit back in my chair and let loose my hatred, embellishing and encouraging it. It's so easy—like going down a slide....

CHAPTER 4: PAUL

THE CHEMISTRY LAB is going well. The kids are in high spirits without that interfering with getting the job done. Claire Wilson had her usual catastrophe near the end, not following instructions, and ruined the whole 14-step procedure. She came to me in tears and I had to salvage the experiment, mostly to help out her long-suffering lab partner. He's pre-med and needs to get a good grade. I've assured him in private we can work something out.

I pause as I put the jars of chemicals back in the storage room. Chemicals and apparatus in the cardboard boxes brought up that old memory again. It seems to be happening more and more. My emotions are closer to the surface. I'm sure it has to do with Cora. She tries not to pry, I can tell, but she wants to know me, know more about my past, and it's harder and harder to deflect her. In the park Saturday, I was trying to get her to think about a long-term commitment, marriage even, but I know she will need to understand....

She keeps asking about Sam, and it's hard to keep him locked in the box I've tried so hard to keep closed. I want to give it one more try, to attempt to apologize, but it's agonizing. It's been a long time since I allowed myself to think about him and it's been several years since I last found him. To say things didn't go well is the understatement of all time. I had called Castro to find out if he knew where Sam was and he gave me the name of a Mexican restaurant in Reno.

* * *

October 18th, 2008

I'd been sitting in the alley, on an old metal fire escape, waiting for Sam to come through the back door of the restaurant. It was like a movie set: trashcans and dumpsters, piles of discarded newspapers in yellowing stacks and bulging black plastic bags in piles. The Mexican music had been turned off and several other employees had already left. I knew Sam was still in there. I could hear his voice from time to time, and each time it sent chills down my back. It was the same, but different, older and joyless. At last the door opened. He pushed through the door with two more plastic bags which he added to the pile.

He turned to leave and spotted me, stopping in his tracks.

"Hello, Sam," I said.

He nodded. His face was a mask.

"I brought news. I tried to get a hold of you earlier, but anyway — I'm here."

"Yes?"

"The insurance settlement money is still in the bank, along with the inheritance money. It's been sitting there untouched for all these years. You should take control of it. The bank sends me notices to keep the account current, but, well, it's your money."

"Fine, I'll call them."

I sighed. I was surprised how he'd changed, somewhat closer to my size and weight, but still thin. We looked moderately like brothers then. "You look good, Sam," I said.

"If you're done?" he said, and started to walk off.

I reached out for his arm, but he quickly evaded me.

"Come on, Sam," I said. "Can't we let this go, after all this time?"

"What part am I supposed to let go?" he said.

"At the time, I felt it was justified. Dad died and no one but me seemed to care. You and Mom wouldn't even talk about him. I felt I was alone trying to make up for Dad's death. I know I was wrong now. I'm sure you cared but...."

"Yeah, I cared, Paul. I'm sorry I didn't remember Dad like you did. I was seven when he died. I grew up hardly remembering him at all."

Sam was growing increasingly livid. "You said you took care of it, Paul, and what did you do? What the fuck did you do? You put it in Mom's car. Mom's car! What the hell were you thinking?" I was speechless, staggered. I screamed at him. "Who do think you are, God? Don't you think I would do anything if I was able to bring her back?"

"Maybe, but I can still remember you saying in the kitchen you wanted us both dead. I asked you before, and I want to know. I really want to know. At the time, were you sorry I wasn't in the car?"

I was taking gulps of air now, trying to calm myself, but rage was welling up. "You asshole. Fuck you! That's it. I've tried. I'm done trying to be your fucking brother. Go rot in hell!"

I saw it coming, but didn't try to duck. He pulled back and punched me on the side of my face and I was lifted off my feet, crashing into the pile of black bags. The pain of the hit, and the desolation I felt, brought tears to my eyes.

He stood over me. He was crying and gasping, still out of control. "Get away from me, Paul," he said, "and never try to find me again."

I lay there settling myself, then slowly climbed to my feet. The rage was gone. I felt my protective walls building back, into their old familiar place, as I brushed off my jeans. The paper with the bank account number was still in my hand. I crumpled it up and threw it at him. Then I turned and walked away.

* * *

The chemistry building has gone quiet. All the labs are over, students gone, and the last footsteps are heard, echoing down the empty hall. The office will be emptying out soon. I sit silently in the old wooden armchair outside the chemical closet. The memories keep rushing back. This wasn't the first time we had come to blows. And, as hard as I try, I can't seem to get up off of this chair.

I know where this is leading—I give it up. It's like I'm there, transported even further back. I start to shake. Okay. Okay. Go ahead—demolish me.

*   *   *

OCTOBER 23RD, 2001

It was late afternoon, and the last of the people were leaving following the graveside service Louise arranged. There was a crowd. Mom had a lot of friends.

Sam and I sat there for a long time on two of the metal folding chairs that someone set up for the burial. We were alone. Even Louise and Rick had gone home. It was peaceful there. I heard a bird chirping some ways away. The shadows of the tombstones lengthened across the close cut grass. "Sam," I said finally, "we should leave."

"And go where?" he asked.

"I don't know," I said. "Home makes me sick."

We sat there awhile longer, both thinking, sighing. "Just don't say you're sorry again," Sam said. "I – I don't understand why— why you need to keep...."

He stopped. I looked over at him. "No, dear God," I thought. I swallowed, hard.

I could see the thought flash across his face. He leapt to his feet.

My body clenched and my hands started to tremble.

I could see his rage building, agonizing second by agonizing second.

"It was you! You killed her! Tell me it isn't true. Tell me." He was screaming by now, at the top of his lungs.

I was motionless, paralyzed—unable to say a word.

He became airborne, flying at me.

Chairs were scattered.

He began punching me. Then picking up a chair, he began attacking me with it.

I fended him off and tried to grab him.

Now we were rolling on the ground, over and over.

He was trying to kill me and I was trying not to kill him.

He landed a good punch and my head started spinning. I had 30 pounds on him, but he was a wild man. I had to defend myself. I rolled up onto my feet.

He leapt at me again.

I punched him hard to get him away from me.

Blood started pouring from his nose.

Again he came at me.

Suddenly, I was on the ground with him straddling me, and he kept punching me, again and again. But he was becoming so exhausted that the blows were useless.

I rolled him off of me and managed to stand up. I bent, leaning forward, my hands on my knees, gasping, too. He tried to get up, but slipped as he tried to stand, and fell back on the grass.

When he could get enough breath, he gasped, "You killed Mom, didn't you? You put that fucking bomb in the trunk of her car. Tell me the goddamn truth."

"Yes," I said. "I'm responsible. I killed her."

"Then you killed me, too, brother," he said. "Were you sorry I wasn't in the car?"

He paused as I searched his face for some hint of forgiveness.

"I should tell someone, but I won't," he gasped. "This is between you and me. Watch your back."

He was now able to climb to his feet. He took one last repulsed look at me and stumbled away.

I staggered to Mom's mound of dirt and lay down beside it. I was virtually dead, too. The only thing that kept me breathing was that my brother was alive.

*   *   *

I sit motionless by the chemicals closet in the cold silent laboratory of Linfield College, taking deep breath after deep breath, trying to loosen the grip of the memory. The chair suddenly reminds me of an electric chair. *Please. I want to have a normal life. Please let me go.*

CHAPTER 5: SAM

IT'S ALREADY LATE when I ask two kids for directions to the chemistry building. I park my car as close as I can and stop by the office where I'm directed to the lab section. I lean against the wall outside the room and listen by the open door, glancing in occasionally. There are roughly 20 kids in goggles working at the black high lab tables. There's a friendly buzz of activity as Paul's voice rises above the din to give directions. His voice makes me recoil hearing it, but I'm captivated, too.

About quarter of four, the room starts to empty out. I wait for Paul to leave, but for a very long time nothing happens. I listen closely, wondering if there's another exit. Then I hear a small sound inside and keep waiting.

It's an hour later when Paul finally comes out and locks the door. He looks ill, grim, and heads down the hall toward the office. He comes out in five minutes or so and heads in the general direction of the back parking lot. I may be in luck here. He doesn't have a phone or address listed in the directory so I'm hoping I can follow him home. I've parked my car in the lot behind the building, but there's no way to know if he drove or if he's parked there. I didn't see his car.

Paul walks around a corner from the lot and there, parked behind another building, is his hot BMW coupe. I hurry to my car and get ready to follow him.

Pulling onto the main campus road, he turns and heads toward the north end of town. Ten minutes later, he turns into a curved driveway and disappears behind a thick grove of trees.

I make a quick loop around a long block and find a place to pull over, about 200 feet past the driveway where I can see his car through the trees. About 15 minutes later, Paul comes out in running clothes and I follow him back to the same park, pulling into a nearby parking slot. *Let's see who's in the best shape.* He does a steady 6:30 per mile pace. I can keep up, but I'm definitely not loafing. He does five miles and heads back to his car. He's not an old man yet.

I follow him to a grocery store and finally back home. *Maybe I'll just stroll up to his front door and see if I can get invited for dinner.* The thought makes me laugh to myself, but it's not a happy laugh.

It's starting to get dark and overcast so I risk a walk through the trees around the perimeter of the house. The structure is a medium–sized bungalow, probably from the early 40s, with a large porch in the front under an overhang with four steps, plus a smaller porch in back. The outside walls are painted light brown with darker trim around the windows. It's gloomy under tall trees, with foliage encroaching on the house.

The house sits on a large piece of property that's been partially allowed to go natural, with a ground cover of ferns. A large gravel turn-around near the house circles a grassy area in the front yard. You can see a neighbor's roof through the trees, but I don't think you'd hear any noise from inside. I sit and indulge in some black fantasies, waiting until long after dark, before heading back to my apartment to think and plan.

I have most of the information I need. It's time to decide if I'm really going to do this or not. I put some soft music on my iPhone and drift. A small normal part of myself says *Just walk away* but I can't. I can't. I know that I may be ending what little ordinary life I've been able to create for myself over the past decade, but it's not enough.

It comes back to me; the homeless derelict who died a few blocks from my apartment last week. He was stuck. He died alone. Who knows how long he had been sleeping in that tattered sleeping bag on the street, begging for food. Circling.

This is not a life either. I'm an amoeba in a petri dish, moving randomly round and round, never getting anywhere new. If I don't break out soon, I'll go crazy. Maybe this is crazy.

I decide to go ahead.

* * *

When I sit down for coffee and a late lunch, I'm ready. I've arranged for the rental to start tomorrow morning at 9:00 am for seven days and an option for up to two weeks. "We'll see how it goes," I tell the landlord. *Right*....

He'll supply some basic food that I've requested in the refrigerator, including a variety of drinks, and will leave a key under a potted cactus by the garage. There's an understanding of complete privacy. I've given him the go-ahead for a hefty deposit on my card, but he agreed not to charge it to give me time to replace it with a cashier's check. I have a lot of cash available and I don't want to leave a trail of credit card receipts.

What else? I go over my checklist: Disposable cell phones that can be used, once then destroyed to avoid being tracked, and several syringes with anesthetic courtesy of a veterinary supply store. I looked up the equivalent human dosage on the Internet. I've added a blindfold, rope, a gag, some bottled water, and food for the car trip. Now all I have to do is find the girl and wait for an opportunity.

I decide to drive back to her apartment to find her. I'll follow her to some isolated location where I can grab her unseen.

*   *   *

I'm back behind Cora's apartment at two o'clock. Around three she pulls up to a front parking space in an older Honda Civic. She carries several grocery bags up the stairs and disappears. Around five she leaves in the car and I tail her to a downtown restaurant.

She goes inside. I follow her in and slouch in a chair behind her so I can see the side of her face. I can hear her easily in the quiet restaurant as she orders a drink. After several minutes, an older man comes in, gives her a hug, and sits down at her table. He has salt and pepper hair, cut very short, and a pale yellow shirt tucked into tan slacks that probably need to be a size bigger. His belt cinches his stomach in. He throws a navy jacket over his chair back.

"Hi, Dad. How are you?" she says. "Where's Sheila?"

"Finishing up a little last minute shopping for the trip. We'll be flying out in two days. She's really excited, and I haven't been on a trip to a tropical beach for decades. I'm looking forward to it."

"That's nice, Dad. I'd love to go to Hawaii."

"Why don't you come over for a visit, honey? You look sort of tired, less optimistic than you usually do. I haven't told you, but we extended the trip for another week. Sheila got a real deal on room rates."

There's no response, so I risk a glance to see what's going on. Cora seems to be considering her answer.

"I guess I am a little tired. You know I've been working hard to save for school. And I don't want you to go into debt paying for me to come over."

"Are you done with the job at Sears? And what about the restaurant? Working two jobs is too much—you can't do everything all at once. And what about school? Why didn't you sign up for the past two quarters?"

"I hated the Sears job. There's a good possibility that I can be a full-time nanny for one of my professors for a quarter. He's even said I could continue the tutoring jobs I have now. I'd save rent, and I could save almost every penny."

"Why don't you take out more student loans to finish?"

More silence.

Finally, Cora answers. "Dad, I have over $20,000 in loans now. It frightens me, especially since I don't know what kind of a job I can get. A bachelor's degree in biology doesn't lead directly into well-paying jobs. I probably should have gotten the education credits, but I don't want to teach. I've told you all that."

"So, when could you finish?"

She sighs, "If I can eat peanut butter for a few months, I think I can start again winter quarter and finish by next summer. I have two weeks to let the professor know. I'm about ready to say yes. I'm dying to start working and get out of debt."

"Boy, you certainly didn't get your penny-pinching from me. Sometimes, kiddo, I think you have to go for the gusto. Look at your mother. We put off trips for our whole marriage to save money, and we never went anywhere. She was always being careful, like you."

"Yes, she would have loved to go to Hawaii. She talked about it."

I'm picking up on a lot of tension between these two. And I'm learning a lot of personal stuff that I don't want to know. All I care about is when I can grab Cora. I'm trying not to listen, but I can't seem to turn it off.

"Cora," her father says, "I should probably take out a loan for you for the tuition. Should I? I feel guilty about you working so hard."

"I know enough about your finances, Dad, to know that you can't afford to do that. Mom wasn't working that last year when she was so sick. That was why I took off time from school, so you wouldn't have to take off work."

More tense silence. "Honey," her dad says, "I know you aren't happy with me for remarrying so quickly. I want to have some fun. I really do. You can understand that, can't you? It was a long pull with your mother's illness and I loved her, but now I want to live. Life should be more than getting up and going to work. I'll deal with the consequences later."

"I was happy to take care of Mom, but I have to do what seems right. I'm trying to take care of myself and I'm not taking on more debt. I know you can understand that, too."

Silence.

"Sheila is a very nice person and she wants to have a vacation, too. I wish you'd give yourself a chance to get to know her. If you don't want to come to Hawaii, at least consider coming up to Seattle and spend some time."

"Okay. Let me get my job situation resolved. When you get back from Hawaii, we'll talk about it."

"I'm counting on that. I miss you, Sweetheart."

I glance over at Cora and see her give her father a half-hearted smile.

At this point, the aforementioned stepmother arrives with several shopping bags and plops down, greeting Cora enthusiastically. She's an unnatural redhead with a very complicated hairstyle. The woman is thin enough to wear the tights she has on, but looks like an older person trying to look like a teenager. They all order sandwiches and Sheila entertains everyone with the trip details. They're going to Maui for three weeks and staying at an upscale hotel on the beach which we hear described in glitzy detail. Then we hear about what a good deal she got on everything, which makes it possible to stay an extra week.

"Why don't you fly over for a visit?" she asks. "Please consider it, Cora. It would really make your father happy."

Cora murmurs a non-committal response.

Finally they start saying goodbye. Cora gives her dad a quick hug, and he promises to call from Hawaii. I notice she doesn't hug her stepmother—almost steps away to avoid it. She thanks them for coming down from Seattle to see her before they fly out, and for bringing down some winter clothes.

I follow Cora from the restaurant and run to my car. Making a quick U-turn, I trail them to a new, expensive sedan, watching as they unload armloads of coats and sweaters and transfer them to Cora's car. I have my duffle bag of clothes and supplies, including the syringes, packed in my trunk.

I hope I can do this. I'm ready. My heart starts pumping. I follow her to the local library and wait while she goes inside and comes out with several books. There are people all around us. No opportunity.

It's getting dark as I follow her to Paul's where I watch her go inside without knocking. I'm thinking how ironic it would be to kidnap her from Paul's own driveway. I'm tempted to look in the windows, but fight the urge. Besides, she could come out any minute. If she comes out alone, I'll knock her out with the anesthetic and move her car back to the entrance of Paul's driveway where it won't be seen. I conceal myself in the trees about 15 feet from her car and hunker down.

* * *

Minutes pass, then hours. I'm chilly and uncomfortable. The wind is suddenly picking up; a weather front is due in.

A little after 10 o'clock the door opens. Cora turns at the open door and calls back to Paul that she'll see him tomorrow. She huddles against the wind, clutching the coat around herself, and walks down the steps alone. I take a step out from behind the tree. My heart is racing so hard that I can feel it in my chest.

Paul doesn't have an area light, just a small porch light, and I know she can't hear me with the wind whipping the trees. The syringe is tightly gripped in my hand. I know that I'll have to cover her mouth and restrain her struggling for a few seconds. Just as Cora places her hand on the door handle, Paul appears in the doorway. I slide back into the gloom. He didn't see me. I gasp in relief.

"Don't forget to let me know about the concert tickets," he says.

She smiles, waves, and gets in the car. He stands outside, watching as she drives down the driveway. I can't follow her because Paul is still on the porch. When I finally get to my car, she's gone down the street. I gun it to her apartment, but she's already parked and inside. Unless I knock on her door, that's it for tonight. There's a light on inside, but I don't know if the roommate is home. I'm tempted to do this anyway. What excuse? What could get me through that door or at least get her to open it?

I decide to wing it.

I walk up the steps in the dark.

As I reach out to knock on the door, I hear voices, girls laughing.

I grind my teeth and go back down the stairs.

* * *

It's late the next afternoon and I'm slouching behind Cora in a downtown cafe. She's sitting at an outside table with a girlfriend who just arrived. The girl's parents live in McMinnville and she's down for an overnight visit from Portland.

I could have waited in the car but I'm hungry, and this is one of my favorite college dives with cheap food and cold beer. I'm sitting close to Cora so I can listen in, plus I'm throwing down a fast Reuben sandwich and a local brew in case they leave suddenly. They're talking about guys. Cora's friend is troubled about Paul. *Join the club.*

"Jeez, Leslie. I'm confused about how hard he's pushing me to make a commitment. He's even starting to talk marriage, maybe in the spring. I mean it's flattering, but...."

"That's crazy, Cora. You've only been dating for three months. Not even considering the age gap, you hardly know him." Her friend pauses. "Here's the thing. He should have a past with history, lots of friends, but he doesn't. Doesn't that worry you?"

"I've asked and probed. He doesn't want to go into his past."

"Okay. Name one good friend he's introduced you to, not someone you were introduced to at a party. He's been teaching here for three years."

"I keep thinking he's so overwhelmed with my wonderfulness he doesn't have time for his friends."

I glance toward them and almost laugh at her friend rolling her eyeballs. I stop myself in time. I don't want to attract their attention. Besides, there are reasons he's weird. I know them all. That's why I'm here with my black thoughts.

"You're right, I know," Cora says. "It's tempting, though. I'm entirely crazy about him and he's so hot." They both laugh. "Seriously, he seems like everything I want—and he's been so understanding about what I've been going through with Dad."

"Just try to imagine him 30 years older and a couch potato and see if his sparkling personality is enough." They laugh some more, but then her friend turns serious again. "Honestly, Cora, there's something weird about him. Susan and I both feel it. He looks so stable, but below the surface there's tension."

"I feel it, too," Cora says earnestly. "Sometimes he says the strangest things, like 'I've put it all behind me.' Another time he said, 'I can get stuck thinking about things at times,' and then wouldn't explain it. It's as if there's a part of his life he doesn't want to think about, a part that's off-limits. But he pushes that underground and we're gloriously happy. Besides, there's something attractive about a guy who absolutely needs you – and wants you."

"Yeah," says Leslie. "Be careful, though. You have a tendency to try to rescue damaged people and it's gotten you in trouble before."

"Sometimes I hate it that you know me so well," Cora says. "The worst was that guy that kept drinking my cooking sherry and stealing frozen meat out of my freezer. I've learned something since then."

"We'll see," says Leslie.

"I think I'll just enjoy the attention for a while. I'm so—satisfied. What's wrong with that?"

"Absolutely nothing," says Leslie. "It's just that you're always giving too much."

I'm wondering if she might give something to me. I picture her, a captive in my car. I force myself not to go there. My soul is dark enough.

Leslie pauses, then asks "What's the latest plan for this year? Don't you want to be out making the big bucks?"

"It's a hard call," Cora replies, and suddenly bursts into tears, surprising both her friend and me.

"Cora?"

"I—I'm sorry. My dad's sort of gone off the deep end. I feel like a financial and emotional orphan."

"Still spending money on Sheila?"

"I'm trying not to be bitter, but the latest is a three-week trip to Hawaii, first class. I could use part of that money to finish up school. I want to start my real life, Leslie. I want to get a real job and start paying off all these damn loans. Actually, I'm furious. And they want me to come visit them over there. Sheila said it would make my dad happy. Crap! I'm sorry to lay all this on you."

"Parents are people, too. They're as stupid as anyone else. I had three sets of stepparents, with merged relationships, standing on the sidelines, watching my soccer games. Bizarre. You never had to deal with that shit."

Cora sighs. "No. I've had no real problems, until Mom...."

"You've had a hard patch, Cora. But I know your dad; he loves you and he's the only parent you have."

"I know. I know. Maybe I just need some time. I'll think about it—about Paul, too."

"Sometimes I hate the real world," says Leslie, reaching for her purse. "Listen, Cora. I have to meet Mom and Stew for dinner. Do you want to come? Please come. They'd love to see you."

"Next time. I'm meeting Paul. It's been so good to see you. I don't know what I'd do without you and Susan. Don't worry about me. I'll be my happy optimistic self in minutes. You know me. I'll just keep pedaling."

"Cora, you're the most positive person I know. Even you can get down occasionally. You know I love you."

They get up and hug. Cora gives her a big smile and her friend leaves. For some reason, she sits back down, alone, with her cheek on her hand. Several minutes later, she gives a big sigh and stands up.

I'm tired of following Cora around. I didn't like that last encounter. I was starting to see her as a person, with problems. I caught myself wanting to give her a little perspective. *Damn it.* I fight down the impulse—that bit about her father. He's alive and cares about her.

I wanted to shake her and tell her that I know what it's like to be a real, honest-to-God, orphan. Damn it. She didn't have a dad who died in Kuwait and a mother in a ball of fire.

* * *

Back behind Cora's apartment, I watch Paul pick her up and drive off. I'm annoyed and frustrated. I want this done. She's not going to be alone until Paul drops her off. I decide to go for a jog, clean up, and come back later. Besides, I need something to reduce stress. I'm tied up in knots.

* * *

It's later that evening and I'm parked by the dumpster behind Cora's apartment. It seems her last name is Foster; at least, there's a C *Foster* on her mailbox. No one has gone in or out for the past two hours other than the probable roommate who left about 15 minutes ago. There are no lights on in the apartment. I'm hoping she's not spending the night with Paul.

It's 9:30 and I'm sitting in the dark listening to music on my iPhone when Paul pulls up with her. I scrunch down in my seat and watch him walk her to the bottom of the stairs, give her a lingering kiss, then leave. She runs up the stairs, unlocks the door with key already in her hand, and slips quickly inside. A light goes on in the apartment.

Cora appears to be alone. Who knows how long before I have a similar opportunity? Will she even open the door if I knock? Maybe I'll pretend to be a pizza deliveryman at the wrong door. Then I'd need to get her down one staircase, through a 15-foot passageway, and across the back parking area and into my car undetected.

It's dark now and no one is around. Still, anyone could come out of a nearby building at any moment. I could incapacitate a person with one of my drug syringes, but I really don't want to be seen for later identification. Although—I do look enough like my brother—he could be the one identified. *That's an amusing thought.*

Any observer would be a complication, though. I need an hour or two to get out of the immediate area. I need to come up with a better idea to persuade her to let me in the apartment. As I'm mulling this over, Cora's door opens. She emerges with a large bag of trash and heads in my direction. The ridiculousness of this unexpected opportunity makes me shake my head. This is too easy. I was looking forward to stealth and danger and here she is, gift-wrapping herself.

Almost regretfully, I step out of my car and approach her.

"Hello," I say, in my most unthreatening voice. "Let me help you with that."

"Oh, thanks," she says. She hadn't seen me until I spoke. She's uneasy.

I lift the large lid easily and hold it up for her while she lifts the bag. As she stretches to push the bag over the high lip, I push the syringe into her thigh.

"Oh," she says, frightened.

She begins to struggle and I drop the syringe and trap her arms to her chest with one arm while I cover her mouth.

It's over in 15 seconds or so, and she slumps into my arms.

I carefully but quickly load her into the back seat of my car, and partially cover her with my coat as if she were merely asleep.

I return to the dumpster and quietly close the lid, picking up the used syringe. I take a moment to exhale and scan the immediate area.

No one is outside anywhere as I listen to a few quiet voices coming from a nearby TV. No curtains are moving or doors slamming. Nothing. I drive slowly out of the parking lot, onto the local street, and on toward the freeway. I'm not worried that my driving will suffer from the adrenalin rush. I'm calm under stress, a cold customer.

Glancing back at my passenger, who appears asleep, I wonder how long before Paul knows something is wrong and how he'll react. I'd give anything to be there. *Ah, well, you can't have it all.*

I plug some moody alternative rock music from my iPhone into the car sound system that I recently installed, my one luxury, and drive on in the deepening darkness toward Nevada.

* * *

I've just reached the freeway when a phone rings. Shit! She has her phone in her jeans pocket!

If I hadn't discovered this, we could have been traced all the way to Reno. Feeling stupid, but grateful, I get off at the next exit and pull off the road. Getting out of the car, I open Cora's door and reach for her side pocket. I locate her phone easily.

I take a second to look at her face and touch her cheek softly with my finger. I feel suddenly responsible for another human being, a very personal reaction that surprises me and makes me uncomfortable. *I'd better think more about this.* I check her phone contacts and take a minute to put Paul's cell number into my personal phone. I crush Cora's phone in the dirt and kick the pieces around with my foot.

Moving back onto the freeway, I drive north again, heading toward the Columbia River Gorge where my route takes a big right turn along its southern shore. I can't stop thinking about touching her cheek. When I knocked her out and put her in the car it was impersonal. That was different.

I look down the black highway and wonder how I got to this place. Dumb luck, really; random chance that I didn't go another way. I have many hours of dark highway to consider that point in time. Was it really only four days ago?

*   *   *

My car continues down the almost empty road onto the darkness. I'm left stewing about what I'd be doing now if I'd stuck around that night at the Hairy Grape Tavern, pursued that girl—maybe had a cup of coffee with her the next afternoon. Not going running in a park when my life diverged, that's for sure. I listen to the soft breathing coming from the back of my car.

In three hours, I pull off the highway onto a side road to top off the tank with gas from a large gas can I brought. It was a last minute addition. I'd forgotten that Oregon has gas station attendants. That could have been interesting, trying to explain why I had a blindfolded girl in the back seat. Or, even worse, running out of gas during a kidnapping.

A little later, I decide I might as well get the ball rolling by giving Paul a call. He picks up almost immediately and I keep the connection in silence for a minute, then hang up. I pull back on the road along the southern shore of the Columbia River Gorge and on into eastern Oregon. This route to Nevada is longer than going through California, but more isolated. It's a beautiful clear night, with a nearly full moon illuminating the black hills. I'm driving with the window down, enjoying the soft breeze against my face. I'm feeling relaxed and peaceful.

Around 3:00 AM, Cora begins to stir. I've been thinking about how I want to handle Paul. I know he's concerned by now and I decide to give him something to really worry about. I pull off the almost deserted highway onto a dirt road and turn off the engine and lights. I pull out the disposable cell phone and get out of the car. I walk to the back door, get in next to Cora, and check her blindfold in the darkness.

CHAPTER 6: CORA

I HEAR SOMEONE calling my name. It seems far away. The voice is new. Strange. I don't want to go there. I lapse back into unconsciousness. The voice is insistent. Okay, I'll listen to it.

"Cora?"

I can't see anything. That's odd. It must be dark, very dark. Oh, there's something over my eyes. I reach up to remove it. My hands are tied.

"Cora." Someone grabs my hands, holds them. "Keep your blindfold on. Talk to Paul."

The voice. I don't know who it is. I'm frightened. I think I'm in a parked car. "Paul? Paul?"

A phone is held up to my ear. Now I'm really scared. I hear Paul's voice.

"Where are you? Are you all right?" I can hear the panic in his voice.

"Paul?" I say, grasping the phone that the kidnapper still holds, "I don't know where I am. I have a blindfold on."

"Are you alone?" he asks.

"No. There's a man here."

"Sweetheart, let me talk to him." I try awkwardly to hold out the phone with my hands tied.

I hear Paul saying, "Who are you? What do you want? Do you want money?"

Then nothing. A tone tells me the phone has been disconnected. Then a grinding sound as if it were being crushed. Silence. Then the car door is shut hard beside me.

I start shaking. I'm afraid I'm going to die. I realize it's out of my control. It could happen any second. "Oh God. Please, no. Oh God."

The man starts the car and drives onto the road. I jump at the sound of his cold and controlled voice. "Cora, you need to know I have no reason to hurt you. This is between Paul and me, from long ago. Try to relax and I'll explain everything you need to know. We'll be driving for many more hours. We won't stop except for gas. Let me know if you need to go to the bathroom and I'll find a place out in the brush."

I strain to remember what happened to me. I recall walking to put trash in the bin. I felt a sting, saw a syringe in my leg, then a short struggle and darkness. I want to throw up, but hold it down by taking deep breaths. I'm able to say, "No, thank you. Not now."

I can't hold myself together anymore and I start crying, but I try my best to control myself. I don't want him to get mad and hurt me. I cry quietly with my fist in my mouth to keep the noise down and try to focus on the sound of the tires on the road.

Occasionally, I see a dim glow and hear the Doppler sound of a car passing us in the night. The tears soak my blindfold and roll down my cheeks. I jump at the sound of a click, but then some low music starts; it's Bon Iver, one of my favorite musicians. It helps me relax a little. If he likes music, he must have some feelings. Maybe he won't kill me. Partially comforted by the music, I find a position to rest my head and drift into a sort of exhausted sleep.

* * *

I wake up and ask to stop to go to the bathroom. It's dark, sometime in the middle of the night. He lets me out of the car with strict instructions to keep my eyes on the ground, and he removes my blindfold. He says he will catch me if I try to escape. He doesn't say he'll hurt me, but I'm terrified of being beaten.

I couldn't run if I had to, I'm so stiff from the car. I finish quickly and he tells me we're going to have to stop for gas and he'll have to tie me up. Now he merely replaces the wet blindfold with a bandana, his fingers touching my face. I get a sick feeling in my stomach.

"Are you going to kill me?" I ask. I know it's a, stupid question because he'd probably never admit it, but I need something to keep myself from screaming.

"I know you are very scared," he says, "but I already told you this has nothing to do with you. I've never harmed anyone in my life. I want to hurt Paul and this is the way I'm doing it."

"Why do you hate him so much?"

"We go back a long ways, him and me. He hurt me as much as a man can be hurt. Something unforgivable."

A voice inside says *Why me? Why should I be punished?* Instead, I ask, "Why don't you just fight it out?"

"We tried that long ago and nothing was resolved. Neither could win. I tried to kill him then, but I couldn't."

Paul couldn't hurt a fly, I think, but I remember what he does to me sometimes, all I don't know about Paul. He won't tell me about his past. I come out of my panic enough to want some answers. "Please. Tell me how you know Paul."

"He's my brother," he spits out.

At that, I feel my heart lurch in my chest. *His brother?*

* * *

Eventually, we pull off the freeway. I hear vague noises that mean other people are around, some distance away. There's light around the edges of my mask. I wonder if I could scream, be rescued. Would he kill me quickly? The door is suddenly jerked open. "Please don't tie me," I plead. "I'm terrified of being tied up. Please."

He grabs my hands and forces them behind my back. The rope is rough on my wrists. I remember the first time; the old feeling of terror returns. "At least don't leave me tied up alone. Oh God! Please don't do that."

A gag is thrust in my mouth and he rolls me onto my right side so that I'm facing the back of the seat. I start to struggle, panicking, thrashing around.

"Stop it," he says. "Control yourself. This will only take a couple of minutes." Then, to my surprise, he says, "I'm sorry. I'll do this as fast as I can."

I gasp through the gag. The memory materializes—in vivid detail. I'm six and left alone in the dark for hours, in a game of cowboys and Indians, tied to a tree. I remember the fear, the panic.

Tears pool in my eyes again. I try to count. He'll be back by the time I count to one hundred, I tell myself, but I reach one hundred twice before the driver's door opens.

He moves back onto the road and drives down the highway. The car is quickly pulled off the road again and stops. I feel his hands touching me as he unties the rope. "You can sit up now and take the gag off," he says, "but leave the blindfold on."

Trembling, I ask, "When can I take the blindfold off?"

"When we get to where we're going. In about six hours, Cora."

"Okay," I murmur. His voice is different, more compassionate. He seems almost apologetic. I remember him saying, "I'm sorry," at the gas station. He knew I was terrified and stopped almost immediately to untie me—two small acts of kindness. Maybe I'll live; maybe he's not a monster.

*   *   *

It's been hours and neither of us has said a word. My thoughts keep circling 'round and 'round. I'm not going to be a helpless victim. I want to do what I can to survive. I eat the energy bars and drink some water from a plastic bottle. I'm calmer now and have started to think and plan.

I decide that if we stop again for gas and I get a chance before he ties me, I'll push past him, screaming at the top of my lungs, and run. Even if I can get only a short distance away, maybe he'll drive off rather than carry me back to the car. Maybe someone will help me. I'm going to do it. I'm visualizing it over and over. I'm strong and loud.

I've been thinking about Paul. I want to spend all my free time with him. I love our long conversations and our sex life—most of the time. But he has a dark side that I can't quite get into focus. Paul's usually confident, brilliant and self-assured, but at times he seems so vulnerable, sad, and emotionally needy. He absolutely will not talk about his past. He's a puzzle, no getting around that, and I would need more answers before I would decide to commit to him. For now, though, I desperately want his arms around me. My eyes fill with tears.

We never stop at a gas station again. Once, we stop in the dark, and I hear him put gas in the tank from a container.

The darkness is different; it's less dark. We drive on and on.

"Cora," the kidnapper says, "I need to make a phone call and it may take a while. I'm going to step away from the car so you can't hear me, but I'll be close enough to watch you. Don't take off your blindfold. Do you understand?"

"Are you going to talk to Paul?"

"Yes."

"Can I talk to him? Let him know I'm okay?"

"I'll think about it," he says.

The car stops and he gets out. I realize from the open door that we're in hot, dry country. I hear the wind blowing and feel the blast of heat on my face blowing away the air-conditioning. We must be in the desert. He wouldn't be stupid enough to stop where there were people around, so trying to run away seems impossible.

I want to hear Paul's voice, just that, something to lessen this nightmare. Some distance off, I hear my captor's voice rising, almost screaming. Sliding the blindfold up so I can peek out below it, I see the man with his back turned away from me, about 100 feet away from the car. He's totally distracted, yelling into the phone. There's a small plastic bag with several disposable cell phones on the floor near my feet.

I see cacti and scrub brush. The wind is noisy, disguising my sounds.

I quietly open the door and start moving toward the man. His voice gets louder as I approach.

"I haven't made my mind up, what to do with her—what would hurt you more? Should I kill her now or enjoy her for a while before I do? Or maybe not kill her at all—maybe she'd rather stay with me if she knew what you are capable of....

"Our family was fine, just fine; then you go off on your own vendetta, the hell with the consequences....

"We weren't victims then, not until you made us victims. You put the bomb in....

"Shut the hell up. My life was fine, just fine until...."

A long pause....

"No responsibility, not after all this time. Well, no matter....

"I hope this girl means something to you. I'll leave it up to you what I do to her. Should I kill her? Or use her first? Think about it. I know you won't call the cops. I have too many stories to tell....

"You can't find me. You'll never find me. In the meantime, I intend to spend some quality time with your girlfriend, if you catch my drift."

I'm horrified. I had lifted my hand, reaching for the phone, but now I let my hand slowly drop to my side. I try to retreat, but my foot scuffs the gravel. The man turns. We're both immobilized. His face is a glare of hatred, evil, anger. I start to shake, looking directly in his eyes. Finally, I'm able to move. I stumble back to the car, get inside and replace the blindfold.

I'm dead.

CHAPTER 7: SAM

I HAD BEEN IN SUCH A RAGE that I'd forgotten to keep an eye on Cora. It takes me a long time to compose myself. I know what I look like—a raging madman. The mask is off the kidnapper. We look at each other for what seems an eternity. I see the terror in her shaking body. I can see she's close to collapsing. *Damn it all to hell.* I never wanted to hurt her. My mouth fills with saliva. I feel sick. The wall I've built to keep her out is beginning to crack. I fucking wish I'd thought of another way.

The dusty mid-afternoon light is turning the desert sky pale orange as I turn off the highway. This winding gravel road supposedly leads toward the house, but I can't see anything up ahead yet. I haven't said anything to the girl since the conversation with Paul, nor has she said a word to me. I wonder what she is thinking, what she might be willing to try. The glow of satisfaction is gone; so much for being the compassionate kidnapper. I know she won't believe a word I say from now on, not after what she heard while I was spitting venom at Paul.

The car makes its way slowly up the last quarter mile rise to a grove of pepper trees, providing a deep shade over most of the house and walled patio. The fall weather hasn't taken the edge off the high temperatures. It's still extremely hot. The structure is cream stucco with a large curved archway, leading to an inside courtyard. The expansive home is capped with a red tile roof. A gentle breeze ruffles the leaves of the trees and a fountain provides background music. All in all, it's a pleasant setting, but the tension and fear that emanates from Cora cancels out everything else.

She believes that I'm probably going to rape her and kill her and I know there is absolutely nothing I can say to make her think that's not true. I'm amazed she hasn't gone completely over the edge into hysterics, and I'm glad I have one more tranquilizer if it comes to that.

I look back at her and again feel disgusted with myself that I've handled this so badly. I've forgotten she still has the blindfold on and say, "Cora, you can take the blindfold off now."

She doesn't move to remove it.

I try again. "Please come into the house," I say, in my most non-threatening voice. She's trembling and I know that she is not only frightened to death, but she hasn't had any food, except for an energy bar, and almost no water for a very long time. She takes an uneven breath, removes the mask, blinks her eyes at the glare and glances at me. I think she's brave, but barely in control of herself, and I'm concerned she might pass out, so I take her elbow to guide her into the house. She shudders when I touch her.

We stand and look at each other. Her eyes are clear greenish grey and full of fear. Her hair is darker in the dimmer light of the entryway, but very thick. But it's her pale face that draws me again. She's looking at me and I see her square her thin shoulders.

For once I'm at a loss for words. What do you say when the other person has just heard you are planning to kill them? Finally, I say, "How much did you hear?"

"I don't want to die," she whispers, "and I have nothing to bargain with. My life's hardly begun. I have people who love me—they'll suffer if anything happens to me."

She could hardly have said anything worse. "I want Paul to suffer," I say. "I loved him once, but I was a fool. The people who you love have all the power to kill you. Paul killed me."

"I'm so scared. Please give me a chance."

"I told you. I don't need to hurt you. And I'm not going to—I'm not going to make you earn your life. I was just saying that to hurt Paul."

She takes a step backward. "No," she says. "I wouldn't do that—I mean—can I have some time—so you can get to know me? Maybe we could connect—I could try to reach you, touch you...." She's pleading and scared to death. Her eyes are starting to tear up and she's not making any sense.

I don't want to hurt this girl, and I'm intrigued. I study her face, "You must be repulsed to even be near me."

"I don't know—I don't know." Her voice trembles. "I want to save my life and there's something about you that does not feel evil. I'm a good person. If you knew me, you couldn't hurt me. I'm trying so hard to understand you. Please. Maybe there's something – something kind that I can reach. I hope so...." Tears start overflowing her eyes.

I feel like I need to hit my head against the wall for a while. This has got to be one of the most god-awful, weird conversations that ever existed. "Let me get this straight," I mutter. "You want some safe time to connect emotionally with me?" I know she's frantically bargaining.

"Yes," she wails, then throws herself face down on a nearby couch and starts sobbing uncontrollably.

My guilt is crushing me. She's so desperate. Other than Paul, I've never hurt anyone intentionally. I feel sick. I don't know what to say or what to do or what to feel. I just stand there.

After many minutes, the sobbing stops and she lies there motionless on her stomach. She must be so exhausted. She finally turns her head and stares despairingly up at me, then buries her face on her arm and collapses again.

"Listen," I manage to say. "I won't hurt you. I know you're shattered. You can sleep for as long as you want. We'll discuss this situation when we're both rested."

"Okay," she sighs, resigned.

"And I'm making you a sandwich and a glass of milk."

"Good," she says.

*　*　*

I lead an exhausted Cora into one of the bedrooms. The air conditioning is keeping the house cool despite the outdoor temperature, so I cover her with a light blanket. I leave the door cracked so I can watch her every second, but I'm going to have to tie her up at some point so I can get some sleep. The adrenalin in my system is wearing off and I'm exhausted, too. I'm not looking forward to doing that to her. She almost lost it when I had her tied up for five minutes in the gas station. I've got the motion sensor attached over the bed where she sleeps, but it's not enough. Maybe I can put a simple rope connection between us, so I could feel it if she tried to get loose. I'm sure she wouldn't mind sleeping with me, or rather, next to me.

I shake my head. *No. She would mind. But there really is no choice.* I suppose I could drug her again but, God, I'd hate to do that. It would seem so invasive, so unfair. *Right! As if anything I've done to her has been fair.*

If she were able to think in the car at all, I'm sure she was trying to figure out what her options are. She's probably looking for every opportunity to escape, so I'm going to have to be very diligent. I'm sure she's trying to figure how to manipulate me to let her go.

I've read hostage stories about captives falling in love with their kidnappers. If I were the captive, I'd fake that, so the kidnapper would stop paying as much attention to security and give myself an opportunity to run. In fact, she's probably already doing that and I didn't recognize it. That's the whole *I'm going to get to know you* shit. This is so much more complicated than I envisioned.

The rental house is perfect, though. *The next time I abduct someone I'll rent it again.* The thought that I am skirting madness crosses my mind. The house is down a six mile long dirt road with low scrub-brush on either side. It would take someone almost an hour to jog it to civilization or even the next house. Since she was blindfolded the entire trip, she has no idea how isolated this house is. Would the seclusion discourage her from escaping if she knew?

She's fast asleep and curled up in a ball under the blanket. To say I've got conflicting emotions is a gross understatement. When I first thought about this in the park, the thought of throwing her body at Paul's feet was a flash of raw fantasy. Now I'm making Cora sandwiches and putting her to bed. Jeez! On the other hand, I can hardly wait to call Paul again and threaten him with potentially killing his girlfriend.

All I had to do was hear his voice to exacerbate the hatred. He destroyed any decent emotions, leaving an empty life of isolation and pain. Long ago, he made a choice, and his brother died because of it. That person no longer exists. But no one took his place. I'm so tired of being a ghost hovering on the outside of life.

But it's hard to threaten to kill someone you made peanut butter and jelly sandwiches for.

* * *

I've slept for hours on the bed next to Cora. She looks like she'll be asleep for days, unconscious almost. I've attached the motion sensor to the wall over her. It will set off an alarm if she moves more than a few inches off the bed, and also trigger an alarm on my cell phone.

I return to the car and start the ignition. I want to be away from the house, so I drive a couple hundred feet down the driveway and stop the car. It's late evening and still hot, almost a hundred degrees in the dark. Dust fills the air whenever there's a gust of wind, which is often, and tumbleweeds roll across the driveway, looking like ghostly animals. I roll up the windows and grab one of the cell phones. I dial Paul's number. It's picked up immediately.

"Is she alive?"

"Yes, for now."

"Have you hurt her? You can't hurt her."

"You know, Paul, I can do anything I want," I say. "Have you made your decision?"

"You're serious," he says, gasping. "You want me to choose between you killing her immediately or raping her then maybe killing her at a later time?"

"Yes, that's exactly what I mean. You choose and choose now." I feel myself falling back into that black place I've been for all these years. I want to hurt him and I want it to last. All the rage comes flowing back and I realize I'll do anything to hurt him. "She's a very cooperative lady," I gloat. "I hope you don't decide to have me kill her right off. I'll let you choose. But if you don't, I will. You have one minute."

"I can't bear either of those choices."

"Choose."

"For God's sake, Sam, are you insane? I can't choose something like that. What have you become?"

"I've become what you made me."

No response.

"You choose to let me kill her then?" I say calmly.

Silence drags on the other end of the line. I wait and wait.

"Please, Sam. I'm begging you. Don't do this to her; don't hurt her, for your sake. You're destroying your life in so many ways. You're killing yourself. Please—bring her back.

"Sam—brother...."

I crush the cell phone and turn the car around and drive back to the house. I'm suddenly drained of emotion. He has literally given me the choice to kill her. The choice of having his brother rape her is so abhorrent that her death is acceptable. That I don't, and never did, intend to hurt her is irrelevant. Only coldness remains, coldness and a sleeping pawn, part of a larger game.

* * *

I've been watching her on and off for hours after talking to Paul. She's beautiful, with very kissable lips softly parted in sleep. I want to brush her long hair away from her face so I can see her better. It's hard to sit across the room. She can't sleep much longer. It's been fourteen hours since she fell asleep in exhaustion, and the sun is up.

I've had a lot of time to think. As I look in the mirror, all I see is a tall man with gray eyes and dark brown hair. I don't look like a monster. The eyes are hollow, though, with nothing to hold onto, a portal into a deep bottomless pool. I make myself smile, but there is no joy. I used to know joy, but it was long ago. I can barely remember what it felt like.

I've also been thinking about her offer to connect with me, so I would care about her and not hurt her. I'd settle for feeling something, anything except this terrible void. So I guess I'll let her try if she wants to. I know in my heart she doesn't want to. *What kind of a bastard would coerce a girl to—let's get real—seduce a guy to save her life?* I'll try to convince her again that I'm not going to hurt her. But I may not try very hard. She does have a point if she's willing to try. I'm hoping she'll try on her own, but I don't want to tell her that. It gives too much away.

I know I'm not making sense either.

CHAPTER 8: CORA

I'VE BEEN AWAKE for a while, but I keep my eyes closed to think. What am I willing to do to stay alive? Should I try to seduce my kidnapper? Could I even do it? I'm not an overtly sexy person.

I squint my eyes to glance at him, but he's preoccupied and doesn't see I'm awake. He's good looking, but I keep imagining him strangling me.

He does look like Paul, the same gray eyes and wavy brown hair. It makes him less scary, but I can't allow that to influence what I do.

Can I put up with some physical contact—lull him into a sense of complacency so I can escape? Or hit him over the head—can I even do that? I'd have to hit hard. If I didn't knock him out, it would make him furious. Maybe he would kill me.

Dear God, it would be unbearable to try to kill someone. I can barely comprehend that I'm thinking about it. If I knew for sure he was going to kill me, I think I could try. I'd much rather try to escape, but where am I? Miles and miles away from civilization?

When we were sleeping next to each other on the bed, he had me tied with only four inches of rope between us. He could feel it if I tried to untie it. I'll have to try to escape when I'm not tied up.

I have an idea. I noticed a small window when I used the bathroom. I think I could wiggle out of it. If I can just make him think I need some uninterrupted time in the bathroom. If I can make him believe that I'm going to let him have me, maybe he'll let me have a shower first—a long shower.

I'll do it. No matter what I have to deal with out there, it has to be better than waiting to be killed. I just can't believe that he won't do me any harm. I can't allow myself to think that. I have to do something to save myself.

* * *

Okay. I'm decided. But I'm scared to death. I keep putting it off; the day is getting brighter. *Shit. Do it.*

I take a deep breath. "Hello," I say.

He gives me a very long look.

"Have you thought about it?" I say. "Are you willing to let me try?"

"To try what?" he asks.

I stare at him.

He studies me quizzically. At last he says, "I'm not going to kill you or hurt you. I'm not evil, regardless of what you heard on the phone."

He doesn't seem like a monster, but I know you can't trust appearances. I remember Ted Bundy and shudder. "I believe that," I say. *Oh God,* I think.

"Then, yes," he says. "You can try—to connect with me."

I swallow. "Can I, um, clean up a little?" I try to look willing, but end up feeling like I'm making a fool of myself.

"Yes, of course," he says.

I grab my shoes and socks, give him a feeble smile, and head into the bathroom. My heart is pounding.

Thank God he didn't question why I needed shoes to take a shower.

I turn on the water, slip on my socks and shoes and quietly open the window. It's next to the john. I step up onto the seat and brace myself so I can get both feet out the window.

I twist and squirm and get to my hips.

It hurts as I push hard. I imagine calling for help after getting stuck.

One last massive wriggle and I'm out. It's about a six-foot drop to the ground, but I'm not hurt.

Go! Go! Go! I start running off to the side of the house, over a small rise and downhill, parallel to the road. It's windy and the sand is covering my footsteps already.

I clutch the small towel I stole to shade my head from the sun. It's horribly hot.

I wish I'd taken a few seconds to drink a lot of water from the faucet. Damn it.

I run as fast as I can.

He'll probably beat me if he catches me, or worse.

I know my time must be running out. I start to look for a place to hide, like a depression or ditch.

I glance at the house over my shoulder.

I must be over a half mile away when I step in a hole. My ankle turns over and I fall hard in the sandy dirt with an explosion of dust. The pain is terrible.

As I hug the ground, I look back at the house. He's coming outside.

I see him run around the house and get in the car. I hunker down in the dirt.

He could probably see me if he knew exactly where to look, but the sand and dust are camouflaging me.

I don't think he can find me.

CHAPTER 9: SAM

THE SHOWER STAYS ON for a long time. I don't blame her. If I were Cora, I'd stay in there forever. This is erotic. I admit it. I'm sitting here fantasizing, enjoying the anticipation. There is something so desirable about her. I'm impressed with her self-control and her gentleness. Okay, I'm impressed with a lot more than that. I want to put my hands on her. No one has intrigued me like this for a very long time, maybe forever. The shower has been on for what seems like hours and suddenly a thought crosses my mind. *Why did she need shoes in the shower?*

I leap out of my chair and throw open the bathroom door. The shower is running, but no one is there, just a small open window and curtains fluttering in the breeze.

I race around behind the house and garage. No one, as far as the eye can see.

I run back to the car and pull the keys from my pocket.

At least I didn't leave them on the floor of the car.

Shit. Shit. Shit.

I drive as slowly as my mind will let me, looking down the road and from side to side.

Nothing.

It's been about 20 minutes since she disappeared into the bathroom. Even if she ran straight down the rough road, that's about two miles she could cover, max.

In two and a half miles, I turn around and go back, very slowly, toward the house.

The scrub brush is low and sparse. Even considering that, it would be easy to flatten yourself down to the ground and disappear, especially if you covered yourself with sand to camouflage yourself.

Damn, it's hot. Even at eight in the morning, it's heating up fast in the direct sun. There is no shade. I take a drink from one of a package of plastic water bottles. It's warm, but I'm parched already and I haven't even gotten out of the car. The humidity is probably approaching single digits. As far as I know, she's only had a glass of milk and a few sips of water in the past 20 hours. I'm starting to get anxious about her out in this heat, along with everything else I'm worried about.

I try to calm down and think. *What are her options and what would she do?*

I make two more complete passes up and down the first two miles of the driveway. I'm crawling along in the car and get out many times to hike up to land swells to get a better look. It's been over an hour already. I'm positive she hasn't gotten around me.

If she were moving through the brush, she'd have to watch the car and only move when I was long past her. She wouldn't make any distance at all, so she must be in the two miles around the house, probably a lot closer.

I drink more water. If I were Cora, I probably would have hidden out near the house and waited until I drove away, or it got dark, and just walked down the road. But she didn't know the house and she didn't know how long she'd have before I discovered she was gone. She also didn't know if she'd have to walk one mile or 20. Most people would have wanted to get away as far and as fast as possible.

She must be so scared, and it's damn hot.

I decide to make a quick search of the house and garage. I gun it back to the house and race inside, half-expecting I'll find her sitting in the living room. Of course not. It takes 15 or 20 minutes to search inside and under every space that seems big enough for her to hide. I'm tipping over furniture, moving frantically. *Damn it. Damn it. Nothing!*

I return to the car and drive up and down the road but see only empty space. There's a spot that seems to be the highest ground except where the house is. I grab the pair of binoculars that I took from the house, hike up to the ridge and scan everything. It takes a long time to search the area thoroughly. I've almost finished the second water bottle and am getting seriously worried.

The wind has picked up, which makes the heat even more unbearable, and the rising dust further reduces the visibility. I have to be careful I don't get turned around out here. It's easy to lose sight of the car and the house. I'm hoping Cora didn't get lost, go off in the other direction and walk farther and farther away into the wilderness.

The thought crosses my mind for the first time that I may have to call 911 to save her life. I make a deal with myself. If I don't find her by two hours before dark, I'll call an emergency rescue squad. I can't let her die. I wonder bleakly how long I'll be in jail. I figure I've got four hours to find her.

I decide to search in a rectangular grid about a half-mile on either side of the road, scanning everything, hoping I'll glimpse something. I start yelling, "Cora, where are you? I'll take you home. I promise. Cora! Cora!" The sound dies immediately in the wind and dust.

I grab two water bottles and start walking. The thought comes to me that this is a military-type search. Dad would have known what to do. I'm winging it as I go along. Even Paul is much more methodical than I am. I shudder at that thought and push it away.

Every five minutes, I try calling. Even if she could hear me would she answer? I suppose not if she thought I might kill her. Of course she thought that. She overheard the damn phone conversation, didn't she? She'll probably decide to take her chances. *Shit!*

* * *

I'm back at the car. I've seen nothing. I've been searching over two hours. I pound my fists on the steering wheel. *Agghh! How could I have botched this so badly?*

It must be 120 degrees or more now in the sun. If she dies, it's all on me.

Suddenly my body starts shaking. This is all to do with Paul. I never meant to cause this, but if she dies I would still be a murderer.

It takes several minutes to start functioning. I'm getting muddled in the heat. I realize I have to focus. I'll think about that later.

I finish one of the water bottles and put two more in the front seat. I'll make one more pass. I'll try closer to the house for another grid, then call for a helicopter. I drive halfway back toward the house and grab the water.

I start walking up the low ridge leading back to the house. I'm starting to think of explanations that I can give rescuers to explain the situation when I call 911.

When I get almost back to the buildings, I reverse and head back in the direction of the car. I'm almost back to the car when, out of the corner of my eye, I see a flash of pale blue through the dust. I race as fast as I can toward the spot where I thought I saw it. Absolutely nothing. Then I think I see it again off to the left, and run.

It's Cora, lying pitifully in a gully just below the ground level. She's half-covered with sand, under a towel from the bathroom, trying to keep out of the sun. It's incredible I caught a glimpse of her. She's not moving. I get down on my knees beside her. I remove the bath towel and put my hand under her head.

She moans and blinks her eyes. She's conscious, but confused. She tries to struggle with me. She's very weak, but alive. I feel a surge of tenderness toward her as I start to gather her in my arms.

CHAPTER 10: CORA

SOMEONE'S ARMS ARE AROUND ME. I panic. I don't know where I am, or who this is. I scream. I hear someone saying over and over, "Thank God. Thank God."

A man kneels beside me in the dust, offering a bottle of water. I grab for it and start gulping. After I drink half the bottle, he pulls it away. "Take it easy," he says. "Just sips now."

"It's so hot," I manage.

"I know," he says.

I begin to know who he is, where I am. I sip more water. He's shielding me from the sun with his body. I focus on his face. He seems glad to find me. He doesn't look like he's going to hit me. It comes to me that he's probably saved my life. I'm—grateful.

"Can you walk if I help you?" he yells. The hot wind is a roar, making it hard to hear.

"I don't think so." I point to my extremely swollen ankle.

"I think I can carry you. The car is close."

With some difficulty, I'm gathered up in his arms and he makes his way to the car, walking carefully over the rough ground. I'm so glad to be alive. I start gasping, leaning on his shoulder.

It's several minutes before he's unloading me at the house. I try hopping on my own, but almost immediately he puts my arm around his shoulders and half-carries me inside. I'm awkwardly lowered onto a settee by the door in the wonderful coolness of the house. We both pant, trying to get our breath.

I look down at my hands for several minutes. "I'm sorry."

When I look up he's glaring at me.

"That was a stupid-ass thing to do," he growls.

I look back down at my hands, but he grabs my shoulders and shakes them roughly.

"You're hurting me," I protest.

"Are you crazy?" he roars. "It's over 120 degrees out there. It was just dumb luck I found you." He's almost screaming. "You could have died. You were almost invisible in the dust. Don't fucking do that again."

"Okay! Okay! I won't," I snap back.

I'm at my wit's end. I don't understand anything. He seems angry that I put myself at risk. Nothing makes sense, and I'm getting mad too. I'm going through hell. At least I want to know why.

"Want to try another shower?" he says with evident sarcasm, glowering at me.

I sigh indignantly, and try not to glare back at him.

He helps me hobble to the shower, gives me a towel to partially hide myself, and helps me take my clothes off. He unties my filthy shoes and pulls roughly on my jeans. After all I've been through it hardly bothers me. I'm so sandy that I don't even feel naked, and I'm angry. He hands me some soap and a washcloth.

"Don't try anything," he says threateningly.

I risk giving him a look. *What in the hell could I try?*

I stand leaning against the wall of the shower and let the water cascade endlessly over my head while I try to think. As the anger wears off, the fear starts returning. Should I be terrified? Should I try to think about killing him? He probably did just save my life.

At last I grab the shampoo and start scrubbing the dirt out of my hair. It takes several attempts with periodic rests to get most of the sand rinsed away.

I finish without passing out, but it's close. I had to keep the water cool because of my sunburn. Even the pressure of the water hurts my bare skin, and my ankle throbs when I move it. I know I'm seriously dehydrated, but I'll be damned if I'm going to ask for help. He throws a robe in my general direction, surprisingly averting his eyes, and I put it on. With his help I limp the short distance to the bed and sit inches from the bathroom door.

He has a fast shower, constantly glancing out to see if I'm still here. I don't move a muscle. He wraps a white bath towel around his waist and walks over toward me.

This is it. I feel the blood drain from my head and I glance quickly up at his face.

He pauses in front of me, standing silently, looking down at me. I look down at my hands and swallow. Several moments pass. I can feel my lips and chin trembling.

He walks on past me to his duffle bag and puts on some jeans.

I can't believe it.

He continues on toward the kitchen.

"I'm making us something to eat," he says coldly.

I sit there, a bundle of nerves.

I hear sounds rattling from the kitchen; a pan slammed down, a refrigerator door slammed and reopened.

I hear his voice, "How do you like your eggs?" He sounds less angry.

"Scrambled," I yell back. Then I think I'm losing my mind. *Maybe I should ask if he has any mushrooms or spinach.* Now I'm sure of it.

"There's food," he says loudly in a few minutes.

I gather my courage, tighten the belt of my robe, and start to limp slowly into the kitchen.

He looks up and comes over to help me walk. I shrink at the contact initially, but then relax enough to let him help me.

He's made us scrambled eggs and toast, with juice. By the time he puts a plate in front of me, I've calmed down some. We empty the entire carton of orange juice, pouring glass after glass. He seems less angry. All of a sudden, I'm starved. I gulp my food. I catch him almost smiling at me, once.

He helps me back to the bedroom. "How are you doing?" he asks.

"Exhausted," I say. Just ginger-peachy, I think.

"Then let's sleep," he says. "I'm exhausted, too."

I lie down on the bed. He turns his back to me, and pulls a shirt and socks from his duffle bag. He puts them on quickly before lying down next to me. He gives me a quick glance, ties my wrist to his with a very short rope, and turns on the motion sensor.

He gives the longest sigh I think I've ever heard, and closes his eyes.

"Thank you for saving me," I whisper.

He answers with his eyes closed. "You're welcome."

"Um—what's your name?"

"It's Sam."

"Just Sam?"

"Sam Thomas, same as my brother."

"Your brother," I say, remembering he told me that before. "What...? Why...?"

"Let it go, okay?" He sighs, "I won't go there."

"I don't understand," I say. "You change back and forth from being a terrifying kidnapper, to a decent guy, and back again. Which are you?"

"Decent." His eyes crack open. "Despite what you think, I never intended to hurt you. You got caught up in a catastrophe that started years ago. I'll take you home unharmed. Now get some rest."

I'm exhausted, but I try to think. I'm lying in the dark room, almost chilly from the air-conditioner, with a soft comforter over me, tied to a man whose name I just learned. Maybe he wants me alive for ransom, but no one's mentioned money. Maybe he's going to rape me. But that doesn't make sense; he didn't have to take me a million miles to do that.

He got mad because he had to hunt for me for hours in the heat. He didn't have to. He could have let me die, especially if he was going to kill me. I hear the air-conditioner click off and take several deep breaths. I feel my heart rate finally slow and almost tear-up at the relief from anxiety. The eggs were great. I think I'm going to live.

The night drags on. I let my guard down and relax, getting some sleep, but then nightmares wake me up and I'm scared all over again.

My thoughts circle endlessly. I realize that I'm not afraid anymore; not much, anyway. He had his chance to kill me in anger, let me die in the desert, or rape me. He did none of those things. He made me scrambled eggs and covered me with a warm blanket. He was furious with me, but didn't take it out on me. On top of everything, he put on more clothes before lying down next to me, allowing me to relax. On double top of everything, he seems familiar in a towel. *Oh, crap.*

He does look a lot like Paul, who's probably going absolutely crazy. Even their voices are so similar that I'm often startled. I don't think I should bring up calling Paul to tell him I'm fine and just had breakfast. I'm very tired and my thoughts are not making any sense. I try to go to sleep, but this time I can't. It's a very long time before I feel myself drifting off.

* * *

The motion sensor goes off in the dark, scaring me.

"Sorry," Sam mutters, untying me before heading into the bathroom.

I sit up on the side of the bed.

"Can you walk alone?" he asks, when he returns.

"I think so."

If I step on the outside of my foot, I can manage to hobble across the room. "I want to wash my hair again. It's full of gravel." I turn at the bathroom door and ask, "What happens now?"

He looks at me evocatively, then shakes his head. Then he laughs to himself.

"What?" I ask.

"How about dinner and a movie?"

I stare at him as he gives me a sheepish grin.

Maybe this is all a dream. Maybe I just need to wake up.

I get inside the bathroom and sit on the john. How do I feel about all this? I take off my robe and limp into the shower. I've left the bathroom door cracked open. There's good shampoo and I take my time, thinking. I can see him glancing at me quickly through the clear shower door to make sure I haven't tried the window again. At least he doesn't seem to be gawking.

What if I refused to—do anything? I could try it and if he got angry I'd have to decide. I'm beginning to believe he wouldn't force me to do anything. He's making jokes for God's sake. I take my time in the shower, dry myself off, put my robe back on, and comb my wet hair.

I walk out of the bathroom and see Sam is sitting pensively on the couch. I go over to the other end. We sit in companionable silence for a few minutes. Finally, he says, "Do you still want to connect with me?"

I'm completely not sure what he could mean by this.

I should say no, but I say, "I can try. I kind of owe you. I could have died out there."

"You don't owe me anything," he says.

After a while, he gently takes my arm and walks me over to the bed. He lies down and closes his eyes.

He seems so normal, so non-threatening. I touch his cheek with the back of my hand. I touch his forehead, his jawline, and his shoulders. He sighs. I stop from time to time to see what will happen. Nothing happens. He smiles slightly with his eyes closed.

"What?" I ask.

"Does this seem as crazy to you as it does to me?" His eyes are still closed.

"Yes."

I search his face, the vulnerable expression. I wait a long time to see if he will push me. He doesn't. He doesn't make a move toward me. It's as if he doesn't want to scare me. Much time passes in this way. I run my fingers through his dark damp hair.

I feel desire for him. It may be terrible, but I do. He seems so familiar. His lips look so soft, so warm. He's a very handsome man. With his eyes closed he looks so young, so uncorrupted by whatever drove him to this desperate situation. Slowly I lean over him and touch my lips to his. My robe loosens around my body. His eyes open. I see desire in his eyes, too.

My fingers glide down his neck. I lean over and make my lips follow my fingers.

"Stop, Cora," he says. "Stop. Now. You don't have to do this. If you don't stop, I'll.... Just stop. Okay? Damn it."

"I don't understand," I say. "I thought I had to...." But I'm not fooling myself. I'm pretty sure, now, that I don't have to do anything.

"You still don't get it. I never intended—to make you do anything against your will. You're just a girl who got caught up in all this. This is becoming impossible. I'm only a man...." He rolls over on his side away from me. I think I hear a moan.

I don't say anything because I don't know what to say or how I feel. I believe he's in some tormented place.

* * *

Time is artificial. We've been awake at night and sleeping during the day. I see Sam stewing quietly, apparently trying to figure out what to do. I realize that the fear I had of him is slipping away. I suppose if he is really crazy it could all surface on a moment's notice and I could be in deep trouble again. But as time goes on, that seems less and less likely.

We haven't talked much, but everything Sam says is meant to reassure me. I've tried not to push him. I understand something terrible and pivotal is going on here. For some reason, I'm willing to remain in the background as some internal fight continues. He looks up after a long silent period and says, "Cora, can you give me some time? Just a little time?"

I smile slightly and nod.

He nods back.

Time passes. At one point, he takes the ropes that he'd had me tied with off the table next to the bed, and throws them violently against the back wall.

"I'm sick about that," he says.

More time passes. He appears to doze. I made a little noise to see if it would rouse him. It didn't. I wonder if I should try to sneak away, but then I remember my ankle.

At last I say to him, "I'd like to go out and get some fresh air."

"Go ahead," he says. He looks at me as if deciding something. Finally, he says. "It's okay. You're not my prisoner. Not anymore."

"You're quitting?" I ask.

"Yeah. Go figure."

I shake my head and limp out onto the front veranda, then a short ways farther along the stone entryway. The sun is just setting over low dry hills to the west. It must be in the low 90s now, but with the dry air and a breeze it's almost cool. The tops of the hills are still sun-lit but the sagebrush and shrubs blend into the dark ground. It's beautiful here. I'm surprised that I can be peaceful enough to enjoy it. I shake my head again. I feel—safe.

*   *   *

We've both dozed on and off. This is such a bizarre situation. A few hours ago I believed my life was over. Either I was going to be killed or die, drying up in the desert. Now I'm lying with my forearm touching my captor, not tied to him. It's three in the morning and it's a beautiful night. He opened the windows and there's a soft desert breeze blowing the floor-length white curtains. I've slept at odd times and I'm not tired. I've thought and thought. Finally, I've given up trying to understand it all. I want to go home, but there's something bizarrely intriguing about this situation, so much mystery and so much sadness.

"Sam?" I can tell he's awake.

"Yes?"

"What are you going to do with me?"

I hear him take a deep breath and then another, and another.

"Cora, I won't keep you here, or anywhere else you don't want to be. I'm damn confused, but I do know one thing. You have somehow succeeded. You have enabled me to believe—I might be able to move ahead; I might risk connecting with someone. I've been alone a very long time."

"I've hardly done anything," I say.

He pauses for several seconds. "When I was out in the desert looking for you, I realized I held your life in my hands. I was terrified. I don't want you hurt, any more than I've already hurt you. I'm so sorry."

I sit up on the side of the bed.

"Cora? Do you want me to take you home now?"

"I'm confused, too. I'm almost dizzy with this. I need some time."

He sits up, too, and puts his head in his hands. "I've only taken what I've wanted, given nothing to anyone. I don't know who I am now."

"Who have you been?" I ask.

"My life has been frozen for the past 10 years. I feel like I'm a 17-year-old boy in a man's body. I need to get you away from my messed-up life."

I bite my lip. I almost don't say it, but I can't help myself. "What if I don't want to get away from your messed-up life?"

He moans, and says nothing.

"Why?" I finally ask. "Why have you been stuck?"

"Because it's been safe to hate. It's a feeling I know. I'm used to it. If I venture out, I might not survive the pain."

I'm trying to put that level of anguish into my life experience. I know I've never felt that kind of agony, even when my mother died.

At last Sam asks, "Cora, are you okay?"

"No," I say. "I don't think I am."

"Why? Did I hurt you again, somehow?"

"No, not the way you mean. It's just that—what am I going to do now? With myself?"

"You can do anything you want.

"Sam," I sigh, "I believe I'm in love with Paul—but there are things I've buried, that keep resurfacing, some cautions from my friends, and voices I've refused to listen to."

I see his hands start to tremble and he balls them into fists.

I search his face in the near-darkness, "And I—I have strong feelings for you, very confusing. Give me some time to understand this."

"Listen to me," he says. "I'm strongly attracted to you. But I have nothing to offer you. Put your blinders on and forget about me. I've seen you with Paul. He's put a life together. You have friends, plans, stability, and someone who loves you. Before you get in any deeper, you need to stop this. I'm a broken person. Without me you've got it all. I've become a—complication."

He puts his hands on his knees, stands up and walks outside into the blackness of the entryway.

It would be the most ridiculous form of idiocy to align myself with a crazy guy who kidnapped me to torment his own brother, whatever the reason. There's a strong physical pull, no use denying it. But I'm not crazy, too, am I?

I'm sitting on the bed, in the darkness, wanting to pull him back in here and make love to him. I can count off many reasons why that wouldn't be sensible for him or for me. Still, this has become one of the harder decisions I've ever had to make. Just one night, just one episode, what difference could it make? But I know it would make a lot of difference to me—to Paul, who deserves loyalty—and to Sam. He doesn't need his head jumbled any more than it already is. I square my shoulders and walk out into the darkness after him.

I find him staring out at the desert.

I walk up beside him in the darkness. "Sam, should I be afraid of Paul?"

He takes a breath.

I wait.

"Look at me—at what I did," he says. "It's not what we say, Cora, but what we do. I've got problems, serious problems. It's probably me that you need to be afraid of. Paul has put together a successful life. I've got to believe that he's done the better job of recovering from our past. I've tried to hide from my anger, and look where it's gotten me. I have nothing. Look at that, Cora."

"If you hate him so much, why won't you tell me the whole story so I can make up my own mind?"

"Two days ago I might have told you, when it didn't matter. I'm starting to look at myself and what I'm capable of. It's been 10 years. Both of us are different men. Only Paul should share his past. He— it's his story to tell. Ask him."

"Did he hurt someone?"

He looks at me as if I've kicked him in the groin, nodding his head over and over.

He's silent for several minutes, then says, "I told you. There are things I can't talk about. And maybe I've been wrong about some things."

I have to let it go. I wait several minutes then ask, "Sam, I want to know. What were you thinking when you paused—before walking past me—when you were still angry? You know, after your shower? That was the last time I was really afraid of you."

"You were probably right to be frightened," he says. "I almost didn't keep walking. It was close."

I need to think about that.

We stand inches apart. The pull between us is unrelenting, almost painful.

We stand silently listening to the night desert sounds. My head and my heart keep whipping me in various directions. My deepest self tells me that I'm unable to make any decisions with what I know now. "You're right, Sam," I say finally. "I need to go home." I adjust my robe and cinch it tightly.

He keeps looking out at the empty space. "I'll drive you back," he says. "I need to talk to Paul." There's kindness now in that voice, what I've started to expect.

I swallow hard. "Won't that be dangerous—if you really hate each other?"

He finally looks at me. "I'm the one who was trying to kill him," he smiles wryly. "And, anyway, I don't think we'll try to kill each other in front of you; messy, turns girls off. I'll call him and let him know the plan. When do you want to leave?"

"As soon as we can."

He hesitates for several seconds, sighs, and pulls out his phone. I can hear Paul answer as Sam puts it on speaker.

"Sam." The word is said with hopelessness. I can hear Paul's anguished, familiar voice and it's heartbreaking.

"Paul. I've made a decision. I'm bringing her back. We'll be there tomorrow night."

"What! Sam, why? For God's sake, is she all right?"

"I'm doing it for her."

A pause, "She got to you, didn't she?"

"Yes," Sam replies without looking at me. "She got to me. I don't want any surprises or ambushes. It would upset Cora. She's been hurt enough."

"Of course, Sam. No ambushes. I don't want to hurt you. I never wanted to hurt you."

What could have happened between these two to cause such alienation? I want to hear Paul's voice directly to keep up my resolve. I walk up to Sam with my hand out and he hands me the phone.

"Paul?" I say.

"Cora? Sweetheart? Are you hurt?"

I want to be home with his arms around me. I do—but I see Sam's shoes kicking the dust with nervous tension. I feel that, too. Suddenly, I'm completely unsettled.

"Paul, listen." I swallow. "I need your absolute assurance that Sam will not be hurt or arrested or anything. It's part of the deal."

"Did—did he say what went wrong between us?"

"No, nothing—it just seems fair. He's been really decent."

I turn and give Sam a small smile. He looks up from his feet and focuses on me. He tries unsuccessfully to smile back. Then looks away.

"Cora. Hang in there," Paul says. "I'll see you tomorrow. I love you."

"Until tomorrow," I say lamely.

I click off the phone. I couldn't tell Paul that I loved him in front of Sam and that frightens me. And I can't bear to look at Sam again, to see alternatives. I say to the darkness, "I want to go home."

Unbelievably, he wraps his arms around me. "Anything you want, Cora," he says. "Anything at all."

I can feel the blood pounding in my hands. They hang loose at my sides, but that's not where I want them to be.

CHAPTER 11: SAM

JUST 48 HOURS AGO we were headed the other way, pulling into the driveway at the rental house. Cora was blindfolded and terrified and I was trying to decide how to torment Paul. Now we're going the opposite direction and my life has been turned upside down. I'm trying desperately to get my head around this.

We're talking a little, trying to get to know something about each other. She's adding to the information I overheard before.

She's 23. I didn't even know that. She has a couple of quarters to finish her degree, but is taking a break to earn some money. Her mom died four months ago of cancer. Her dad remarried, the infamous Sheila, a month ago and he works for a local Seattle television station as an assistant program editor.

She's an only child and her two best friends, Susan and Leslie—the girl I recently sort of met—have graduated and moved out of the area for jobs, although they communicate frequently. She likes to ski, when she can afford it, and loves to hike in the mountains and backpack. She might teach, but would really like to work on water conservation issues.

It's hard for me to say much. There's a lot of history that I don't want to go into. I don't have much of a recent life story to share, but I do tell her about my music, and my favorite singer-songwriters, Sam Bradley and Bobby Long—how they motivated me to learn their style of playing, how much inspiration they've given to me. I'm starting to write some songs. I describe my favorite bands. She even knows several of them: The Decemberists, Fleet Foxes, and Death Cab for Cutie—all from the Pacific Northwest. I feel like she knows me a little. Music is so personal.

I mention that I make a living repairing computers and even say I'm good at it. I can't help it. I don't want her to think I'm a loser. I even tell her I have money in the bank and I put more away every month. I can tell she's surprised, but tries to cover it up.

We're going to have to stop somewhere to get Cora something to wear. I've put our filthy clothes in his-and-hers garbage bags in the back seat. Also in mine is a small blue bath towel, a keepsake.

I'm wearing my last pair of jeans and an old faded black t-shirt. Cora's wearing one of my old blue button-down shirts and a pair of my cutoffs held up with the all-purpose rope. I hadn't gotten around to planning a kidnapped person's wardrobe. Her hair is loosely tied back with a rubber band. We've hosed off our shoes and are both barefoot while they dry.

She's adorable.

Dawn is just breaking over the horizon in southwestern Idaho, all pale yellow colors. When she was awake, she kept some distance between us. But in her sleep, Cora is curled up with her head on my shoulder, her arm thrown casually across my lap, totally unafraid of me now. *If she only knew how close I am to abducting her all over again.* What I feel for her is tormenting me, but I can't let her see it. This is hard enough on her already.

I believe I should do this for Cora. I believe Paul loves her. I saw them together. If I didn't, I wouldn't take her back to him, but anxiety is just below the surface.

I remember Paul. He was an idealist. Sometimes idealists hurt people, really hurt people. I of all people should know that. Right and wrong are never as simple to figure out as idealists imagine. It's the old "I'm going to kill you to save you" idea. If I thought Paul would pull this crap on Cora, he'd never see her face again.

But we're not kids anymore. Surely we've grown up and learned.

But then again, look at me. Music alone kept me in the real world, but 10 years out I'm just beginning to heal, and that's probably because I ran into Cora. My head is spinning with things I need to think about. I want to start thinking like an adult. I've been isolated for so long, and during all that time, I haven't had anyone to talk seriously to. How do you grow if you're stuck circling in your own head? *Shit, I hope I'm doing the right thing.*

I glance down at her face for the thousandth time. She's so lovely. There's so much I want to say and almost none of it appropriate. It's happiness to look at her. I know that emotion now, something you can't force, and something that just is. Cora stretches, looks up, and smiles at me. The what-ifs are killing me.

"How far are we?" she asks.

"We've only done four hours or so of driving and we need to stop for food, and I could really use a nap. We're sort of ahead of schedule. Do you want to drive?"

She looks at me. "No," she says slowly, "I'm in no hurry."

"What are you hungry for?" I ask. "The sky's the limit. I'll buy."

"You bet you'll buy. I didn't bring my purse." She smiles impishly at me.

I smile at the road.

"Hmm? It's such a beautiful morning," she says. "Let's get juice and doughnuts. You know, the kind with a really long shelf life, and eat outside." *It's such a normal conversation for an ex-hostage.* I shrug my shoulders agreeably and pull into the next large truck stop, which probably has a small clothing section.

Cora goes in to use the restroom and clean up a bit, then get some food. I go into the gift shop and buy a tourist blanket in green and yellow that says *GO DUCKS* on it, plus a football logo.

Cora's found some blue nylon swim shorts and a white tourist t-shirt that has a large trout across the front.

Back on the road, I turn off on a local side road that looks like it will head up into the hills, and drive until we finally find a spot with a view of the valley among a grove of poplars. The grass is soft and warm. I spread out the blanket and lie on my back, put my elbows behind my head, and look up at the sapphire blue sky through the bright yellow leaves. Cora lies down beside me, curls up on her side, and we both drift off to sleep before we get into the food.

It's so peaceful here with the sound of the wind in the leaves and an occasional meadowlark. I've had a great nap. I don't think I'll ever have doughnuts with powdered sugar without thinking of this spot. We've been laughing about getting the sugar on our clothes and faces, shoveling them in and drowning them in juice. There's no expiration date. I looked.

I set about making a mental picture to remember, looking at her face smeared with the white powder. Without warning, I'm hit with the realization that soon I'll be dropping her off with my detested brother, handing her off like a relay baton, and I fall apart. There's a contraction in my chest that grabs me so hard I moan out loud in pain. Of course she notices.

"Sam?"

"It's nothing," I say. "Probably indigestion from year-old donuts."

"What's going on?"

"I'm just worried. Is there anything I should know before I return you? You know what I mean."

"Paul is a good guy, Sam," she says softly. "He's been very good to me. He loves me."

"Do you think you can talk to him, about who he is? What you need?"

"Paul is so smart. Sometimes he gets impatient with me—when I'm slow to take action on something. He seems to have my life figured out, and he tells me what to do. Don't get me wrong, he's usually right. And he's critical about my attitude with my dad. He just remarried and I don't like her. Paul gets angry about that—says to give her a chance."

Despite myself, I remember thinking that exact same thing. "What else?"

She takes a few minutes, thinking.

My head is spinning with a new picture of Paul. If I truly believe he killed purposefully, then there's no way I could return Cora. It's been a possibility that I never wanted to closely explore.

An accident should have made it impossible to hate as much as I do. Yet for some reason, I can't give that up. I need that hate. But as I look over at Cora, so concerned about me, I wonder....

Maybe, I could let some of that go.

"Cora, I haven't said much about Paul. What happened between us was long in the past, but it was dark stuff. It appears he's healed, changed from what he was. Suffice it to say he was obsessed and he hurt people. He couldn't let hatred go. I used to believe that what he did, the risk he took, was on purpose—but now I just need some assurance that he's safe, that he hasn't hurt you."

Cora is quiet, thinking, maybe thinking what to say.

"Is there something...?"

"Sometimes he's too rough with me," she says, looking down.

I roll on my side with my head on my hand and look at her seriously. Suddenly I feel queasy. "How often?" I ask.

"Almost every time we get together. He says it—turns him on." She's embarrassed.

"Do you like him to do that? Does it hurt?"

"It does hurt a little," she says, "and no, I don't really like it, but it's something I can do for him."

"If he knows it hurts you, why does he keep doing it?"

"He doesn't know it," Cora says. "He's never asked."

I feel a chill. We're quiet for a while.

"If you told him, what would he do?" I ask. "Why haven't you?"

She sighs, "There are places we don't go—things off limits. If I pressure him, he gets so closed off and sad. It scares me to ask him about it—but now I need to."

I can guess the places he doesn't want to go. "Are you afraid of him?"

"No."

We sit in silence for a bit. I try to let it go. I've pushed hard enough.

Cora takes a deep breath and asks, "Sam, what will you do after you return me?"

I'm about to say I'll do what I've always done. Find a place to make some money, move on when it suits me. But I realize it's a lie. I'm not the same man I was four days ago. I've been stuck for years in a two-dimensional existence.

I accuse Paul of making things black and white, but isn't that what I've been doing? I want a life. I want to feel more. I'm hit with the idea that, if I became more, I might not have to return Cora to a man who needs to hurt her to get turned on. It's an overwhelming idea.

"Suddenly, I'm considering changing the way I live my life. I care more about you than about hurting Paul. Hating him has been the focus of my life for so long. It's become such a heavy load to carry. I'm so tired. Maybe I could put it down."

She takes my hand.

"I might find a place I like, settle down, find a real house and live there. You know, get to know people, build a life. Do you think I could do that?" I look over at her and there are tears in her eyes. "Yes, Sam," she says. "I know you could."

* * *

We've not talked much for the past four hours or so, each lost in our own thoughts. Every once in a while I reach down and tuck a lock of hair behind her ear or stroke her forearm with my thumb. I can't help myself. I'm trying to frame what I want to say to Paul and I'm trying to think what to say to Cora.

There are things that I want to say to my brother, things that I don't want her to hear. She'll need to love him and feel safe, especially after this mess. But she deserves better. I want her to know that so she can fight for better.

She hasn't said anything to indicate she's changing her mind. I want to ask her every other minute if she's changed her mind, but I don't quite do it. I don't want to shake her confidence in him. I care about her too much. But I think that she needs to have her eyes open. Maybe her confidence is blindness. She could get hurt. That's what I've begun to worry about big time.

I want him to know that, if he hurts her, the world won't be big enough. But what if he still can't control himself? If only he'd gotten professional help years ago, maybe things would have turned out differently. I wish someone had been paying more attention.

* * *

OCTOBER 12TH, 2001

It was late October and my life was fantastic. I always smiled to myself when I thought of that word. When I was a little kid, Paul would razz me for using it over and over. Our soccer team was 8 and

1 for the regular season and everyone said we'd go all the way to State. I was into my junior year in high school and had started to think about colleges. There was the GI Bill money to use for tuition and it was a given that I'd be majoring in computer science. I was already making a couple hundred bucks a month repairing the computers of my friends' parents, and the school had recently hired me to keep the computer lab afloat.

My problem, of focusing on school, was Gloria's fault. She was a senior and hot for me. She wasn't the brightest girl in school, but she did excel in one thing—softball, the inside variety. Paul was always kidding me about not knowing what to do with a girl. If he only knew....

Gloria and I had been hooking up for the past two months and she'd taught me everything I needed to know. What they always said was true—learning can be fun. She was always saying, "Sam, I've got a new idea for tonight." *Damn.*

The only significant problem in my life was my brother. It wasn't just that we were getting older and had separate lives; he'd gotten weird, seriously weird. All he wanted to talk about was the possibility that we might invade Iraq. He kept saying, "Finally we'll get the SOB who killed Dad."

Women chased Paul and he took advantage of their interest. That was one thing we had in common. But their names changed often; I could never keep up.

I heard Paul's motorcycle pull in the driveway. He had a sweet little Honda that he rode to school and back. I kept bugging him about putting a girl on the back, but he shook his head.

"Hey, Paul," I said as he came in the door.

"Hey, dork-head. How's the love life?"

"You never believe me when I tell you, but I could probably teach you a thing or two."

That got a real smile out of him. "Maybe you could. We'll have to compare notes after Mom goes to bed."

"I need to do some more research. I'm meeting Gloria after the game. Are you coming?"

"Duh. Is Mom going to make it?"

"I don't know. She's been putting in extra hours of vacation relief."

"Why?" Paul asked. "I mean, I guess she could use the money, but both of us are self-supporting. Maybe we should talk to her about it."

"Let's do it. She's always so tired or not here." I threw my soccer shoes and shin guards in my duffle. "You want to shoot some baskets? I've got an hour before Castro picks me up for the game."

"No. I want to catch CNN. They have 24 hour coverage of the coming invasion. They're even talking specific dates."

"Paul. They're gonna' do what they're gonna' do. Don't you ever think about anything else?"

He gave me that disgusted look.

I sighed, "Paul, please. Can't you let it go? It's starting to mess up your life."

"Let it go? That guy killed Dad. Don't you care anymore?"

"Of course, I care. But Paul, I've got my own life now. I can't do anything."

"Fine, Sam. Go do some more research with Gloria. I'll do something. I'll be damned if I just forget it."

"I didn't say to forget it, Paul," I sighed. "Let's drop it. Okay?"

"Fine."

Paul was starting to scare me. We'd always been different personalities. When kids teased me, I laughed, made it part of a joke we shared. But not Paul. He took everything personally. He was such a good athlete that no one taunted him, but if they messed with me, it was the end of the world. When I was eight or nine, one of the kids pushed me on the soccer field. It was nothing. But Paul got so angry that I thought he was going to punch the guy. I had to throw myself at him to get him to back off. And I was the little kid, for crap's sake.

But something was seriously wrong with him. My fears had become too persistent to ignore. The thought crossed my mind, again, that I should bring it up with Mom.

* * *

It was the following Monday night and Mom and I were eating dinner together. I hadn't had a chance yet to talk to her about my brother.

She'd been working and I'd been with my friends all weekend. "Mom," I said. "I want to talk about Paul."

She looked surprised. "Is he okay? She asked, handing me a plate of chicken casserole.

"I'm worried. All he wants to do is talk about going to war to avenge Dad. He comes home every weekend, never talks about any friends, and he's angry at me, at CNN, at the world. He says I don't care about Dad because I don't care about the Iraq thing."

"Sam. I think he's okay. He's doing well in school. Off the charts really."

"But, Mom, you're the one who's always talking about balance. All he does is study and come home weekends and hide out in the basement."

"I was talking about your balance; you know, some school work in addition to sports and playing around with Gloria."

I gave her an innocent look.

"Don't give me that look, Sam," she grinned. "You've been pretty cheerful recently. How's that working out?"

Mom and I always had an easy relationship and talked about everything. "It's working out well, Mom. You ought to try it."

"Well, I just might. If I wasn't so tired, I just might."

She did look tired, hair pulled back in a hair clip, with the same sandals she'd worn for two years, at least. "That's another thing, Mom. Can't you cut back working? Paul and I are doing well, making our own spending money. And GI Bill money is pretty much covering our college. Are you short? Money, I mean?"

"You always did worry about me, Sam, more than Paul. He tends to be in his own world." She got up, went to the refrigerator, and poured me a second glass of milk.

"Mom, Paul brought this up. He wants you to have a little fun, too."

"Really," she said. She picked up my plate and kissed my cheek. "I'll think about it. I sort of got on that treadmill when your dad died. I'll think seriously about not taking any more overtime. It's horrible to miss out on anything like your soccer. You'll be gone in a year and a half." She smiled wistfully at me, and reached across the table to take my hand.

"About Paul?" I asked again.

"Oh, yes. I got sidetracked. You're really concerned aren't you? He's the one that always worried about you. All right, I'll corner him when he comes home next."

"Paul needs help. Don't forget, Mom. Okay? You have a lot going on."

"I always have a lot, Sam. Obviously, I like it that way. But I sure lucked out with my boys. I've gotten used to not worrying about either one of you."

* * *

I didn't like that memory. It made me feel sort of sick. Why? I'm damn worried about Cora; I know that. There is almost nothing I could say to her that will help either of us, unless there is real danger.

Oh God. I can't make small talk with her. I imagine she feels the same. This doesn't seem like the time to ask what her favorite movie is or whether she likes bowling. On the other hand, I can't shake her hand and walk away. Can I?

"Sam," Cora breaks the silence, "can you find a place to pull over?"

I find a small rest stop and park, way down at one end. An elderly couple is walking a dog, far past the rest rooms. We are essentially alone.

"Sam, can you...?"

And I had been doing so well. My self-imposed isolation crumbles. I wrap my arms around her and pull her to me and she starts to cry. I rock her gently in my arms trying to soothe her. I feel like sobbing myself and a part of me is angry because she didn't let me keep my wall. This is a knife twisting in my gut. She made her choice, damn it. This will never do, but I can't think of another thing. I keep swallowing, over and over.

"This is terrible," she says.

"I know," I say. Time passes. Finally I tip up her chin so I can look her in the eye. "Cora, listen...." She nods.

"You are not trapped here. We've both agreed that this is the place you should be, for now, anyway. But if things change, and you don't want to be with Paul, or even stay in Oregon, you can contact me and I'll come back for you. Do you understand?"

She nods.

"And one more thing. Paul was impulsive and driven in the distant past. I don't know him now, but I want you to keep your eyes open. If he starts to seem dangerous, then you need to make a move. Talk to him. Really get to know him."

What I don't say, what I can't quite articulate or want to say, is that maybe Paul is not deserving of the extreme hatred I've been directing at him. And if he's not, maybe I can let some of that go, at least enough for me to try to get better.

"Yes," she whispers. "I'll stop avoiding that. I'll talk to Paul."

"You deserve the best. I'm not that person yet, but I'm going to try to learn to be. I'm going to try very hard."

We sit there in silence for a while.

"Sam, I want to remember you. Can you kiss me? I – please...."

I feel the blood pounding in my lips. I can't resist her. I touch her lips with mine and hear her gasp. I slip one hand under her shirt. Her skin is so soft, so warm. I wind the other hand in her hair. I am so close to being lost in her. She is so beautiful. I ache for her. I pull her face to mine and feel her warm breath on my cheek, then bury my face in her thick hair. The pull is so strong. God! How I want her. I'm beginning to believe she wants me, too, not just for the moment. The anguish of giving her up is almost beyond enduring, but I pull away.

"Cora, I care—deeply." I'm trying not to say the word out loud for both our sakes. "As ridiculous as it seems, after three days, I do. Look on me as an insurance policy, Okay?"

"Okay," she whispers.

"I want to make love to you, but I can't. I can't do that and give you back to Paul. It would break me apart. Let me do the right thing. I need to feel good about myself. I'm trying my hardest to grow up here. Can you understand that?"

She nods again. I believe she is tortured, too. Finally, she takes a deep breath, gives me her bravest smile and says, "Take me home. Please hurry."

I take a deep breath and start the car.

"I'm sorry," she says.

I'm never sure what she means when she says that. But I do know it means she hasn't chosen me.

I turn my head away as she straightens her clothes. I thought I knew the depths of feeling in my hatred. Now the longing I feel, the desolation of losing her, is another expression of unendurable pain.

*   *   *

I drive the last, final hours. I haven't been able to talk much. Cora's spent the past hour leaning against me. We both know it would be better for both of us if we sat on opposite sides of the car, but we can't. Cora finally straightens up and slides over toward the window. It's dark now and I'm pulling into Paul's driveway. I stop the car across a large grassy area in front of the house about 100 feet from his porch. Paul is waiting under the outdoor light, watching us.

I keep my eyes straight ahead, but say to Cora. "I'm going to East Glacier, Montana, a small town near the entrance to Glacier National Park, and I'm going to build a life there. I'll get a mailbox at the post office and I'll check it regularly." I thrust a piece of paper in her hand with an e-mail address and my cell number. "Call me if you need me. I'll be there."

"Yes, Sam," she says simply, slipping it into her pocket.

I pick up my last disposable cell phone and ring my brother. I can see him stand up from the front steps and put it to his ear.

CHAPTER 12: PAUL

I'VE SPENT THE PAST 12 HOURS OR SO in a state of confusion building toward horror. I originally thought that if I had Cora back, safe and sound, everything would be like it was. But then I really started to think. What has my brother told Cora? What poison has he filled her mind with?

I know I've been totally evasive with Cora about my past. I was going to have to deal with it eventually, but I kept putting it off. If I'd told her some or all of the truth, whatever Sam told her would have had some of my point of view to temper it. Could he have been able to convince Cora that I killed Mom intentionally in a state of rage? Could he believe that?

I've never specifically denied that to Sam because we always end up in shouting matches. I never believe he could actually think that until I replay our conversations in my mind. It seems conceivable that he does.

I've done all I can do. I've spelled it out in a letter, how much I loved Mom, how it was all such a horrible tragic accident, how the guilt is never-ending, how much I miss him in my life. I've been sitting with the letter in my hand under the porch light for hours, waiting to try to connect one last time, thinking about how much I love him, have always loved him. I've been thinking back to that last day, so long ago, when I was completely happy—the exact minute.

* * *

AUGUST 3RD, 1990

It was over 20 years ago. Sam and I were playing. It was warm in our backyard, but the big oaks provided a lot of shade. Glendale, California, was hot in August, but it would be great that night, outside, sleeping in our tent. We had a flashlight we used to read ghost stories. Sammy was trying to get his soccer ball past me, into the small goal net I had set up. I laughed at him as he pretended to be angry, then gave me a kid grin. For a little guy he wasn't bad, but after 10 or 15 minutes, he was done. I would have practiced until dark or until Mom made me come in for bed.

At his age, I would have looked like him. We were both tall for our ages, with dark hair and skin that tanned well. Which was good, since we spent a lot of the summer at the community pool.

"Come on, dork-head," I said to him. "Mom's probably got dinner waiting." We headed in through the kitchen door at the back of the house.

Summers in Glendale were the best. We had a neighborhood gang of friends and it was still safe enough to roam around after dinner from one house to another, playing outside until dark, then settling in at one house or another to watch movies or play video games. We hung out at our house a lot because Mom always had good snacks.

"Wash your hands, gentlemen," Mom said.

I raced Sammy to the bathroom and grabbed for the soap. We had a scuffle over it and I ended up splashing water on his head, and he shrieked with laughter. I was 10 and becoming a cool dude. Obviously, little brothers were beneath me but, to tell the truth, Sammy was cool too. We'd moved around, being military brats, and had to make new friends, but we always had each other. Dad was active-duty military, which meant he was gone a lot, so I considered it my job to keep an eye on the kid.

We were having spaghetti. Mom knew we loved it so we had it almost every week, even though I was sure she was sick of it. She was a great mom; let us do anything we wanted, as long as it was reasonable. I tried not to cross the line or to worry her. It was hard on her when Dad was gone.

"How was the pool?" she asked.

"Fantastic!" Sammy said.

It was his new word. Everything was fantastic.

"I dove off the high board. Paul said I'd never do it, so I showed him."

"He did," I said. "Not bad for a kid. I owe him an ice cream cone."

"I'm almost seven now," he said automatically, as if that made him grown up.

Mom smiled. "See any cute girls, Paul?"

"Right, Mom. Like I was looking."

"Castro Kincaid was looking," Sammy said. "All he ever does is talk about boobs."

The doorbell rang.

"I'll get it, Mom," I said.

I opened the front door and saw two military men on the porch.

"Hello," one of them said. "Is your Mom at home?"

They were so serious. I got a queasy feeling in my stomach. "I'll get her," I said.

* * *

We were sitting together on the couch in the dark. No one remembered to turn on a light, or wanted to. Mom's best friend had come and gone and now there was just us.

Dad was dead. My mind kept repeating that over and over. It wasn't possible. Not Dad. He knew his way around. He took care of himself and other guys. I knew that because some of them came here and told me so.

Sammy finally cried himself to sleep in Mom's arms. He'd been hysterical, holding onto Mom for dear life. We've all been sitting together. Sammy and Mom had always been so close, but I was Dad's son. I wanted to be just like him. I wanted to be a soldier—take care of people and our country. Now I just wanted my dad. I was lost. I couldn't cry. I wished I could cry. I felt like gasping for breath.

Finally, Mom picked Sammy up in her arms and walked with him into her bedroom. In a minute she was back.

"Paul," she said. "Can we all sleep together tonight?"

"Sure, Mom," I said. "We'll be okay."

"I love you, Paul," she said.

* * *

It had been over a month and school had just started. I was trying to do the old things; get my homework done early so I could go hang around with the guys after dinner, get to soccer practice, sleep. But everything was so hard. School was usually easy for me, but now my head was always somewhere else. For the first time in my life, I was forgetting things, almost everything. I tried making lists, setting things out the night before, but I was in a fog. Everyone had been — understanding.

Without trying, I did well on the tests, even if I forgot to turn in homework. I thought that they were making it easy on me. All I could seem to focus on was Sam. I wanted to know where he was, who he was with, if it could possibly be dangerous. Mom didn't seem to worry, but she was so busy trying to work. She upped her nursing hours and was tired at night. Or probably she was depressed like me. Everyone asked me, "Are you feeling depressed?"

Duh. No. I was as happy as a lark. I just didn't want anything to happen to Sam. I never used to think like that, but now I saw danger everywhere. He didn't even look sometimes when he crossed the street. I tried to get him to tell me where he was going, but it bugged him, so I tried to spend a lot of time with him so I could keep watch. We were still sleeping out in the tent most nights. Mom understood that it was our thing.

My friends kept asking me to come over, watch movies, talk about guy stuff. But I didn't want to horse around anymore. Suddenly, it all seemed so stupid. They were burping and saying stupid stuff and punching each other and....

My dad was dead. How was I supposed to deal with that? It was easier to hang with Sam and some of his dorky friends. At least they didn't notice if I were different.

Sam and I were good, though. I could tell how much he needed me. He wanted to do everything with me. I watched all his kid soccer games and took him to the movies. Mom thanked me over and over for putting up with Sam. She didn't see that it helped me, too. Sam was proud of me and happy when I was around. I liked to see him forget, especially when I couldn't, all that had happened to us. It was enough. It was everything.

* * *

I finally see Sam and Cora pull in the driveway. The memory of what we meant to each other evaporates like water on a hot griddle. If Sam knows the explosion was an accident, then he's the most unforgiving bastard on the planet. I'm sick with it. The brother I love is destroying me by not giving me a chance to redeem myself. I've suffered and grieved in a world of loneliness. If he could meet me a little, forgive me just a little....

I realize my hands are trembling and jam them in my pockets.

And what about this turnaround with Cora? I keep replaying it over and over in my mind, the phone conversation with her. She didn't even sound frightened. She said he'd been fair, decent. What does that mean? Was he more than decent? Did he decide to seduce her, to hurt me? It seems almost logical. He's a big, good-looking guy. Suppose he turned on the charm, and convinced her I was dangerous. I remember him as a 17-year-old, with girls hanging on him. *Just how decent was he?*

I'm very unsettled. Disturbed. I'm hoping against hope that Cora will fling herself into my arms and that I can comfort her, reassure her, make things okay. I guess I'll have to see how she seems. The car door opens and my phone rings.

I swallow. "Sam, what do you want me to do?"

"Meet me."

We both walk to the middle of the yard with stone masks. I tighten the straps of my straitjacket. We stand there for several minutes, grimly looking at each other. I try to organize my thoughts. I know this may be my only chance.

He has the most incomprehensible expression. This is the first time we've looked each other in the eye since Reno, three years ago. I used to always know what he was thinking; now he's unreadable to me. We stand in silence, trying to begin.

"She's an extraordinary person," he finally says. "You do know that? She made me start questioning my entire life, made me feel something."

I swallow.

"I want you to know, if you hurt her, I'll make it my mission in life to end yours."

"Sam. I love her. I'd never hurt her."

"If I didn't believe that, I wouldn't be here, and she'd be on the other side of the planet. But you've been capable of doing bad things to people you love. Just tell me. Are you in control?"

I wince. My whole life is in the tightest control.

"Can't you forgive me, Sam? I was wrong, so wrong. It was all a mistake, a tragic mistake. I lost everything, that day. I lost my brother."

He looks at me for a long time.

My shoulders droop. I see no compassion there. "Sam," I say, "this hatred is destroying your life and mine. Please...."

He shakes his head looking down at the ground. "I'm going far away, as fast as I can," he says. "That's the best I can do, now, for all of us."

"Is there absolutely nothing...?"

"Just take care of her, Paul, for all of our sakes."

I can hear the anguish, the tight control, in his voice. For whom, I wonder?

"I'll try my best to protect her. Always. I promise."

"All right then." He turns to leave.

I reach out in a last attempt to connect and grab his forearm. "Wait, Sam," I say. My voice is cold, a touch of rage. "If you leave like this, that's it. I'll never grovel for forgiveness again. Just be sure. Be very sure. You're not the only one with something to forgive."

"Look, brother," he says, pulling his arm away, finally letting his anger loose. "She's yours now. Make violent love to her on a piano; dance naked in the moonlight. I don't fucking care. I. Don't. Care."

He returns to the car, and opens the door for Cora. He doesn't look at her. He walks her slowly back to me. She's limping and carrying a little garbage bag.

He almost runs back to the car without looking back, climbs in, and slams the door so hard the car shakes. He makes a tight turn into the yard, and punches the gas pedal. The wheels spin in the grass before catching, finally allowing him to make his escape.

As he leaves the driveway, I take one last look at the back of his head. Cora is still standing motionless, watching him, watching me. She's not flinging herself into my arms.

I make a fist around the letter and shove it back into my pocket.

Cora stands at my side. I want to comfort her, but I'm so afraid, I can't look at her. Three days ago, she adored me, loved me, and was my salvation. I believe that if I look into her eyes I'll see doubt, maybe fear.

I know my hands are icy. Finally, I put my arm around her shoulders. "Cora," I say. "I've been so worried. Are you okay?"

She turns to me. "Paul. Please tell me what this is all about."

I pause. "What did he say? What did he tell you?"

She looks up into my eyes. "He said to ask you; that you needed to be the one to tell me."

I wince. I can't help it. I want things the way they were. I want fun and laughter and warm affection. I desperately need that. I hid that so well. I know that innocence is over. I frantically try to figure out how much I need to tell and how much I can keep her from knowing.

"Let's go inside," I say.

Somehow I get her into the house, fumble with a corkscrew, and settle her on the couch with a bottle of wine and two glasses. I fill both our glasses and drain mine in one long swallow. I take a deep breath.

"Paul, tell me. It can't be so horrible."

"Oh, yes it can," I say to myself. If I could be the man I'm pretending to be. If I could make a small joke and pull her to me—kiss her gently. I try.

She takes her hands and puts them on my cheeks and turns my face to hers. "Paul, just start out. Tell me something; start at the beginning."

I know there's almost nothing I can tell her—that I can bear to tell her. I guess I'll start the story; try to tell her about Dad, how much I loved him. Then I'll figure out where I can diverge from the truth. "Give me a minute," I say, as I think back over the point in time that it all started going wrong—and the last point in time that everything could have turned out differently.

* * *

OCTOBER 19, 2001

When I came home weekends, there'd been a lot to deal with, starting with Mom's broken leg. She fell off her bicycle and did a job on her lower tibia, breaking it in several places. It seemed to be healing well and Louise, our neighbor, drove her to doctor's appointments in Mom's old car, an ancient Chevy.

Sam and I were tense around each other. Since we had that fight about my obsession with the war, there'd been a distance. I wished to hell he'd get off my back on that. If he wanted to pretend that Dad's death was in the distant past, fine. But I couldn't forget it. I kept replaying that last day; Dad putting his arm around my shoulder, telling me he was proud of me, how I was going to be a fine man one day. Finally, he gave us all a hug, kissed Mom big-time, slung his olive-green duffle over his shoulder, and was gone.

I kept seeing him walk through that terminal door, over and over, like repeated five-second reruns. Sometimes I sank down on my bed and let the picture go on for a while until I could manage to turn it off. Maybe Sam had a point. On some level, I knew this wasn't good for me, but thinking about vengeance felt so good. I kept thinking that if Saddam Hussein was dead, maybe I could let it go.

But that damn weapons inspector had been trying to tell the world that there weren't any weapons of mass destruction. I couldn't believe that some CNN producer was going to give him his own half-hour special to make his case. Hussein was a murderer, and crazy, and he killed my father.

Dad had been an army engineer, stationed in Kuwait City, just before Saddam Hussein and his army invaded that country. It was peacetime and there was no warning. In the middle of the night, planes dropped bombs on an unsuspecting city and Dad was killed trying to get to the embassy. Of the four engineers, only one young lieutenant survived.

I wanted Hussein dead. Fuck the weapons inspector who stood in the way of the coming invasion.

And my bomb was ready.

I knew where the guy lived, only five miles from my house. I was going to scare the guy off, enough that he'd pull out of the CNN piece. My plan was to place the bomb in a safe place in his neighborhood, then call to tell him when and where. I'd blow it up and warn him not to go on TV, or the next one would be closer to his house.

I was making absolutely sure no one would get hurt, I wasn't that crazy. But maybe I could make a difference.

I heard a noise on the stairs and turned.

"What the hell is this?" Sam said.

"What does it look like, smart guy?"

"It looks like a bomb."

"Bingo," I said. "What do you think about that?"

"What the fuck. What are you doing with that?"

"Why don't you mind your own business, little brother?" I said.

"You're completely over the edge. You're nuts. Someone's going to be hurt or killed. I'm calling the police. And I'm telling Mom!" He turned and ran up the stairs before I could react.

I hyperventilated for several seconds then raced up after him. By the time I reached the kitchen, Sam was yelling and Mom's mouth was open in horror.

"I told you! I told you before! He's crazy! He needs help! What are you going to do about it?"

I staggered into the kitchen and grabbed Sam's shirt. He started struggling, but I pulled his arm behind his back and held it.

"Let me go, you asshole," he screamed. I twisted his arm harder.

"Paul. Paul. Let him go. You're hurting him," Mom yelled.

"Neither of you care," I screamed. "Dad's dead and you just want to forget it. Well, I'm not forgetting it. Someone's going to pay."

Sam managed to struggle free and I shoved him violently away from me. He stumbled across the kitchen into Mom who was leaning on her crutches. They ricocheted together against the counter and Sam fell hard against a sharp corner. Blood started streaming from his head. He leapt to his feet and lunged at me, screaming, "What are you trying to do, kill us both?"

"Yeah," I screamed back. "I want you both dead. As dead as Dad, asshole."

Mom shrieked at the top of her lungs. "Stop! Stop! Stop!"

Everyone froze. We all stood there panting, glaring at each other.

"Just stop," Mom said in a more normal voice.

We all stood immobile for a long time. I started to be able to think. These were the only people who mattered to me on this Earth. I tried to pull myself together. They were scared. I was scared, of myself. I'd been on a treadmill of rage.

Maybe Sam was right; maybe I did need help. At the very least, I could see how worried they were. And I fucking didn't want them to get authorities involved.

They were standing, looking at me, waiting for me to say something, explain something. Minutes passed and I calmed down some more. "You're right, Sam. I've gotten crazy. I probably do need help. You're right."

"You're fucking right I'm right. I should call the cops or the guys with the straitjackets."

"Please, Sam. I'll quit this. I promise. I'll get rid of the bomb stuff."

"Now," Sam yelled. "I want it gone now."

"Yes. Yes. It will disappear tonight."

Sam turned and looked at Mom, "Say something."

She looked stunned. "Paul, I never thought...."

"I'll get rid of it all. I'll do it now. I promise." I looked at Sam; his eyes were filling with tears. I caused that, too. "I'm sorry, for all of this," I muttered, and retreated down the basement stairs.

* * *

I'd gotten all the bomb materials packed neatly in two large cardboard boxes. It seemed a shame. The bomb was ready. It was so simple that I didn't need to test it. It had a simple acid switch. If the acid interacted with the two chemicals—boom. All I had to do was position the thing and run.

I hadn't completely decided what to do next, but I was beginning to see that I needed to give this all up and get help, like Sam said. This was all I'd thought about for months. I'd managed to compartmentalize my schoolwork, and most of my classes were in my major, so I'd kept my grades up. Chemical engineering was so easy for me. It was so logical. I read the textbooks like novels and laughed at the simplicity.

But something had to change. I was sick with how I'd hurt Mom and Sam. I decided to do what I could to reassure them and try to make things right.

The basement door opened. Sam came partway down the old wooden steps and sat underneath the bare bulb.

"How are you?" he said, looking down at me.

"Better. How are you, Sam? I'm sorry."

He nodded. "Yeah, that was pretty bad."

"I'm getting the stuff out of the house tonight. I'll get rid of it permanently. I guess I needed a wake-up-call."

"Are you going to be okay? Mentally, I mean?"

"I'll get help. I promise."

"Okay, then," he said, getting up. "Please. You're the best big brother I have."

"I'm the only big brother you have," I smiled weakly at our old joke.

He nodded and walked up the stairs alone.

I looked at the empty stairwell and wondered where to take the bomb. I couldn't exactly load the boxes on the back of my motorcycle with bungee cords and drive off—plus the bomb material wasn't all that stable.

Then I had an idea. Mom wasn't driving her car because of her leg in a cast and, anyway, the last time Sam checked, her battery was dead. Louise had been using her own car to drive Mom to the doctor's office.

Okay. I'd put the boxes into the trunk of Mom's car until I decided what to do. It'd be fine for a week and in the meantime I'd charge her car battery. Next weekend I'd drive the bomb out in the country, disassemble and dump it—or go ahead with my original plan. I'd have a week to think it over and calm down.

* * *

I look over at Cora, sitting by my side. Her eyes seem older, deeper than I remember. I see sadness there too. I swallow. I search my past for a safe place to start the story. There is no going back. And for the love of me, I can't figure out how we're going to go forward, either.

"Cora," I say in desperation. "Let me tell you about my dad...."

But something is very wrong. When I try to tell her how much I love Sam, how much my life revolves around keeping him safe, I can't pull up the feeling anymore. My brain keeps shifting back to that phone conversation—the one where he told me about her being *cooperative*. Then I hate him. I can't feel the love anymore. I try and try. I feel something different, something cold and sinister.

I look at her by my side and also feel fear—all-encompassing fear. She's not mine anymore, if she ever was. I try to rehearse what I want to say, but can't think of a thing.

CHAPTER 13: SAM

FOR THE PAST FOUR HOURS, I've mostly been breathing in and out. That's all I can manage. I need to face the fact that feeling something can be a lot worse than feeling nothing, in the short run at least. Maybe it's because I haven't felt anything for so long that this is so devastating. I'm waiting for the crushing pain in my chest to get better. I've had to fight throwing up. I feel overwhelming guilt and I'm not sure why.

Maybe I'm sick with what I put Cora through. I'm trying not to think that it was a mistake to bring her back—*for her or for me?* I don't know.

It took me all of a half hour to pack my worldly possessions into my car. I filled three trash bags with everything I didn't need, and threw them in the dumpster. It reminded me of the dumpster behind Cora's apartment. Everything reminds me of Cora. I lock the front door and walk away. I'll send the keys to the landlord and arrange to have the apartment checked out. I know one thing. I can't stay in the same town with her, always looking for her, defining my every movement, letting my shadow existence become even more divorced from living. I need a life of my own.

I throw my old army duffel in the back seat, take a last deep breath, and pull away from the shell of my life in my old beater Toyota.

* * *

I'm driving again after a short nap on the side of the road due to complete exhaustion. I am absolutely not going to think about Cora. I'm going to think about my plan.

I'm moving in the right direction roughly, I think. I should check a map.

I've driven all the rest of the night, stopping twice for gas, and am pulling into a small cafe in East Glacier, Montana, population 600. The town where I've decided to restart my life hovers outside the boundary of Glacier National Park on the Blackfeet Indian Reservation. The choice of this area was easy. I've been here before and spent a summer working in one of the lodges, washing dishes and waiting tables. I've tried to swing by northern Montana on the road to anywhere; the last time was a few summers ago. I know how stunning the area is. The base elevation is much higher than near the coast and winter is approaching faster. Even here, in the foothills of the Rockies, it can take a little getting used to, close to 5,000 feet. Mountain summits rise to well over 10,000 feet, plus we're only 10 miles, as the crow flies, from the Continental Divide.

I'm fascinated by the concept of the Divide. You can stand with one foot where the small trickle of water flows into the Missouri river then on into the Gulf of Mexico, the other foot placed where the water ends up in the Pacific Ocean.

It's a severe climate in the winter, and I moved south when it bothered me. Even smaller places like McMinnville can ultimately make me feel claustrophobic; out here you can breathe. The landscape was sculpted during successive ice ages, leaving steep valley walls gouged out of uplifted bedrock. I've always been able to forget my problems in its dramatic beauty. And besides, it's as good a place as any.

I can do construction if all else fails and I'm good at it. I like doing that kind of work—outdoors, physical, and uncomplicated.

It's not hard turning down offers of beer afterwards; I have a list of excuses. But I want connections, don't I? It's going to take a major effort not to close down and push people away. What's the old idea, just pretend to be someone else, and pretty soon you become that person, more or less? Okay, I'll practice. I'm motivated now.

East Glacier is just as I remember it: no new shopping malls or expansive housing developments. I pull into the crowded parking lot of a local restaurant that I've eaten at in the past. The Wilderness Cafe has been here for generations. The wood of the booths has weathered to a dark chestnut color with green Naugahyde seats that will need replacing again soon. The walls are covered with local art renditions of Glacier Park vistas and wildlife, mostly bears and elk. Most of the waitresses look like they've worked here for decades, and enjoy it. I sit down, order hash and eggs and think.

First, I need a place to stay. My waitress, the only one who looks under 50, brings my order and I ask her if there's a place in town that advertises rentals. She tells me to check out the post office bulletin board and I get directions. It's pretty easy—north end of town and look for the flagpole.

I've decided to try and interact with the locals, so I introduce myself. I tell her I'm new in town and ask her how she likes it here. She says she was born here and just got out of high school. Her uncle owns the cafe and she likes working here, although she's trying to save a little money and move to a bigger town where times aren't as hard. She's a little plump, in a comfortable way, has chin-length blond hair and says her name is Lola. She tries flirting with me, innocently, and smiles a lot when I pay my bill. *There. That wasn't so bad,* I think.

The town is rustic in a relaxed, welcoming way. The commercial area faces the main road and consists of a continuous bank of one-story structures, some with false fronts. The buildings are occupied by small businesses on one side of the elevated railroad tracks. There's a vintage railroad depot where an occasional passenger train stops. Lots of small clapboard houses, built long ago, angle off from the main highway. Many of them have small, well-tended lawns, some with low wooden fences defining the front grassy areas. Fall flowers dot the yards and decorate narrow concrete walkways. Old trees line the residential streets and cast a welcoming shade.

I find the post office easily and find the bulletin board to the left of the door where I find there are three rentals advertised. I pick the most promising one and pull my cell phone out of my pocket. Yes, it's available; a small, unattached one-bedroom, furnished with a country look, three blocks away. Before I leave to check it out, I approach the local postmistress, and I like her immediately.

She's at least 80 years old with curly grey hair with a bluish tinge. I guess they're flexible on age requirements on the Blackfeet Reservation. She's wearing a navy corduroy jumper that's seen better days, and a faded aqua cable-knit sweater that doesn't match anything. She calls me 'honey', and looks like she should be home baking oatmeal cookies. Her name is Lavinia, but everybody calls her Vinnie. She hopes I'll stick around because the town needs new blood. I arrange for a post office box and promise to stop by regularly.

As I drive over to the rental, I'm feeling better. Two blocks down and one block to the left on Meade Street, I pull up to a small, white, clapboard house. I can see the rental behind the house, looking like a converted garage.

The owner is Jack Erickson, mid-70s, and talkative. He has buzz-cut white hair, and I bet he hasn't changed the style for fifty years. He's also lived in the area all his life and was happily married until his wife died last year. He has two kids in their mid-40s who have moved to Missoula and Helena respectively, and three grandkids. He visits them often and may spend a few months with them this winter. He informs me the winters can be harsh and that the road leading into Glacier Park will close for the year after this coming weekend so if I want to see the sights I should hurry and go.

I know he's fishing for information as to why I'm locating here. It's pretty isolated, and not much going on, especially in the winter. I'm obviously a single guy and there's not much here in the way of nightlife. I tell him I'm looking for property and want to start building a vacation cabin to rent out and use sometimes. I'm trying to impress a future landlord and I think I've at least convinced him there's nothing too weird about me.

We walk back behind his main house and take a look at the rental. It's nothing fancy, but homier than I expected, with old cedar paneling and a red calico quilt that I suspect his wife made, consisting of three inch varied red squares, covering the double bed. Jack points out a peek-a-boo view of the mountains from the bedroom window. The apartment includes cable and Internet and a very small kitchen. Jack says it's well insulated and utilities are included. We decide I'll pay two month's rent on a month-to-month basis and I'm in. Jack even has some old sheets and blankets and an extra pillow.

We go back to his house and I pull out my wad of bills. Jack gets the sheets and blankets, we shake hands, and I walk back to the cabin. I turn on the heat and collapse on the bed. I congratulate myself; I've gotten to know three people in East Glacier, Montana. My last conscious thought is that I really like Jack's old, red-checked, flannel sheets.

* * *

When I wake up, it's the middle of the afternoon. I'm disoriented and really thirsty. The kitchen has a few basics, and I throw down two glasses of water. I glance at the snow on the mountains that I can see out the small back window. It's a beautiful sunny afternoon, but there's a chill in the air, and the sunlight has that slanted light of late fall. I decide to drive around and see the area and maybe stop in at a local realtor's office to see what's available.

I've seen the entire town in fifteen minutes or so, just the basic sort of small town, including a crowded grocery, a laundromat and car-wash combination, two or three taverns, two clapboard churches to balance those out, a lumberyard, and a hardware and sporting goods store that emphasized fishing. There are twice as many trucks as cars and most of them are Fords or Chevys. There are a few aging cowboys sitting in chairs outside the hardware store and they watch me, all heads turning together, as I drive by.

I've seen several closed real estate offices, but one has a car parked out front, so I pull in. A paunchy man in his mid-50s staffs the office. He drops his feet off a cluttered desk when I walk in the door.

"Hi there," he smiles. "Come on in. I'm Charley Ruggles, not the actor."

He's said that before, I bet. I have no idea who Charlie Ruggles the actor is. He holds out his hand.

"I'm Sam Thomas." We shake.

"What can I do for you? We're pretty slow this time of year so you have my undivided attention."

"I've recently inherited a small amount of money and I'm looking for some property to build a cabin on," I explain. "I'm temporarily between jobs and have some time on my hands."

"Yeah, half the town is temporarily between jobs," Charlie grins, "and property values are really depressed; the recession, you know. What price range are you looking at?"

I have no idea. "What's a nice five acres on or near a creek sell for around here?"

"Well, the problem with raw land is that you usually have to buy it on a real estate contract and put twenty-five or thirty percent down."

"So what's land going for?" I ask.

"Well, there's land and then there's land," Charlie says evasively. "Realistically, you want something not too far from an access road, especially if you want to use it in the winter. We've got a couple of pieces that are listed for sixty or seventy thousand so that'd be about fifteen or twenty thousand down."

"Ouch," I say. "That wouldn't leave much for a building fund." I hadn't considered owning real estate until late yesterday and know nothing. "I sort of figured it was like buying a car and that they'd finance the whole thing." I'm thinking out loud here.

"Besides that," Charlie informs me, "you really couldn't start building until late spring, the weather here being what it is."

Shit. Maybe I should have gone back to Nevada, I think grudgingly, but I've sort of locked myself in here in case Cora needs me. Like that's going to happen.

Yet I realize, despite all my efforts to wall off thinking about her, that is exactly what I'm hoping. I could let her know if my plans change, but I've sworn not to let myself interrupt her life. On the other hand....

"Hello," Charlie breaks in. "Earth to Sam."

"Sorry," I mumble. "Guess I got lost there for a minute."

"Now wait a second here," Charlie says. "Let me think."

"You know," he continues, "I have an idiot brother-in-law who got himself in a pickle. He's started a cabin up Walker Creek, which dumps into Two Medicine River. It's about eight miles from here and about a mile off the main road. He lost his job six months ago with no prospects."

He looks up to see if I'm following along.

I am.

"The cabin is rough-logs, but weathertight, and you could work on it all winter on the inside. It's on a real nice five acres and I bet he'd let you take over the real estate contract, if you'd slip him $10,000 or so."

"When can I see it?" I respond. There's something like excitement welling up in me. It's been so long since I've been excited that I hardly recognize the emotion.

"How about right now?" Charlie grins.

I grin back.

"We'll have to hurry," Charlie continues. "It's getting dark earlier. Let's take my car; I have four-wheel drive. I'll call Walter and see if it's locked up and get a key if I need to."

"So, do you have family in the area?" Charlie asks.

"Nope, I worked here years ago. Always loved it."

"How many do you want to sleep in the cabin? Do you have a lot of friends who like to hike or fish?"

"Doesn't have to be very big, you know, room for three or four in sleeping bags."

"Got a girl that's going to have to hike in? You'll need a snowmobile. We can get a lot of snow."

"Nope, no one special. Maybe someday."

It takes a long fifteen minutes to get to the turn off, onto Walker Creek Road. Charlie's pretty easygoing, but I'm tense handling personal questions. I've made a spur-of-the-moment decision on this and haven't thought through any details. I must sound like a flake to Charlie and I'm sure he doesn't want to get his family involved if this is going to implode. As he asks more questions, I'm trying to sound stable, but I'm having trouble focusing enough to tell a believable story and I'm still exhausted.

I look absently out the car windows as Charlie drives. The Rocky Mountains rise dramatically off the left side of the road. Far away to the north is the St. Mary's entrance to Glacier National Park and the eastern beginning of the infamous Going to the Sun Road. The mountains are a deep dusky blue in the late afternoon light with a crowning of white snow. The aspen leaves shine so brightly yellow that it makes you squint looking at them, contrasting with the dark green of the fir and pine climbing up the lower mountainsides.

I find myself sighing deeply, over and over. I've been tense for so long and I feel my shoulders relax into a normal posture. Maybe I could be happy here, happier anyway. Maybe I could put all this hatred behind me and find some peace.

Charlie breaks into my thoughts, "Here's the turn, Walker Creek Road. The property starts right after we cross the bridge in about a mile. It's on the right and goes on another 500 feet or so. The land slopes back about 450 feet up the hill to a ridge top with a nice view."

We come around a bend to the left. Low but heavy wooden guardrails line a long, substantial wooden bridge standing far above the creek. Underneath is a trickling stream in an enormous streambed. Flat rocks are exposed and the water meanders among them interrupted by occasional larger pools. Yellow and red leaves are falling in the light breeze and become boats, moving gently downstream.

"Don't be fooled," Charlie explains. "There's almost no water in the creek this time of year, but this baby can become a wild lady in the late spring when the runoff starts."

The roof of the structure is showing through the trees, 200 feet along a gentle switchback trail. The cabin rises from a flat plateau, about 60 feet in elevation above the creek bed. The building is made of caulked six-inch logs, still yellow because they haven't had time to age. The cabin is topped with a steep brown metal roof, and a chimney—made of gray smooth river rocks—leans against the right side of the house. Best of all is a porch, extending the whole length of the cabin, about eight feet deep and covered with the extended roof.

Charlie starts being a realtor. "Yep, this is a really nice place, has real potential. It's about 500 square feet divided into one small bedroom and bath and the rest a common room plus a storage area for gear off the kitchen area. You could even put a loft over part of the area under that tall roof. Come on inside."

The rooms inside exist mostly in Charlie's mind. The floor is rough plywood and rooms are defined inside with two-by-fours. There's no plumbing started and electricity is still in the fantasy stage. A hole in the wall awaits an eventual wood stove. I absolutely love it. My experience in construction gives me a pretty good idea of what I'm getting into.

"Let's go outside and walk so you can see the lay of the land," Charlie encourages.

He's got this *just wait 'til you see this* look. It couldn't be a nicer afternoon, about 50degrees out, perfect for a shirt and my down vest. The trees are second-growth timber, about twelve inches in diameter. There's little rain on the east side of the Rockies so there's almost no undergrowth, which makes for easy walking. The creek sound is diminished this time of year, but gives a subtle background sound as we hike up the trail. As we walk up the dirt path, I can see the ridgeline materializing up another 300 feet or so. I'm wondering what the view will be. Charlie's told me there is one, but it may be in his imagination like the cabin interior. It really wouldn't matter. I love the whole setting of the cabin and the creek and the fact that it's ready to work on this winter.

The land levels off gradually at the top and we step out in the clearing on the ridge and turn around. I can't believe it. The land continues sloping downhill beyond the creek all the way to Two Medicine River, then flattens out all the way to the sharp upslope of the Rockies. The sun is almost ready to set behind the mountains that are navy blue in the early evening light. The first major snow of the year covers the top half of the mountain ridge.

"Pretty nice," Charlie understates it.

I stand there taking it all in. Charlie, the professional realtor, knows when to shut up. We stand there for a very long time. I want it so much I ache.

"Charlie," I say. "Do you really think I could get into this for $10,000?"

"Well, kid," he says. "I just might be able to work this out. My brother-in-law's going to lose it anyway and another brother-in-law holds the real estate contract, which I bet he'd be delighted to transfer to you. Like I said, times are tough."

I have to ask. "How many brothers-in-law do you have around here?"

"Two, both married to one sister. Not at the same time, of course; small town."

I smile back. I really like Charlie.

"What do we do now?" I ask.

"Let's go back to the office and write something up. We need to discuss what Walter had planned for utilities so you know what to consider in the contract. You can come by tomorrow about noon and I'll let you know what's what. Okay? I bet I can get a free dinner out of this if I play my cards right."

* * *

I'm back at my rental after getting a quick dinner at the cafe, the same corned beef hash. I didn't have enough energy to deal with anything else new. I've turned up the heat—it's getting chilly outside, supposed to get down to freezing tonight—and curled up under a new flannel-lined sleeping bag that I got at the hardware-sporting goods store. I'm too tired to even think about unpacking the car.

I'm finally calm enough to try to get a handle on all this. If I can get into this place, it won't completely trash my bank account. I know I'm making important decisions on the fly here, but damn it, this feels so right. I just don't want to make any terrible mistakes. The small inheritance I got from my mom has been sitting unproductively in that bank account for 10 years. Besides, buying a cabin is better than blowing it on a fast sports car or throwing it at loose women.

I'm going to let myself think about Cora. I've been fighting it since I left her. I'm exhausted from not thinking about her. The thing I keep going back to is how terrible and wonderful it felt to hold her in my arms in that stupid rest area and her crying. I really want to go back and kidnap her all over again....

Stop it! I can't do that. She made her choice. Maybe that asshole of a brother can make her happy. But I know I don't want her happy with him. What I want is for her to come and find me, and make me happy. I'm definitely a fucked-up bastard. Surely, I'm not what she deserves now. But maybe I can work in that direction. This seems as good an area as any to try to reconstruct myself. I'll start figuring out details tomorrow.

One thing I do know is that I have to get back in the mainstream with humanity, not lurk out in the fringes as I have for the past 10 years. Well, now I can include Charlie as an acquaintance, at least. That's a total of four people I've met in East Glacier. I wonder when I'll stop counting.

I fall asleep thinking of Cora in my arms. I wish I had a picture of her. That's what cell phones are for, stupid. Why didn't I think to take a picture? Maybe I could sneak back and take a quick snapshot. I tried Facebook, but I'd need to friend her and I don't want Paul to have any connection with me, so I put it off. Besides, I don't want her life to be trivial to me.

This is probably not healthy, but I can't fight it anymore. I dissolve into a variety of fantasies from the past few days.

*   *   *

Twelve o'clock on the nose. Charlie's car is there plus two trucks. I walk in and I can tell by his smile it's good news. And he's not alone.

"Hello, Sam. This is my brother-in-law Walter Roberts and my other brother-in-law Stanley Locklear." We shake hands all around. "Looks like we can all do each other a favor."

Walter is short, round, and a non-athlete if I ever saw one. He says he likes to fish, and I bet he knows all the good fishing holes in the county that are 50 feet or less from the car.

Walter's going to be permanently retired unless they get a new local newspaper that will keep him on as a classified ad person, but I don't think he cares. He says he looks everything up on Craigslist like everyone else.

Stanley, on the other hand, is an outdoorsman. He's married currently to Charlie's sister Roxy. He's got on a faded reddish flannel shirt, with rolled up sleeves, and I bet he's got 20 more at home just like it. He probably gets two new ones every Christmas. He's about 5'9" with a balding, high forehead and a small beard. He has eyes that sparkle with good humor and intelligence. Stanley runs large equipment for hire, bulldozers and backhoes, and even does a little well drilling on the side. We've talked about what needs to be done on the property and Stan can provide heavy machinery to do it. Charlie does a good job explaining the terms of the contract and, with a few minor changes, we all agree. It's about as simple as any land transaction could be. And that's it. We all sign the papers and, barring any title problems, when my money gets transferred to the local bank, I'll be a property owner. I like Walter and Stanley.

"Tell you what, Sam," Charlie offers. "Let's talk some about what needs to be done to get you in, building supplies, before the weather breaks. In three weeks, four on the outside, you'll be getting in and out on a snowmobile. You'll need to get any big stuff delivered by truck soon."

Stanley says, "I'm not busy. Want to go over and talk to Bob at the lumberyard? Then we can see Bill at the hardware store and start making lists of what you'll need. When the property closes, you'll be ready to roll." Then he laughs to himself, "Unless I'm appearing overeager here?" He looks over at me.

"No. It's a good idea," I smile.

Charlie, Walter and Stanley walk me over to the lumberyard. This is probably the biggest thing going on in East Glacier.

Later, as I go to sleep, I realize I've stopped people counting.

*   *   *

I'm using my rental as home base, but what I've accomplished in three weeks astounds me. The brothers-in-laws have rallied around me, probably due to boredom, but I'm grateful. Thanks to Bob Waters, who owns the lumberyard, and Bill Forester, who owns the hardware store, my cabin is stocked with flooring supplies, electrical supplies, plumbing supplies, cedar interior siding, cabinets, a counter top, wood burning stove, stove pipe, nails, screws, and tools. There's so much stuff I have to keep moving it around to clear space to work on various projects, but I'm good humored about it.

There's been a regular caravan of trucks picking up supplies in both Kalispell and Great Falls. No wonder Bob and Bill love me. Bob's wife even bakes me cookies. I have a gas generator hooked up to provide power for light and power tools, plus a pump and a decent-sized interior water tank. I might even have a shower someday if I can figure out how to hook all this up together. The water system is way down the line, and it's possible I was a sucker for a good sales pitch, but I've been assured that it was the deal of the century. Besides, I needed more stuff to trip over.

I have three old wooden chairs purchased at the local thrift store, mostly so my new friends can sit down while they volunteer advice and drink beer. I've purchased a used snowmobile so I can get in and out when it starts really snowing, but it's held off so far. I've been told I can get six to eight feet of snow at the cabin.

I'm most proud that I've made a big effort to get to know people. I go to Peggy's Cafe, a small barebones breakfast place, with decades-old linoleum and waitresses you don't want to aggravate, which is the local boys' hangout. I have breakfast every morning, plus all the coffee I can drink for a dollar-fifty extra while I shoot the breeze before going out to the cabin and working all day. I still have to be a little guarded about my past, but they seem very accepting of people with vague histories and don't pry. I've even been invited over for dinner several times.

The leaves are really falling off the trees now, but I've got the wood stove temporarily hooked up and functional in my cabin so I'm warm while I work. I keep looking out the window for Willie Long's truck. He's one of the morning coffee group at Peggy's. He's blond, six foot three, and attracts women like flies. He's becoming the first real friend I've had since high school.

He's also Vinnie's grandson and shares her generous easy-going personality.

Willie's making a last run out with a table saw before it starts snowing and I expected him a half hour ago. We're planning to get it unloaded and headed back to town before the first big storm of the year hits. The wind is picking up fast and the late afternoon light has suddenly dimmed with the clouds rolling in. It's predicted to be a major storm, with temperatures due to fall 40 degrees overnight.

I haven't been in this part of the country in the winter and am a little apprehensive, but excited, too. It makes you realize what a safety net friends are if things get dicey. I'm working hard on developing friendships. It was tough the first week, but now I can hardly wait to have breakfast with the boys and hear all the local news. I'm volunteering to help my neighbors out on any projects because it's a good, non-threatening way to get to know people.

I hear Willie pull up with his pick-up and I throw on my coat to go down to help bring the heavy saw table up. We'll have to manhandle it up the switchback trail, but it shouldn't be a problem. Willie's built like a linebacker and in top shape.

"Hey, Willie," I yell, running down the hill.

"Sorry I'm late," he calls back. "We had to stow all the canoes for the winter and organize the gear in our storage building. It took longer than I thought."

"Hell, I don't care," I reply. "We can drink my thank-you beer back at my rental or have a few at Carson's. The beer is still in the car."

"Let's go to the Moose," Willie laughs. "Hurry. I'm thirsty."

We untie the rope, flip off the tarp, and slide the table saw off the truck bed. Then we start stumbling and laughing, hauling it up the tight switchbacks. You'd have thought this was the most fun thing to do on the entire planet from Willie's perspective. I've never met anyone who enjoyed life more; it's totally impossible to be depressed around him. It's starting to snow as we reach the porch. We move a couple of boxes, around and throw the saw inside. The fire in the stove is dead for the night so we run for it. It's snowing hard by the time we get back to my car.

"I got the snowmobile tuned up yesterday," I inform Willie. "I'll exchange it tomorrow morning at Jamison's so I can get into the cabin, and I'll leave my car in their outbuilding on the highway."

"It's a good thing you got that load of dry wood on the porch," he says. "Tomorrow you're going to need a fire going before you start working. Your life's about to change from tourist to resident," he grins.

I'm sure Willie's right. This is not like living in downtown U.S.A. You have to pay attention out here. If you don't, you can get yourself in a lot of trouble fast. Not that I'm way off the grid, but I'm glad I have some time living in my rental to observe and learn.

Sometimes, I go three or four hours without thinking about Cora, but the nights can be bad. I'm sure this gnawing longing will diminish. All those years, I didn't crave what I couldn't imagine. Occasional sex aside, what I really want, what keeps me up at night with longing, is intimacy with a desired woman. Okay, and sex, too.

I feel better, though, more normal. I really like my new life, both in East Glacier and my cabin. If only I could stop picturing her here.

CHAPTER 14: PAUL

I'VE HELD IT TOGETHER, barely, for most of the past six months. I've alternated between passion, pretended indifference, and angry fear. And I've had a lot of alcohol. Cora has been progressively horrified. It's become a pattern. I make up my mind to forget the past, hers and mine, and try to make it work on a day-to-day basis.

I pretend to be loving and worry-free and simply appreciate her; then I get frightened, drink too much, and start getting sarcastic about everything. Finally, when she's had enough of that she calls me on it. I accuse her of everything imaginable. She denies it, cries; I beg forgiveness and we start it all over again. I'm sick of it and I'm sick of myself.

I think she's becoming frightened of me. I'd never hurt her, but sometimes my rage scares me, too. I buy wine by the case now and start drinking when I get home from teaching. I got a call from Susan, her best friend, yesterday and she asked me directly what the hell was wrong. She said she's never seen Cora so secretive and tense.

I put her off the best I could. I hadn't had much time to drink before I got that phone call so I sounded fairly reasonable with Susan, but I've been dwelling on that call all day. Damn it. Cora's been talking, or at least her friends have been asking, demanding, to know what's wrong. It's Friday and Cora's coming over and she told me on the phone she wants to talk over our problems. *Fine!*

And she said she wants me sober; that this is important. *Great!* I can do sober—if I have several drinks so I can pretend to be sober.

What a fucking disaster. I love this girl. I should have gone to some mental health clinic. There's a lot of mud to dredge up, a whole lot. Once that door is unbolted, can I ever shut it? Or would it blow out in a rush like a smashed airplane window? If they look at how close I am to losing all my control, they may have to put me away. Shit!

One more drink—then maybe I can face her. I know she cares, or used to. But I keep having waking nightmares of her having sex with my brother. Maybe they're seeing each other? Maybe he lives near here? I know Sam wants to hurt me. That would be the way to do it.

But then I think how loving she is; how she's tried, over and over, to understand and help me when I go to these dark places.

All I ever wanted to do was help and love my family. That's all. I wanted Cora to be family. If I could only have that one thing, I'd dedicate my life to trying to be who she wants, but the harder I try to pull her to me, the more she slips away.

I hear her car in the driveway. One more drink—the bottle's empty. When did that happen? I've only been home an hour. I hear the door.

"Paul? I'm here."

"Come on in, sweetie, sober as a judge."

She takes a close look at me and sighs deeply.

"What?" I say.

"You said you wouldn't drink, Paul. I can't go on like this. I want to help, but I can't keep trying if you won't."

"That sounded like an 'or else'." I slur the words.

"It's—maybe it is."

A sliver of fear lacerates me. "Just tell me, honey, is Sam around? Did you stop off for a little cozy conversation before you got here? Or maybe a more intimate connection?"

"Paul. I've told you over and over. I've never seen him. I've never communicated with him. Never."

I look at her. "Honest?" I slur.

"Honestly, Paul. Please believe me."

"Well, I don't." I make an awkward grab for her and she easily evades me.

"I quit," she says. "That's it. I won't do this anymore. I'm done. It's over, Paul. I'm leaving, for good."

A blinding rage overpowers me. I step over to her and push her hard and she falls against the couch. It horrifies both of us.

She tries to get to the front door, but I block her path. "You're leaving me?" I say with a mixture of terror and anger. "For good?"

"Please, let me by," she says.

Something snaps. I grab her around her waist and start hauling her toward my closet. She starts screaming and kicking, but I'm enraged and she's unable to get free. I grab a handful of my ties and drag her to the bed. I start tying her up to various bedposts, all while she's struggling, trying to get loose.

"Stop it, you—you...." I say.

Even as drunk as I am, I could never call her that.

She's crying and screaming, pleading, promising to stay. I finish and return to my kitchen table for a drink. The bottle's empty and it was the last one.

"I'll be back in 20 minutes," I say, "and then we'll talk about you leaving."

I run out the door and trip and almost fall on my front steps. Damn, I really am drunk. Well, it's only four blocks to the liquor store. I'll drive real slow. I get in my car, make it down the driveway, and turn left. I know the way.

CHAPTER 15: CORA

I STRUGGLE USELESSLY for several minutes, straining, pulling—screaming. Finally, I collapse and try to think. I look up at Paul's ceiling. I'm flat on my back, not even a pillow. I struggle for several more seconds in fury. Damn. The old terror of being tied up comes back. I beat it down, over and over, taking deep breaths, trying not to scream.

I can't believe it. I simply can't. *How in horrible hell did it come to this?*

I figure out the time frame. There's an electric clock on the dresser across from me. 6:30. Okay. Five minutes to the liquor store, 10 minutes max in the store, and five more back here. He should be back by 6:50, 7:00 at the latest. I wish I could straighten my left arm; it's in an awkward position. Okay, that's better. *Damn him. Damn him.*

I look at the clock. It's only been five minutes. I'm furious. When he gets back, I won't say a word. I'll let him untie me and I'll calmly walk out, get in the car, and I'm gone.

But what if he won't untie me?

Okay, I'll plead forgiveness, promise to try harder, say it's mostly my fault, and then when he's relaxed, I'll leave.

Could he be a stalker? I never even thought of the possibility. He's a college professor, for God's sake. I swallow hard.

I look at the clock. It's been 15 minutes—any minute now. I want out of here. I'll do anything, say anything, get away and call him later. I'll be very contrite.

I think about how Paul's been the past few months. He's been emotionally like a ping pong ball. I should have paid more attention.

What's wrong with me? I'd forgive him, over and over. Even though he never hit me, there should have been red flags all over this situation. *Stupid. Stupid. Stupid!*

Where is he? It's been over a half hour. I start to cry. I'm scared.

* * *

It's been an hour and a half and it's dark. Really dark.
I finally stop crying and try to think. Does anyone know I'm here? Who would raise the alarm? I talked to Susan last night and she's given me the weekend to talk to Paul, insist he get help. I told her to let me handle it, and I'd call her Sunday night with a progress report. She even promised to give me that long and not bug me. That's two days and she might not worry for another day or so.

My left shoulder is really hurting again. It's completely quiet here. The house is set off the road in a thick grove of trees.

At least there's heat on. I'm not cold, thank God. He's got to get back here soon.

Apart from Susan, who would get worried? Dad usually calls on Sunday, but it's not a scheduled thing. Sometimes we go for several weeks without speaking. Leslie, my other best friend, is working in Portland. We usually talk or text daily—unless we're very busy. I don't know how long before she'd get worried. Susan is probably my best bet.

I look at the clock. Its red-lit numbers shine out in the darkness; 10:30. It's quiet. I can hear hard rain on the roof. It's a dismally lonely sound. I want to go home. I want my father. I want my mother. I'm so alone. *I want....*

I know who I want, but push it under.

I've dozed from time to time, but I wake up often. I'm not in real pain, but I'd give anything to put my arms down and roll on my side. I'm coldly frightened now. What if he's never coming back? What if he's so out of control that he takes off, leaving me here?

Surely Susan will get worried enough to come find me. I've never thought how dependent I could be on a friend knowing where I am. I never, ever considered that. She's so reliable and she's worried.

I figure by Monday she'll start making noise. She lives an hour away, also near Portland. She'd probably drive down after work Monday.

How long could I live? People are found in earthquakes after 10 days alive. I'm strong. I could probably last a week or more. Surely Susan will find me.

What if Paul tries to kill me? That's crazy, but then this whole thing is beyond belief. Maybe he thinks if I told anybody he'd lose his job and he'd have to kill me. He pushed me, hard. I never thought that was a possibility, either. My God. I start to cry again.

Sam tried to warn me. I allow myself to think about Sam for the first time tonight. I've spent a fair amount of time trying not to think about Sam, but he's broken through.

I shake my head at the situation. Sam had me tied up, too. But not like this. Maybe both brothers are crazy. It's possible. But now, Sam seems like the normal one. He didn't hurt me. Sam didn't leave me. He searched and searched for me in the desert. He didn't drink a drop; he needed all his faculties. He constantly tried to reassure me, to make it better. I mean, maybe he was crazy, too, but somehow he seemed a lot more in control when the shit....

I've spent weeks, months, trying not to remember Sam. I've said to myself that I need to keep that all compartmentalized, keep it a separate issue, try to make it work with Paul. But the subconscious always wins, doesn't it?

Paul acted lovingly, but Sam did the loving thing. I know he didn't want to bring me back, wanted to tell me things that I didn't want to hear about Paul. It's clear now. I can't hold back my feelings any more.

Paul must have felt it. In a crazy twist, this is probably partly my fault. Paul is brilliant, but he's also desperate. He probably sensed my conflict, but was so needy he buried that, too. But it always surfaces. *Oh, hell.*

What I want is Sam. He would understand. At least, I want to try to talk it all out with him. I wonder for the thousandth time how he's doing. Did he make friends? Has he found happiness? He needed to remake himself on his own. We both knew that. He needed the confidence of doing it himself.

What about me? Do I need to make it on my own, too? Mom had confidence in me. My dad leans on me. Where did that person go? I have to find the strength I used to have—if I ever get the chance.

I dissolve in tears.

* * *

He's not coming back tonight. I need to face that. It's completely dark. The clock says 4:00 a.m.

I'm very thirsty. At least I don't have to go to the bathroom. Not yet, anyway.

I can't get my head around this. Paul, who are you? What happened between you brothers?

I thought I loved you. I try to remember you at your most caring. You seemed wonderful in the beginning.

I think about Susan and Leslie. I know I can explain all this craziness, eventually. We're a family, too. But it's hard to imagine any discussions about Paul that would make them understand. They won't want to hear anything redeemable about Paul, not after this.

The overwhelming sadness and waste of it all consumes me. It's not as if Paul couldn't love, but his neediness left me breathless at times. When I tried my hardest to love him, he turned his back—but not in indifference.

I can't get my head around it. What is causing this? What? I realize Sam has the answers. And more. The connection I've fought against so hard and so long envelops me. I want to go to him.

Suddenly, the fear resurfaces. I start thrashing around on the bed. I wrench my arms; kick my legs uncontrollably as far as I can, straining against the ties. Finally, I dig my teeth into my lower lip and let the pain distract me. It works, but I taste blood. I need to live through this.

CHAPTER 16: SAM

I'VE SPENT THE WINTER adjusting to my new life. Many of the people in town have become much more than acquaintances. For the first time in many years, I had Thanksgiving dinner with friends and met their kids. I shared Christmas Day with Vinnie, her son and daughter-in-law and their family, including Willie and his half-sister Tashi. I helped set off the small local fireworks display on New Year's Eve.

This year was the first time in a decade that I've spent much time in rooms with Christmas trees that weren't in restaurants or bars. Everyone seems proud of me. I sense they know that my life hasn't been normal for a long time and I'm so excessively appreciative that it stands out. Also, I never talk about any family or friends, but they don't pry. Just being given a second chance to have an actual life, it's everything.

After New Year's, Vinnie invited me over for a Sunday dinner, just the two of us.

This didn't start out to be such a chest-baring event, but there's something about Vinnie that allows human weakness. Vinnie now knows some of the truth. We've been sitting in Vinnie's warm living room. She keeps the house warmer than I'm used to and it makes me sleepy, especially after a huge meal of chicken and dumplings. We settle in and start telling each other stories.

I'm learning about Vinnie's past. She was born in Oklahoma in 1930, but her family migrated to northern Montana when she was seven, escaping the dustbowl that devastated the south. Her parents managed to acquire a small farm near East Glacier and started farming, harvesting hay and raising cattle. They did fairly well, at least Vinnie never remembered being hungry, and she got a decent education starting in a one-room schoolhouse.

She was smart, but opportunities for women were limited back then, and she married at the age of 20 and had two kids fairly quickly. The man I met on Christmas Day, Willie's father, was one of them.

According to Vinnie, her husband was a good-looking guy with plenty of charm, but had a problem with alcohol. After putting up with him for 10 years, she divorced him, loaned her kids to her parents for a year, and got a teaching certificate. After supporting two kids on her own by teaching for 25 years, she retired to work part-time at the post office in East Glacier.

I ask her if she's bitter about raising her kids all by herself, and she looks at me like I'm crazy.

"Sam," she says. "I've been lucky every day of my life. I had loving parents, enough to eat, an education that allowed me to dream, and I determined my own destiny. What's better than that? I'm not saying there weren't difficulties, even near disasters, but like I said, I was lucky."

"Why do you think luck has so much to do with it?" I ask. "Besides, I always thought you made your own luck."

"Don't you believe it," Vinnie says. "Good luck is never having something terrible happen that you can't overcome.

"How's your luck these days?" she asks, looking at me with the sharpest eyes I ever saw.

And so I start in telling her enough about my past that she understands what I've had to deal with. I don't go into detail about Paul and me. She knows something terrible happened to make me hate him, that I've been overwhelmed with hatred for years, and that I've been trying to overcome it. And I'm starting my way back.

She's proud of me. I get hugs. I think I need someone to feel proud of the person I am, down deep, more than I need air. The last time I felt that emotion was when I said goodbye to my mother the morning she died.

I've come to love Vinnie. It's what I don't say that gets her going. She knows my heart has been touched in a major way, and that's what started this progress; that there is a special girl involved. I want to talk about Cora so much, but how can I tell that part of the story? Vinnie doesn't press me, but she knows enough.

We talk again about hatred, how it can keep us locked in place, how it isolates us from feeling and love and all that's beautiful in the world.

"Keep working on that, honey," she says. "It's the key." She walks me to the front door and turns to me, putting her hand on my arm, "Your luck has turned, Sam. I know it."

I believe her.

I'm still thinking late into the night about what Vinnie said. I've come so far in the past three months since I arrived in East Glacier and allowed myself time to think. If not-hating is the key, and I'm beginning to think it is, then why can't I forgive, if only to help myself? My mind circles round and round. I am better. I know it.

But I'm not at peace.

*   *   *

I stand and survey my accomplishments. It's late March and even a rookie like me can feel the winter weather loosening its tight grip. The bathroom, including the shower, is finished and ready to hook up, along with the kitchen, as soon as I get water. I'm still flushing the john with a bucket of water and showering at Vinnie's or Willie's, but I live here now.

Fortunately, Walter had a small drain field put in last summer. I'll need to drill a shallow well on the property, plus protect the water lines below ground.

Doing the indoor plumbing was the worst. I exchanged friggin' plumbing parts every friggin' day for two weeks, but it's done.

The loft sleeping area was the easiest to construct and I have a double bed up there with a red and blue crazy quilt that Vinnie made. The electrical wiring could have been a problem, except that one of my morning boys is an electrician and he offered to do some basic wiring in exchange for a few days' work delivering firewood, which is his winter occupation.

The downstairs is all one room, except for the bathroom and tiny bedroom which are now drywalled in the back to the left. To the right is the kitchen area and through that, the back door. I've put a few shelves and cupboards in the kitchen and I'd kill for a sink that's hooked up.

I've built a fold-up dining table, hinged to hang down on the wall, and had three more dining chairs donated. In fact, most of the stuff here is donated. I have mismatched glasses, pot and pans, silverware and dish towels, all contributed by my new friends. I feel like the ladies are treating my cabin like an oversized doll house, but it makes me feel valued.

I even have an old brown couch, with the one rip on the right cushion, covered with a green and yellow blanket with "Go Ducks" on it. It's my most prized possession, with the possible exception of my beloved guitar. When my resistance is down, I wrap my blanket around myself and remember.

Bringing the couch in on a tiny trailer, pulled by a snowmobile, was a Kodak moment. The only thing more picturesque was Willie and I hauling in the mattress looped over our heads, a mile through the snow on snowshoes. We could have brought it in on the trailer, but sometimes a man has to do things the more challenging way, and deserve a few beers as a reward. Actually, we had quite a few before we started and it's amazing we didn't drop it more. We laughed a lot, though. Willie kept walking blindly into trees.

My life has settled into a pleasant pattern, and I do some computer work if Steve MacIntyre needs me in the repair shop. I replenish supplies, drop by and see Vinnie, then work on the cabin the rest of the day. Sometimes one of my coffee boys or either of Charlie's brothers-in-law comes out to help.

Once or twice a week, I have a few beers at the Dead Moose tavern which is owned by Carson Hitchcock, who also doubles as the local tattoo artist. He's not very busy tattooing, probably because he's not very good at it.

Sometimes I even pack in my guitar and entertain a bit. I'm not that good, but here they think I'm a genius. Most evenings, though, I stay home and practice my guitar picking, read, and keep the fire going. I'm content and pleased that I chose this place to start over.

When I think of Cora, it's not with the pain of those first months. I believe she would be proud of me. I hope she's happy. I haven't heard a word from her since I gave her my e-mail address and cell phone number, which is just as well. I don't want to be just a friend. A chatty letter about the weather would be painful. Sometimes I notice a girl in town, but they never get beyond being a face in the crowd.

* * *

My plan for today is to go in for breakfast, then stop by the lumberyard to get some more flooring and nails. Then I'll check in with Steve to see if there's work stacking up, and stop by and say hello to Vinnie.

After getting the snowmobile from under the lean-to, I drive to the main road and park it at Jamison's. I exchange it for my car, which is stored in their outbuilding near the highway, and start the eight mile long drive into town.

Several times this winter I've had to wait a day or two for the plows to clear the road. And the temperature bottomed out at minus 31 once last month. But I've made it through my first winter unscathed.

Arriving at the cafe, I settle in solving the world's problems with the boys. I stay longer than usual because some friends I haven't seen for a while are in and I need to get caught up. I finally leave around 9:30 and, after picking up supplies at Bill's, amble over to the post office to see Vinnie.

Just as we start catching up, Pete from the Amtrak station across the main road bursts through the door.

"There you are, Sam. Glad I caught you."

He stops to catch his breath. "Train got in and a girl got off. She collapsed in our waiting room. All she said was, 'Do you know Sam Thomas?' Walter saw you leaving the lumberyard. I hoped you might be here."

It takes me a few seconds to take this in, and then I'm running toward the train station. It's three blocks, across the tracks. I don't even think to get my car. I crash through the door and see a crowd of people surrounding a wooden bench seat. She's sitting slumped over, with her head on her right hand, eyes shut.

It's Cora.

She's as pale as a ghost, hair unkempt, and thinner than I remember. She has circles under her eyes and a big cut all along the length of her lower lip that's only partially healed. I push through the crowd and kneel down in front of her.

"Cora, can you hear me?" I ask softly.

Her eyes flutter open and she looks at me like a rescued drowning victim. Tears well up in her eyes. "Oh, Sam," she says.

"Are you okay?" I ask stupidly. She's obviously not okay.

"Yes. I haven't eaten for a long time. I—I wanted to get here, to find you."

"I'm here. Don't worry about anything. I'm so glad to see you. You're safe."

"Here's some juice," someone offers, and I hold up the bottle to help her drink.

I slide in beside her and support her with my left arm while holding the juice. We sit there looking at each other.

Suddenly, Vinnie pushes through the crowd and takes this all in. "Sam, why don't you take her over to my house until we see how she is?"

That seems right. I haven't even gotten beyond astonishment that Cora's here. I certainly can't put her on a snowmobile.

I throw my car keys to Pete. "Can you go get my car? It's at the post office," I ask.

"Sure thing," he says.

Everyone wants to help. Vinnie says she'll meet us at her house.

We sit there quietly. I want to get some food into her. She's sipping the last of the juice when Pete comes in with the car keys. I help her up and take her to my car. In five minutes, Cora's on Vinnie's couch and I'm smiling at her.

"What sounds good, honey?" Vinnie asks. "You need to eat."

"Soup, maybe, please?" Cora asks.

"Homemade chicken noodle? I have some in the fridge. And how about a muffin with homemade blackberry jam?" Vinnie loves to feed people.

"Really wonderful," Cora says. Her voice is already stronger.

"Cora? Can you stay for a while?" I ask.

"As long as you'll let me," Cora answers.

I have to remember to breathe.

Vinnie is hovering in a nice way. I look up at her. "Thanks, Vinnie. We're okay here. Do you have to get back?"

"I closed the post-office for two hours. It seemed like a national emergency to me," she smiles.

*   *   *

I'm slowly starting to tell Cora a bit about my life here. Most of the soup has been eaten, the muffin and the glass of milk, although it took a while. She had to rest every few bites. Her eyes are drooping and I'm sitting with her on the couch with my arm around her. It's become apparent that Cora needs to rest for a few days before I take her to the cabin. Vinnie won't hear of a motel room and already has Cora's suitcase unpacked in her guest room.

"I've got to get back to work," Vinnie interrupts. "Will you kids be all right?"

"I don't know how to thank you," I say as I get up and give her a hug.

"Sam," she says, "you're welcome to sleep on my couch for a few days until we get this young lady back on her feet."

"You're the best," I say, and she hustles out the door.

I walk over to Cora, help her to her feet, and walk her into the small extra bedroom. I lay her on the bed with the white chenille bedspread and lie down beside her and hold her hand. The old mattress sags a bit, but this feels like heaven.

Finally Cora speaks, "It's a very long story and I'm too tired, okay?"

"You're here and we have all the time in the world," I say quietly.

She smiles and rolls on her side toward me and goes to sleep.

I'm overcome with emotion. I'm so glad there's no one to see me. Something awful has happened and I know it had to do with Paul. I'm overwhelmed with guilt that I gave her back to him. I should have known. People don't change, not really. I'm sick with it.

But she got through whatever it was and decided to come to me. I'm so exhilarated she's here that I want to run around doing fist pumps in the air.

I tuck a blanket around her and watch her sleep. I know I'll make it my mission in life to try to protect her from anything like this again. I know I've just been waiting and hoping. I hope I can begin to deserve her.

* * *

Vinnie's back from work and we're talking quietly in the living room. Without going into any details, I'm trying to explain that I've only known this girl for a few days and that she was in a bad relationship.

"Sam," Vinnie says. "This thing you have may not be very old, but you're involved with each other. It's as obvious as night and day. She went through something real bad, and took all her last energy to get to you, and you certainly don't look like you're sorry she's here."

"Vinnie," I say, "I'll take care of her to my dying day if she'll let me."

"Oh, Sam," she laughs. "You're a goner."

"Don't I know it?" I reply.

* * *

Vinnie's happily basting meatloaf and I'm sitting in an old recliner in the bedroom watching Cora. Her eyes open a crack and she smiles wistfully.

"You're back with the living," I say.

She slowly swings her legs off the side of the bed and holds her head on one hand, testing her lightheadedness. I jump up to steady her as she tries out standing.

"Whoa," she says, "head rush. Do you know where the bathroom is?"

I help her down the hall and into the tiny bathroom. There's something different about her eyes, sadder, older—something.

I want to ask about the bruise on her cheek and the cut on her lip, but I don't know how to broach it. She looks so shaky. I'm hoping she's not sick. Her thick hair is a tangle. I'd love to sit and brush it for her.

"I'm fine now," she smiles.

"I'll wait outside the door, okay?"

"Thanks," she says.

"How are you feeling?" I ask when she opens the door. "Do you want me to help you walk?"

"No, but stay close just in case."

She makes it to the living room couch and sits down. "I bet you're surprised to see me," she says.

"I'm so happy you're here. I can't believe it."

"I want you to know you're under no obligation to me. I didn't know where else to go to get away from questions—to think. My dad's such a...."

"Anyway, I needed a little time to get my strength back," Cora says quietly.

I sit down on the couch next to her and pull her close to me. "You need to know I love you," I say simply. "I've spent the past six months hoping for you to come to me. I can hardly handle my happiness."

She starts to cry, but these are happy tears. She's laughing and crying at the same time.

Vinnie appears at the door. "Dinner," she announces. She looks back and forth between us and starts laughing herself.

*   *   *

We're sitting around Vinnie's table, making small talk. It's comfortable. Neither of us wants to get into the heavy stuff yet. Cora's answering a few of Vinnie's questions about herself. I'm struck with how little I know about this person that I'm in love with. I watch and listen fascinated, like I'm watching a classic movie unfold in front of me.

I get up to wash the dishes. Vinnie doesn't have a dishwasher and I fill the split sink with hot soapy water. It's a small house and I can see them at the table and hear most of their conversation.

Vinnie's going on and on about me—what a wonderful boy I am, how hard I've worked on my cabin, how well I've fitted in with everyone, and how well liked I am. I feel like she's talking about someone who I don't even know, but it begins to dawn on me that I am that person, a part of the community. I feel proud of myself and could kiss Vinnie for making me sound so normal to Cora.

I finish the few dishes and put them on a rack to dry. When I return to the dining room, Vinnie is getting up.

"Well," she says, "I'm off to bed; early day at the post office and I'm old. You kids cuddle as much as you want to. I'll be dead to the world in a few seconds," and she gives me a big wink.

I sit down beside Cora and take her gently in my arms. We sit there for some time, not talking, just being together. This is pure joy and I don't have to give her back to anyone. Every once in a while I pick up her hand and kiss it.

Cora breaks the silence. "I've had a long time to think about things, Sam" she starts out. "I'm trying to put all that's happened to me in some sort of context.

"I believe that what's happened to me, since I went back to Paul, is part of something larger that I can't figure out. I need it explained to me and I need to know what happened between two brothers that started all this. You need to trust me and tell me."

"Do you trust me enough to tell me what Paul did to you? I promise not to go crazy, out of my head, but I need to know."

"What if you can't handle it and I lose you to this? I'm really not sure what I would do if I lost you now."

A spasm of fear passes through me. I take a moment before responding.

"How about this idea," I say. "Let's give this some time. If it drives us crazy, we'll have to get into it, but wait 'til you're ready. You need to get rested and recover a bit. I want to get you healthy enough for the trip to my palatial cabin."

Her eyes darken. "I want that, too."

"All right, then. Let's get you some sleep."

We walk into the guest room and lie down. I hold her until she drifts off, trying not to show her how cold my hands have gotten.

*　*　*

Cora is making a rapid recovery. I'll be taking her to the cabin for the first time. I've been fantasizing over that almost every minute since she got here.

I have all sorts of noble reasons for wanting her at the cabin, but the blunt fact is I've been waiting to seduce her. It's been wonderful at Vinnie's, but it's like feeling up your high-school girlfriend with her parents down the hall.

It's a cold but beautiful day and spring is in the air, although it's still below freezing. I've left Cora in the car at Jamison's and have just returned from turning up the heater at the cabin so she'll have a warm welcome. She's bundled up in everything she brought plus an extra sweater and scarf from Vinnie.

We haven't had any serious discussions yet but it's getting harder to put it off. We both know some pretty horrible things happened. We're both spoiled, acting uncomplicated and happy, but I know it can't last. My jaw hurts from grinning and I find I can laugh out loud without being half-ass drunk.

Cora is eating everything in sight. Sometimes I catch her with food in both hands and tease her about it. She's taken so many baths that I wonder what she's trying to wash away, but bury that thought. I sit and watch her brush her hair. There's a reason so many painters have painted that.

She's so beautiful. Every time I point that out to Vinnie she about doubles over with laughter, like I'm the first guy to ever say that about his girl.

Is she my girl?

* * *

It seems only a few minutes and we're at the bottom of the last roll of the hill approaching the house. I've offloaded Cora so I can get a run at the last bit and park the snowmobile under the lean-to. I slide down the hill to Cora and find her looking awestruck at the cabin. Her mouth is open in wonder.

"I can't believe it," she says. "It's magical."

"Wait 'til you see the inside," I say. I can hardly contain my excitement. Willie and I spent most of yesterday afternoon finishing the flooring, hanging the last lights and final wiring connections, and finally stowing all the extra building supplies in the spare bedroom.

I help Cora up the last hill and open the door. We walk into the front room. I've put the tabletop down and have placed the mismatched chairs around it. The couch with the green and yellow blanket is facing the wood stove that shows the fire through a large glass face. There's a thick wool rug on the floor in front of the fireplace. The new wood flooring looks great and my old guitar hangs on the wall, as do two pairs of snowshoes.

"Welcome home," I smile at her.

"Our own world."

"Yes," I murmur, and take her in my arms. I've waited so long, dreamed about this, given up, then hoped many more times. Before I allow myself to get lost in passion, I take a moment to give thanks for where I find myself, how far I've come.

She's so beautiful, so willing in my arms. My gentle kiss turns harder and more demanding. She doesn't seem to care. The thought crosses my mind that she's been seducing me all along. The passion we began, that night so long ago in Reno, has been lying there, combustible, like firewood stacked, waiting for the match to be struck. It streaks down the grit of the matchbox.

I'm on my back and she's straddling me, her breasts pressed into my hands as she moves on me in an ageless rhythm, on and on, toward the inevitable end.

* * *

We doze together on pillows in front of the fire. I feel desire again. I start to play with her hair, kissing it, moving to her neck, her ear lobe. She moans in response. I glance at her to see if she's coming along with me.

"Don't expect me to stop you," she murmurs. "I can't ever imagine stopping you."

Passion overwhelms me. I'm lost in it. I wrap my hands in her hair. I kiss her lips open with my tongue. I search her mouth, thrusting with my tongue, over and over.

She moans and pulls me against her. I stroke her arms, her shoulders, her breasts. My hands move urgently. I try not to hurry, to build tension, but she wraps her legs around me, pulling me to her. I listen to her sighs, loving them.

My hands move urgently down her belly, between her legs. Her body rises, pushing harder and harder, rubbing against me. I'm crazy with it, helpless. I can't contain my desire any longer. I roll on top of her and bury myself in her. I feel Cora's tension building and breaking around me, surrounding me. I let go and we collapse again into each other's arms.

CHAPTER 17: CORA

IT'S BEEN OVER A WEEK and Sam and I haven't gotten around to any serious conversations. It's too easy to enjoy learning about each other and fixing up the cabin. It's been an untroubled, joyful time—except for me thrashing around in my sleep. Sam keeps asking about that and I've managed to put him off.

My life has been a rollercoaster, for nine months at least, starting with Mom's death. I catch myself sighing contentedly, smiling and hugging my man. That's exactly how I feel, like he's mine and I've known him for months, extending back through that long darkening period with Paul. Sam's open to questions about himself, how he feels, what he's thinking, like he's on a personal journey of discovery and welcomes it.

We're looking forward to tomorrow night at the Dead Moose. Sam's bringing his guitar and I'll hear him play in public for the first time. He says, immodestly, that it can be a real turn on, as if I needed any help in that department. He's going to be supporting the headliner, George Williams, who used to play with a well-known blues band. His friend Willie is threatening to back him up with a tambourine. Dave Miller, his other best friend, will be there to harass him.

Dave is the assistant police chief in charge of the tribal police station centered in East Glacier. It's somewhat unusual for a non-Blackfeet to have that role, but Dave's credentials were so impressive, including 20 years in charge of an army medic unit, that they bent the rules. Plus, he's such a dedicated, quality guy that the whole community has bonded with him.

I'm laughing at Sam doing dishes in a ruffled yellow apron that Vinnie forced on him. He keeps making faces at me and blowing handfuls of bubbles in my direction, when my cell rings.

I glance at the phone to see who it is. "Hey, Susan."

"Hi, pioneer woman. Shoot any cougars recently?"

"No, but I've been thinking about it. How's everyone surviving, or more specifically, how's Jeff? Is he on again or off again?"

"Oh, off. There's really no passion on either side. Listen—I have some news of Paul, from Jeff."

"What?"

"You know that Jeff's majoring in chemistry and knows Paul as one of the associate professors in that department."

"I'd forgotten. So...."

"So, Paul's disappeared; left the department suddenly with a story of his mother needing him, that she was seriously ill or hurt or something. I thought I'd snoop around a little."

"Susan, please, I don't want you anywhere near him. Stay away from him."

"Why? You haven't told me much about your sudden escape to the wilderness."

"No, I haven't told you everything, but you need to trust me on this."

"What if he contacts me to find you? Should I keep it a secret?"

"Yes, absolutely. I don't want him to know where I am."

"You sound scared."

"I'm not scared. Okay, I know I sound frightened, but I haven't told you all that came down and I want to tell you in person after you meet Sam. It's complicated."

"Jeff says even the other professors are worried."

"What about his mother? What's everyone saying about him leaving?"

"Cora? I thought you said Sam told you his mother was dead?"

"I understood she died a long time ago." I give Sam a questioning look.

Sam gives me a *What's happened?* look, and I hold up one finger.

"God, Cora. This is an absolute mess. Should I say anything to Jeff?"

"No. Don't say anything to anyone, even to Jeff. Just ask him to keep listening for any new information.

"Would Paul hurt you or Sam?"

"I don't think Paul means me any harm, but we had a really bad ending."

"Everything I worried about, Cora."

"Yes, you were right about him."

"So now what?"

"I'm trying to figure out if he could find me, but I don't know how."

"Cora, I love you. There's so much you're leaving out. You can trust me."

"I'd trust you with my life, Susan. Things have gotten so far away from ordinary. Just know that Sam is everything I'd hoped he'd be. He's been beyond supportive. He has good friends here. I feel safe. I promise to tell you everything. Soon."

"I'm calling tomorrow. I will 'til this is settled."

"Can you give Leslie a call? Tell her I'll e-mail her."

"Sure. Listen. Someone saw a tall guy going through my trash a few days ago. Could it have been Paul, looking for phone records or an address?"

"Oh, crap. I'm hoping it's not connected, but shred everything if it's connected to me. Call me later, Susan. I really need to talk to Sam."

"Let me know what I can do. I love you."

"Love you, too. Bye." I turn to Sam. "Paul's disappeared."

"When?"

"Right after the quarter ended; right after I left. Jeff is one of Susan's oldest friends from her hometown. He's majoring in chemistry and knows some of the chemistry staff. They don't know anything except that Paul told the department head his mother was very ill and he needed an emergency leave of absence. No one's heard anything else and they had to replace him a week into the new quarter."

"What did you mean when you said to shred something?" he asks.

"One of Susan's neighbors saw a guy going through Susan's trash last week. I'm pretty sure it was Paul. And what about your mother?"

"Paul and I don't have a mother. She died 10 years ago."

"I don't...."

He sighs deeply. "I think it's time you heard the truth about my past, whether I'm ready to tell it or not. Do you think you're strong enough to hear my story?"

"Do you think you can handle mine?" I ask back.

CHAPTER 18: SAM

I'M AFRAID I'VE SEEN the last of carefree Cora, although that was really over when she met Paul.

"I'm more sorry than I can say that I'm not a normal guy with ordinary problems like paying for student loans or something." It's a stupid way to start. She scoots next to me, but her smile dies on her face.

"I haven't thought about this stuff for a very long time," I say, putting it off one last moment.

Finally....

"I was about to start first grade in Glendale, California. Our family lived in a white frame house with huge shade trees in the backyard. My dad's name was Vince. He was tall, a man's man, and there was nothing on earth that he couldn't do. He'd grab me and we'd roughhouse on the lawn, but I remember how careful he was not to hurt me. I'd run full-speed across the yard flinging myself at him and he'd laugh. He was career military and 41 years old in 1990. He'd started as a buck private after enlisting in the Vietnam War in 1968, just after the Tet offensive. He was smart and ambitious and moved up the ranks quickly."

"What did he do in the military?"

"He set his mind on a degree in engineering and the military put him through college at USC. He graduated in 1985 with a BS degree in civil engineering and the rank of captain. He was sent to Panama in 1989, after Manuel Noriega's government was toppled, to help restore water and electricity. I remember looking Panama up on a map with Dad before he shipped out. He told me about the Canal and we put in a pin to mark the spot. I was five.

"He met my mom, Elisabeth, in the late '70s, when she was an army nurse. They got engaged after dating three weeks." I smile at Cora.

"Mom was always putting on funny hats and pretending to be a storybook character or making tents over the clothesline for us. She made the best Halloween costumes by hand out of felt. Paul and I were giant ninja-turtles one year. I adored my mom." My throat locks up and I try to talk three or four times before I give up entirely.

She waits patiently.

I wait until I can finally exhale and take a deep breath, then several more.

"This is difficult," I manage.

We sit quietly for several more minutes.

"Okay," I say. "Paul was a daddy's boy. He wanted to grow up just like him, go into the military and be brave and save the world. Everything was good and bad to Paul, good guys and bad guys. He became totally absorbed in what interested him or he couldn't be bothered to lift a finger.

"The biggest problem Dad had with Paul was convincing him to study things he was bored with. He was bored a lot. He was brilliant."

"His mind works like a three-dimensional chess game," Cora says. "He was two or three steps ahead of me, always. He'd take a complicated problem and outline multiple solutions like a computer. Sometimes he'd say his imagination was a curse."

"He was right, Cora."

She gives me a confused look.

"Paul was my hero. He could do everything better than I could and he always watched over me. Mom was much more relaxed about me, let me fall out of trees, go farther away in parks, that sort of thing. Paul, on the other hand, felt that disaster followed me like a tracker and it was up to him to protect me. God help any kid who shoved me. Paul was in his face with fists raised.

"Our favorite thing was camping out in the backyard all night in the summer. I was never afraid with Paul around. We told ghost stories. Paul would go outside in the dark, pretending to scare my friends and me, moaning like a ghost."

"He must have loved...."

I give her an aggravated look until she stops talking.

"Mom made us bologna sandwiches and gave us a thermos of milk when we slept out. She always put in Cheetos and Hostess Snowballs, you know, the ones with coconut sprinkles, the pink ones and the white ones." I grimace. "To this day I can't think about them without getting sick."

"Those snowballs were disgusting. I was a Twinkie fan myself."

"I'll remember that for our next road trip."

"Go on," Cora says, gently.

"Okay." I take one more deep breath. "I was seven when Dad was deployed to Kuwait in early 1990. We put another pin in the map. He was part of the Army Corps of Engineers and was sent there with three other engineers to plan an upgrade of the Kuwaiti water system. Saddam Hussein had been threatening to take over Kuwait on a number of pretexts, but his actual goal was to control the access to the Persian Gulf and eliminate billions of dollars of war debt owed the Kuwaitis."

"I was too young to understand much except that Dad would be gone until fall and I missed him terribly. On August 2nd, 1990, Dad was there in the initial bombardment when Iraq bombed and invaded Kuwait City. An air battle developed over the urban area and a plane was shot down. It crashed where Dad was. He was killed instantly."

I hold up my hand. I need a moment here. Cora doesn't say anything and I can't look at her. When I can, I say, "Our world collapsed. I remember sobbing in Mom's arms when she told us and I remember Paul sitting there like a statue. He let Mom hug him, but he was never happy after that."

"There was sadness," Cora says. "Several of my friends mentioned it, but whenever I broached that topic with Paul, he'd deflect me. He started telling me about your dad, one time, just after I got back, but he didn't get far. He couldn't. It was too upsetting. And then he started drinking...."

"It's been a long time," I say, "and my memories of that time are pretty fuzzy. I got over the worst trauma fairly soon. I was seven. But it was worse for Mom and Paul. Mom was tough and she had two young boys to make a life for. She put all her energy into trying to make a normal home life for us. The military community helped."

I try to shake off my mood. "Let's stop for tonight," I say. We walk out onto the porch and look out over Walker Creek, which is growing daily with the spring runoff. The mountain air smells of pine and we listen to the song of the river in the dusk for many minutes until I feel her shiver.

It's getting chilly in the cabin and we stand silently for a while in front of the dying fire. Cora moves over and puts her arms around my chest. "Why don't you build up the fire in the fireplace and let's go up to the loft. I bet I can help you focus on something else for a while."

I do as she suggests and we climb the ladder to the bedroom. "Just lie down," she says, "and close your eyes."

"I can do that," I say.

"How's the refocusing going?" she asks in a few minutes.

"Amazingly well," I say.

*   *   *

We're lying in each other's arms. "What are you thinking about, Sam?"

"I'm remembering the time we spent together when I stole you," I grimace. "You were so brave. I still don't understand how you could have been so forgiving. Back then, I mean."

I can feel her smiling in the dark.

"You were so hot," she says.

"No, seriously, I want to know."

"You kept trying to make the situation less frightening for me. I was so scared when you tied my hands, terrified really, and you pulled over the first moment you could to make it better for me and untie me."

I give her a sardonic look. "Yeah. I was a real hero."

"And then you found me when I ran into the desert. I almost died in that heat. You must have searched for hours. When I realized I had more to fear from the heat than I did from you, it was almost too late."

"You didn't really know it, Cora. I could have been your worst nightmare. Spraining your ankle aside, you were right to try it."

Cora rolls onto her side, reaching over to touch my cheek. "You took care of me when you found me, even though you were furious. I was afraid you might have beaten me for trying. That's why I was afraid to call back. When the heat got life-threatening, I was too confused to think."

"The whole kidnapping thing was despicable, idiotic. Did I ever tell you that I was going to call 911 if I didn't find you in that last hour?" I moan into my hands.

She smiles, "I would have loved to hear you explain to the helicopter crew how I got lost. But you found me, I'll never know how, covered with that little blue bath towel in all that desert."

"It was close, Cora. The wind was blowing sand all over you. I'm not sure even the emergency guys could have found you in time. I dream about it over and over. I'm looking for you in the blowing dust and I can't find you." I shudder.

"I remember you saying over and over, 'Thank God! Thank God!'"

"I thought I was just thinking that."

"And then making me scrambled eggs even though you were angry. God. If you hadn't been as caring as you were, I would have been paralyzed with fear. But you know what finally made me care about you?"

I hold her question with my eyes.

"It was after you made me breakfast and we went back to the bedroom. I didn't know what you were going to do to me; you had just your jeans on, remember? When you laid down next to me on the bed, you'd put on more clothes so I wouldn't mistake your intentions — so I could relax and go to sleep."

I smile as I remember.

"Okay, now I've got a question for you," Cora says.

"Hmm?"

"When did you begin to get interested in me?" Cora asks, "I mean, when did I become a three-dimensional person?"

"When did you become more than a helpless victim and sex object?"

"That's not precisely what I mean, but yes."

"I remember exactly when," I say. "I've thought about that a lot. It was when I sat you on that bench by the door, after I carried you into the house covered with sand. You were dehydrated like a prune and half-dead. I was furious that you had put me through all that anxiety, those horrible hours. Not rational, I admit, but true. Remember...?

"I was shaking your shoulders and yelling at you. You were almost comatose at the time. Instead of cowering, you basically told me to stuff it. It took me a while to recognize it, but I was in awe of you, your courage. That's when I started falling in love with you."

Cora shakes her head, "If they made a movie about us, no one would believe it."

* * *

We're sitting at the table finishing Cheerios and toast, early the next morning. It's projected to be the warmest day of the year, spiking to the high 60s. Walking out to the deck, we sit down with large mugs of coffee, our legs dangling over the edge.

"I'm glad it's such a sunny day. It helps with my mood. Are you ready for me to continue?"

"Yes," she says. "I'm anxious, though."

I smile to encourage her, but I can't help her now.

"After Dad was killed, Mom went back to work full time as a nurse. I was in the second grade and Paul was in the sixth grade. I made friends easier, mostly on sports teams. I played mid-fielder in soccer and second base in Little League. If I'd had my wish, I would have quit school and just played soccer.

"Paul also played soccer. He had the killer instinct that I didn't have and would plow through anyone, anytime, for goal shots. The challenge with coaching Paul was getting him to be a team player. He got it, though. He was smart enough to know that was the way to win and winning was everything to him—that and keeping me away from danger.

"He avoided trouble by figuring out the likely outcomes. He was a very strategic thinker and could push any limit right to the edge. I on the other hand messed up continually. Anyone giving me advice,

I had to test it. I had to learn by making mistakes. Nothing serious, but I really gave Mom heart palpitations at times.

"Paul seemed happier with me than with kids his age. He was the acknowledged soccer star as long as he played, but the joy went out of it when Dad died. I think he played just to see Mom happy. The other kids his age were joking around, acting like normal crazy teenagers, and Paul didn't fit in. He finally quit soccer senior year.

"As I grew older, I made my own friends. Paul and I were four years apart and I liked having kids around me constantly. I spent years hanging out in the backseat of other kids' vans, being transported up and down freeways to games."

"Both Paul and I loved it when Mom was in the stands, although she embarrassed us by yelling too loudly." I stop for a second, thinking back. "She had a bright orange sun hat and I'd scan the stands to see if she was there. She'd get there, usually at the last minute, and it would make my day when I saw that orange hat. She said her proudest moments in life were when I'd make a goal, look for her in the stands, and yell from the field, 'That one was for you, Mom.' When Paul hit a grand slam in baseball, she called his fifth grade teacher and had him announce it in class." I smile, remembering.

"Paul was working toward a master's degree in chemical engineering. He became obsessed with the war plans to invade the Middle East, hoping to avenge Dad's death. It started to drive a wedge between us for the first time. My life had moved on in a way his never had. And then 9-11 happened.

"As early as spring 2002, the military focus shifted to Iraq. There was real war fever in the air and Paul couldn't talk about anything else.

"By early summer, the only people standing in the way of public opinion supporting the war were a few vocal weapons inspectors who kept saying that there were no weapons of mass destruction left in Iraq.

"Paul hated one guy in particular who was getting a lot of press coverage. He started talking about shutting his friggin' mouth for him. As he became increasingly obsessed, I tended to avoid him more and more. That weapons inspector was going to go on CNN, and Paul went ballistic. He started talking about setting off a bomb near the guy's house to scare him away from appearing on the special."

"Did you ever think he was serious, about a bomb?" Cora asks.

"Never. Not in my wildest dreams. Not until I found Paul with some bomb materials. He assured me—he promised me—to quit it all, get rid of it."

Cora looks at me. We both know it's coming.

"One day Mom was driving herself to the doctor and she was in a terrible accident. There was a huge fireball. She was killed instantly. I could—I can still imagine her face—in flames."

The horror breaks through. I'm in Cora's arms and I'm gasping. I've never been able to allow this. It's overpowering; an eruption of pain and grief. It all comes rushing back, a tidal wave crushing over me, demolishing me, my beloved mother, the center of my world, all that was warm and good and loving.

The world is spinning and I grab for something to stop the spinning, and it's Cora. I grab onto her like a dying man, taking a last gasp of breath. I need her so much. I know that I'm probably hurting her, but I can't help it. I can't stop crushing her to me and she's saying over and over, "It's okay. It's all right. I'm here. I'm here."

I'm starting to experience the agony that I couldn't allow since the day everything changed for me. Grieving like this feels like water pouring down a waterfall rather than being trapped behind a dam. I can bear it now. I have an anchor to reality, something good left in my life.

In time Cora asks, "How does this involve Paul? I don't understand."

Some of the rage threatens to resurface and I beat it back, attempting to make my voice sound normal. "Paul had been serious about trying to scare the weapons inspector into silence. He had finished the bomb and was storing it in the trunk of Mom's car—after he promised to get rid of it."

"So that was what made the fire so huge," Cora says.

"Mom's car wouldn't have exploded and burned. It was left in ashes."

"But didn't the police investigate the explosion and find traces of bomb materials?"

"The fire was so hot almost no traces were left to examine. The police explained that the old guy, the driver of the other car that plowed into Mom, was hauling fertilizer. That helped explain traces of ammonia, and he had a history of mild dementia, including several recent accidents, so it all seemed obvious. He also hadn't renewed his automobile insurance policy so the only insurance policy in effect was Mom's and she was driving illegally with a cast on her leg.

"Since they were both partly at fault, there was no big settlement and the insurance company let their in-depth investigation slide. I'm sure it was in their financial interest to let the whole thing settle quickly. Paul or I could have fought it, but there were extenuating circumstances."

Cora and I sit there in silence for a long time, both trying to get a grip on the information. I haven't thought about this for so long, it's almost like I'm telling myself the story too.

"Did you know Paul was involved?" Cora asks.

I take a deep breath, and then another, before launching into this part. "Not immediately. It was later at the funeral. I remember sitting there beside Paul in a fog. Lots of people came up to us, patted our shoulders, and said comforting things. I don't remember much."

"It was when we were out at the gravesite after the service. People had drifted away until only Paul and I were left. Finally the way Paul was acting broke through my fog. It was as if we weren't feeling grief the same way. He kept apologizing to me over and over, like it was his fault."

"At first I thought he felt responsible because he was older, and he always felt responsible for everything, but suddenly I got it. It all flew together like a picture puzzle in fast forward. I knew there had been a bomb; I knew it was in the car; I knew it was what caused the explosion and I knew Paul had killed Mom.

"I flung myself at him. I wanted to kill him. I was screaming my lungs out, punching, tearing his hair, kicking, anything I could. But he was bigger and stronger and defended himself until I was blown out. I remember lying on the grass trying to breathe.

"I didn't even think of turning him in to authorities. I wanted him to feel my agony, my sense of loss. I didn't want to look at his face again, ever. I walked away, from school, from him, from my life in LA. I saw him only twice in the past 10 years until I saw him in that park in McMinnville."

"You never mentioned you saw him," she said. "How? Why?"

I take a few minutes to remember that last time. "It was horrible in a lot of ways. He found me through my best high school friend, Castro, with whom I'd stayed in contact. He tracked me down washing dishes at a restaurant. He appeared one night as I got off work, waiting for me in the alley.

"Mom had left us a small life insurance policy plus the accident settlement. He wanted me to know who to contact when I wanted it. He had it written on a piece of paper and held out his hand to me. I stood there. I didn't take the paper—to show contempt."

"He was hurting, Sam."

"I don't want to hear that," I say angrily. "Not now."

My voice has a harsh sound to it as I go on. "Paul said something like, 'Couldn't I let it go? That he was justified at the time....'"

She looks at me, asking the same question silently.

"I told him I hated him. I told him not to find me again. As far as I was concerned, he was dead. I—I punched him. He dropped the paper and walked away. I did pick up that goddamn paper, though. I still feel guilty I did." I look over at Cora.

She reaches over and hugs me with her head on my shoulder. I groan softly. I feel a little relieved, telling her the truth, but sick somehow.

"Where did you see him that last time before McMinnville?"

"It was in the Reno area, not too far from our childhood hideout," I shake my head. "He tried to defend what he had done with the bomb, gave me reasons why he was justified in the first place. That's the main reason why I lost it again. If he had come to me and started with a real apology, some understanding of how he had destroyed our lives, maybe I could have begun to forgive him."

Cora's unwavering support gives me strength. I feel her warm against me, and it lowers my defenses, allowing me an uncomfortable thought.

The look of despair that I remember on Paul's face, when he was lying in the dust in Reno, reminds me of the look he gave me when I stalked off in McMinnville. In spite of myself, that last haunted stare on Paul's face causes me some real concern. I wonder if hating him hasn't been easier than feeling the pain. I look at my life and wonder if I haven't let opportunities be lost, doors be left closed. I wonder if I put a permanent lock on that door.

I admit to myself that I've liked Paul out there, pleading to be forgiven. It was some sort of connection. If he didn't try anymore.... Is that what I want? Really? And that look on his face, of agony and desolation—I don't want him dead—do I?

* * *

We sit there in silence for several minutes and I finally ask Cora, "What are you thinking?"

"A lot," she says. "Forgiveness is hard, maybe one of the hardest things. I have things to forgive and be forgiven for, too. I was about to offhandedly tell you to try to forgive Paul and then I thought of my own situation. I can't forgive Paul either, not yet. But maybe I could wish he got help. And I have something to forgive that's so much smaller and relatively minor. I haven't been able to forgive, either, so why would I expect you to do what I can't?"

I'm amazed. "What else could you have to forgive, to be forgiven for? You've never spoken of that."

She sighs. "It's my dad. When my mom got sick, he gave up. Left me to care for her, pick up the pieces, talk to the doctors. I wanted to be a grieving child and I had to be the parent. After she died, he rushed into a marriage when I was in the middle of mourning Mom. I didn't like the new woman, never gave her a chance. I probably wouldn't have liked anyone.

"I've been mad at him, polite but distant. I never go home. I hardly ever call him. He calls me and I look for an excuse to hang up. I came here, for God's sake, never told Dad about all that happened between Paul and myself. I wanted to punish him.

"I guess I didn't want to give him the gift of sharing my life. Maybe he was doing what we all do; try to avoid pain and search for happiness. I've punished him for that. That's something to be forgiven—isn't it?"

In spite of my hurt, I can feel hers, too. I can feel her dad's loneliness. I sense my perspective changing, some empathy being born. I sit there in silence trying to get a grip on this.

"I think you are a living, breathing human being," I say. "Who can see all of what we are, what we do to others? But maybe we can learn."

"Sam," Cora says. "It's an act of courage when you share a part of yourself that is damaged. If we can trust each other to show who we are, deep down...."

"I tried one time to connect. It was a long time ago. I met a girl one night after playing my guitar in a bar. She was cute, not threatening. I was a little drunk. I took her back to my place and she asked a lot of questions about my life. And I started answering them. She was so vulnerable herself. She had been on the streets for years and wasn't that old. I thought she was like me. We shared a few more beers. I told her some of what happened between Paul and myself. Somewhere along the line I passed out, and when I woke up she was gone, along with several hundred dollars that had been in my wallet."

"Sam...."

"It's okay. I wasn't even that surprised, but that was the last time I opened up to anyone, until you. You've brought me back, given me a chance. I hope like hell I don't blow it."

"I won't let you blow it," she says.

I give her a small smile. I don't feel like dancing in flower-covered fields yet, but I can allow myself the pain of missing my mother. Even more than that, I can start to feel the loss of Paul and what he meant to me. Hatred of what he did is still there, but maybe a part of me can see his face in my mind as we were together as children and be grateful. At least I don't want him bloody anymore. Maybe the gloom of hatred has lightened somewhat. That for me is progress.

I sit there and allow Cora to hold my hand and comfort me. I breathe a heartfelt sigh, and another and another.

I risk a smile at her and she smiles back. "Thank you," I say, "for everything. I can't even begin to count the ways I mean that."

Finally Cora says, "What should we do about tonight? Can you still play? Do you want to?"

"Playing's not hard. It's second nature and the music mellows me out. I guess I feel like doing something ordinary. What do you think?"

"That sounds good to me, too. So, yes, let's go."

"Also, I want to talk to Willie and Dave about Paul disappearing. We haven't gotten to your story yet. What do you think? Should we talk about this alone first? It's up to you."

She mulls this over in silence for a minute, then says, "I think we ought to get their opinion soon. We're both so close to this. I don't have a good perspective."

"Cora, you know him better than I do. Hell, I don't know him at all, or who he's become. Share what you think is reasonable to help them understand."

"I hate to tell them some of this. I hardly know them."

"You know them both well enough to know how reliable and loyal they are. They'd do anything to help and protect you. Also, we might be running out of time."

* * *

We'll have to stop at my old apartment at Jack's to get cleaned up. I rent it for a paltry 75 dollars a month so we have showering facilities until we get water hooked up.

"Let's eat something," I say, "and we'll just have time to get there by 8:00. I'll play a 35 minute set and then we'll pull them off to the side and talk."

Cora hustles into the kitchen to cook and I pick up my cell to call Dave at the police station. He's 40-ish, slender with observant brown eyes, and thick dark brown hair. He lives his life looking for wrongs to right or people to help, making you wish you had a sister so he could be your brother-in-law. He's East Glacier's only tribal policeman, the assistant chief by default. He has the recently retired chief, Lester Harbinger, to call in times of emergency or when he needs time off.

"Chief Miller here," Dave's usual greeting.

"Hey, Dave. It's me, Sam."

"Why aren't you over at the Moose warming up, hotshot?"

"Just checking to make sure you're going to be there to cheer me on," I say. "Also, something's come up with Cora and I could use you and Willie tonight. We need to run something by you guys."

"Willie's coming by in a half hour or so and just try to keep us away. What's up?"

"It'll hold 'til we see your pretty face. Save some Indian Pale Ale for me."

"Not on your life. I've got Les covering for me this weekend and Linda's out of town at her mom's 'til Sunday night. I intend to get shitfaced!"

I grin to myself. Dave never gets shitfaced. He considers himself always on duty.

We get to the Moose with five minutes to spare. I plug into the establishment amplifier for a test note or two and adjust the mike. Willie and Dave are already teasing Cora about how the bar staff will give them all free drinks, but only if I play well. Carson gives me his usual mumbled introduction and I'm on.

Everyone is used to my varied music preferences and I start off with a couple of familiar R.E.M. songs and even a Doc Watson foot stomper. Then I tone things down with a Neil Young cover. With a few beers downed, everyone is in high spirits and I'm pretty damn happy. Cora is glowing with what I hope is pride. Either that, or she's a little drunk, which also works for me.

I move on to one of my favorite blues song, Johnny Flynn's "Brown Trout Blues", and close with one from each of my favorite singer-songwriters, "Penance Fire Blues" by Bobby Long, and a new Sam Bradley song, "Not My Kind." I turn the floor over to George with a nod to the crowd.

Everyone's still clapping when I sit down, and I gratefully accept a large IPA from Cheryl behind the bar. I know George is doing two sets and I suggest we enjoy his music for a while. Cora is looking at me with satisfying adoration and I take a minute to enjoy it. I'm really feeling good and want it to last a little longer. George is exceptional and playing like he's entertaining a big city audience. I put my arm around Cora and we drift along with the music.

After forty minutes or so George takes a break and it gets quiet enough to talk.

"Okay, folks. What's going on with our girl?" Willie starts out.

"Well, you both know some of it," I say. "Cora had been in a relationship with my brother, Paul. I've had a long-standing serious dispute with him. I don't know him at all now. I hadn't seen his face in years and hadn't wanted to. I stumbled onto him with Cora last fall and was forced to deal with my past. Cora got caught in the middle of it."

Willie and Dave look soberly at each other.

"Paul had a dangerous past that Cora had no way of knowing. I only told Cora about it last night. I don't want to say more about that now, but Paul was volatile and unstable years ago. I didn't disclose that to Cora when we first met because it appeared he'd changed. He seemed like a professional guy who had created a good life. She'd been in love with him in a brief relationship and appeared to be happy. I made a decision not to interfere. Cora and I knew very little about each other. I became involved with her before I knew it was happening."

"Is Paul evil? Is he a psychopath?" asks Dave, drawing us back to the real concern.

"No," I say deliberately. But if he's not evil, I think to myself, what does that mean? "Cora, you know him much better than I do. What are your thoughts?"

"I really need to tell you my story," she says. "See what you think. But, no, it's almost like he feels things too much—blows them out of proportion and they overpower him. He's not bad, but he can be dangerous. That's why I want to get your opinions."

"She decided to stay with Paul, and tried to make a go of their relationship," I say. "I had my own problems. I moved here, to see if I could become someone—healthier. She knew where I was, but we didn't stay in touch. I told her if things went bad this was where I'd be."

I take a sip of my beer and continue, "I've spent the past five months hoping she was safe with Paul. But also hoping—well....

"And then she turned up and things had obviously gone very wrong. Cora hasn't shared any details about the past few months before she came here, but now there's a new development. Paul has vanished. He told his department head that his mother was sick, but our mother has been dead for more than 10 years. We're afraid he may be coming here to do harm. Cora's decided to share some details of her time with Paul because we honestly don't know what to do."

Dave breaks in, "Sam, I think we really need to know what caused the bitterness between you brothers. You know it won't go further than this table."

I take a minute, considering....

"All right," I say. "This is a tribute to the trust I have in you guys." I take another swallow of beer. "Paul went crazy, 10 years ago, as a result of our father being killed in Kuwait. He was trying to intimidate someone with a bomb and it went terribly wrong. It was the direct cause of our mother's death. I've never been able to forgive him. He decimated my life."

We all sit there silently for a while. Willie finally says, "The poor bastard. He caused all this heartbreak and destroyed both your lives. I wouldn't want to live in his skin for anything."

I give Willie a shocked look, "Fuck it, Willie. He keeps causing pain and worse."

"Is he all bad, Sam? Nothing to redeem him at all?"

"I don't want to go there, Willie. Get it?" I have trouble controlling my voice.

Willie gives me a hard look, then sighs and nods his head, letting it go.

"Let me say something, Sam." Cora says. "I never even saw him cause anyone anxiety, even students. He was always so considerate, careful to a fault. He pulled back from any confrontation if he could. He tried so hard with me.... You need to hear what happened."

"Are you afraid of him, Sam?" Dave asks.

I never completely thought about that question before. "Yes, I guess I am," I say. "It's that now I have so much to lose. I can't trust him to act rationally. That was the underlying worry, when I brought Cora back...."

"Brought her back?" Dave asks.

"Let's skip that part for now," I say. "I was scared that he would go off on a crazy tangent and Cora would be hurt. Yes, I'm scared. Not for myself, but that people I care about could get hurt—that it could happen again."

We all take a minute, thinking about what I said.

"Cora's going to tell us what happened between her and Paul after I left." I put my arm around her shoulders.

"I'm not a good storyteller like Sam," Cora apologizes.

We'll ask questions if we get confused," Willie says. "Just start off."

She nods. "After Sam left me with Paul, I thought it was going to be fine, just like it had been. There had been a few things before. Not enough to seriously worry me. But now he was changed, nervous and suspicious." She looks down at her hands. "I was different and Paul picked up on it. I hadn't felt the pressure to make a serious commitment in a hurry, but that was what he began demanding."

"Did he know you and Sam were, you know, involved?" Willie asks. "I guess I am confused. Were you involved?"

Cora sighs. "It's difficult," she mumbles and looks sideways at me. I sigh and then nod at Cora. "I mean really complicated," Cora continues. "If you're asking me if Paul had a reason to be jealous, well—some things had happened that changed the way I felt about him. There's blame to go around. That's for sure."

"That's not the truth," I point out. "Cora got caught up in a larger cataclysm than she could possibly have known. I'm not defending her. That's just the damn truth."

"Okay," Dave says. "We understand a lot about extenuating circumstances and we know you Sam. There were reasons for what happened. Go ahead with your story, Cora."

"One more thing and then I'll shut up," I say. "Cora made a definite decision to go on with Paul. We, Cora and I, had no contact, no e-mails, no nothing for six months, until I found her at the train station. It's important you know that."

We exchange tense looks. "Okay, Cora," I say.

"Well," she says. "It was sort of like his imagination was working overtime. He started interrogating me more and more, never believing anything that I said. He...."

Cora stops and can't talk for several minutes.

She starts again, "He'd be okay for...." She stops again, swallows a few times and starts to cry.

"Okay, Sweetheart," Willie says. "We're moving this to my place."

"No, we're not," Dave says. "Your bachelor apartment would scare her to death. Linda's gone and I've got beer in the fridge. That's where we're going."

Cora gives them both a tearful smile and we leave with three sets of arms around her.

CHAPTER 19: CORA

WE MAKE IT TO DAVE'S HOUSE in less than five minutes and regroup in his comfortable living room. I spent the entire drive dreading what I still had to say.

Sam keeps squeezing my hand as we settle in Dave's living room. "Cora, we don't have to do this," he says. "You and I can talk this over and I can fill these guys in later."

"No. No. I feel safe here with you guys. Besides, if you go bananas, Sam, they can handle you."

Now I can see they're all about as worried as they can get. I keep taking deep breaths.

Dave says, "Cora, there is absolutely nothing on this planet we can't handle. We're all strong and we'll all take care of each other. Just take your time."

I look at the encouraging faces and nod. "One thing first—when I was a kid I lived in a neighborhood that was so safe our parents didn't check up on us much. We played hide and seek, cowboys and Indians, the usual. We girls got tied up to trees a lot by the Indians. One evening everyone got called in to dinner and I got forgotten, tied to a tree. I was about seven. No one noticed for an hour or so and it got dark. It took my parents another hour to call around and find out where I was and get me. I was scared to death and never got over the terror of being tied up."

Sam groans out loud. I can guess what he's thinking about. "It's okay. Honestly, Sam, you didn't know."

Dave and Willie gape at us both.

"Anyway," I go on, "Paul and I tried to keep the relationship working. There had been some uncomfortable things earlier in our relationship that I had tried to ignore, but it seemed to get worse and worse. It was as if Paul believed that Sam had told me things—about when they were kids, and he wouldn't believe me when I denied it. He also suspected I cared more about Sam than I did about him. I tried to convince him I wasn't interested in..."

I look at Sam, then continue. "But I was, and I'm sure he could sense some—some connection. I'd tell him that I wanted to be with him, to make it work, and he'd seem to believe it. Then a couple of days later it would all start up again."

"Were you frightened of him?" Sam asks.

"No, not in the beginning. But he started drinking more and more. He'd say things when he was drunk like he'd never let me go and that without me, he'd lose everything he'd managed to put together. By this time my friends were starting to get scared and there were things I couldn't tell them. I was drifting away from him." I look down at the floor. "I was getting more and more scared, and ashamed, too."

"Ashamed?" Sam asks.

"I wanted out, but I was afraid to tell him. He'd sober up and apologize and he'd try so hard to be the old Paul—it almost broke my heart. I started thinking more and more about you, Sam, and then I'd feel even guiltier. I wanted to be sure that if I left it wouldn't destroy Paul, but he kept getting worse."

"Did your friends tell you to leave?" Sam asks.

"When it got very bad, I stopped talking to friends. I was embarrassed with what I'd gotten myself into. They had already been telling me to end it. It was so irresponsible, looking back...." She sighs. "Sometimes when you're in the middle...."

"It's okay, Cora," Sam says.

"No, Sam. It's not okay. He'd started calling at all hours. Checking to see if I was where I said I'd be. I even caught him driving by my apartment several times, very late at night. Once...."

I pause.

"Once what?" Sam asks.

"Once I considered calling the police. I told him that the next day and he almost started to cry."

"Did it get worse then?" Willie asks.

I look at them all. "No. It got better. It was almost as if he was using every bit of his strength to try to be okay. He said he was sorry—that he'd get help with an old problem. It did get better. I assumed he was telling me the truth—about seeing someone."

"Did he ever physically hurt you?" Dave asks.

"Never. But the heavy drinking started up again. That's when I finally told Paul we had to have it out. He was already drunk when I got there. The minute I walked in the door, he started accusing me of God knows what. I'd had enough. I told him I didn't want to continue. He pushed me, hard, and I fell."

Sam's face is black. It's a minute before I can continue.

"I got up and started for the door. He leapt over, grabbed me, and hauled me kicking and screaming to the bed, tying my hands and feet to the bedposts with neckties. He muttered that he was going to the liquor store and he'd be back in twenty minutes. He was already horribly drunk—and raging—out of control."

Sam starts to stand, but I hold his arm with my hands.

"Wait. Wait, Sam. Let me get this out fast. I waited the best I could. He never came back—not for two whole days."

Willie's glaring into space.

Dave's a statue, his face a mask.

Sam collapses back into his chair with his head in his hands. "I let this happen. It's my fault—my fault. I should never have returned you—I should have at least told you the truth."

"Let me finish. When Paul finally got back he had a huge bandage on his head and was greenish white. He was crying as he untied me and saying over and over how he'd destroyed everyone he ever loved."

"It turned out that he'd tripped, stepping up the curb by the liquor store, and he'd fallen, hitting his head on the bumper of a truck. He split his head open and knocked himself cold. They'd taken him to the hospital in an ambulance and he'd been more or less unconscious the whole time. When he came to and remembered me, he left the hospital without permission and rushed home in a cab."

"I was dehydrated and hallucinating a little, but pretty much okay. When he got some water and juice in me, I was able to stand up and walk. I had some abrasions from the ties and my shoulders hurt a lot for a while." She looks at us. "The worst is the nightmares I keep having, but it's getting better."

"How did you get that cut on your lower lip?" Sam asks quietly.

"Please, Sam...."

"Tell me, Cora."

I look at him for a moment and reluctantly say, "When I was alone and getting hysterical, I'd bite my lip and let the pain distract me."

Sam puts his hands behind his neck and moans.

"Don't blame yourself," I say. "Neither of us knew Paul could be out of control like this. When I suspected—I should have left long before I did. Don't go and try to get revenge. I can't lose you. I can't."

"Don't you see, Cora? I should have known. It's what I've been afraid of all along, but couldn't quite get in focus. He can be out of control, dangerous."

I can see Sam taking deep breaths, forcing himself to calm down. Finally, he looks at me, "Don't worry, sweetheart. I'm not that stupid, 17-year-old kid anymore. I'm learning at warp speed now. I'm going to stay in control. I'm staying right here to keep you as safe as I possibly can. You are everything I want in my future, and I'm not blowing it." He leans over and puts his arms around me.

We sit there silently, struggling to manage our emotions.

"Cora," Dave finally asks, "how was Paul when you left? What did he say? How did he act?"

I'm quiet for a few minutes, thinking back. "It was like he had died; that he had nothing left to lose. He didn't plead with me to stay. He knew it was useless. He sat there on the floor mumbling that he'd lost everyone. He kept staring at his empty hands and saying, 'It's over, Sam. It's over, Sam'. I had nothing left to help him. I got cleaned up quickly in his shower and helped myself to some— you know—clean clothes so I could get home. He hadn't moved an inch off the floor the whole time; sat there staring at his hands. I quietly stepped outside and closed the door."

I look at Sam. He doesn't look angry; he looks terrified, sick.

"Cora," he says. "He's going to do something—something big."

I look back at him, scared too. "He has all that emptiness, plus he has to live with all that guilt. How could anyone go on living with that?"

"I'm scared," Sam says, turning to Willie and Dave. "What do you think? How worried do you think we should be?"

"It's hard to figure," Willie says soberly. "He's surely a risk of suicide, but he wouldn't have to disappear for that, unless he went somewhere to.... But we wouldn't know if he has already done something. Do you think you could try to get in contact? Diffuse the despair, hold out a lifeline?"

We're all thinking what has suddenly become unbearable. Sam starts to shake. It's several minutes before he can get control of himself.

"Willie," Sam says, "I finally hear you. For God's sake, I don't want him dead—not anymore. I want him to get help...."

"It seems like he's unrecognizable when he gets in a rage," Willie says. "He might want to hurt Cora for leaving him. As far as we know, he doesn't know Cora came here to be with you, or even where you are. If he does know, or finds out, he might want to kill Sam, or kill you both. What do you think, Dave?"

"The fact that he was violent in the past increases the possibility he might be again. Having a brother seems to have meant a lot to him. On the other hand, if he suspects Cora told you what he did to her, he may completely give up on any chance of being a brother to you. It's hard to know what he'll be thinking after he settles down a bit. I just don't know."

"I'll do anything to protect Cora," Sam says. "Should we leave, go on the run?"

"I think that's a very desperate last resort," Dave says, "always looking over your shoulder. Here, we can get the word out. If we give a description to Vinnie of who to be on the lookout for, the whole town will know in a half hour. We can pass the word that anyone we don't know, who asks about either of you, gets reported to Willie, Les or me. We can notify you and come out and help."

"Should I leave?" I ask. "Would it be better if I lived away from Sam for a while? 'Til this gets settled?"

"No, that won't work." Dave says. "What if you're a target and there's no one to protect you?"

Willie adds, "I agree. I want you both here, where we can all be in this together."

"Tell you what," Dave offers. "Let's get some sleep and we'll meet at your place tomorrow around ten. Willie and I'll bring donuts and we'll talk specifics."

*   *   *

Sam and I are on our way home in the car. He pulls me up against him. Despite everything we've discussed tonight, I feel better. At least we're not floundering alone in the dark. This is bad, and could be horrible, but having Willie and Dave on our side means everything. I know Sam feels the same way.

We haven't said much on the way home. The more I talk out loud about who Paul is, and with all that Sam has told me about their history, the closer I come to understanding and forgiving Paul. But then images come of being tied to the bed....

We know we're vulnerable. I hardly know Willie and Dave, but I trust them, profoundly. I can hardly believe I've been here less than three weeks. Our relationship is new. I feel like my life started when I got off the train.

"Cora?" Sam says. "You were inspiring tonight; telling that horrific story, still holding onto some compassion for Paul. I need to keep my love for you as my primary emotion rather than revenge. For the first time, I believe I'm thinking like a man, not a furious child. I have you to thank for that."

"Don't put me on a pedestal, Sam. I've made mistakes, too."

He starts to disagree, but I put two fingers against his lips. I know I'm right.

We pull up to the base of the hill. It's beautiful in the starlight, bright enough that we can walk up the path without the flashlight.

"I love this place, Sam."

"Our place," he says.

We reach the cabin porch and stand under the roof overhang, leaning on the railing, looking up at the stars. There's one huge star just setting behind the mountains in the park. It's so brilliant you can see a stream of its light reflected in the creek.

"How do you feel about tonight, Cora?"

"I've been doing a lot of thinking—about myself. I have a tendency to see the good in people...."

"That's one of the things I love about you."

"Yes, but when I was tied up, I realized I could die—that trusting people, carelessly, can get you into trouble. I thought I could ignore what could happen—ignore the darkness of human nature. I had all the warning signs and kept coming back for more. That's disgusting. Worse than that, it's stupid."

"Cora, I...."

"Wait. I want to follow this thought. Love should be based on something other than dependence. Not that anyone's perfect, but maybe two mentally healthy people could do better. I want to take better care of myself."

"It's been my struggle ever since I arrived in East Glacier."

"And look at you. You've created a whole new world through force of will. Be proud of that. I am."

"Cora...."

"One more thing. How I feel about myself is not dependent on Paul. God! I'm learning that the hard way."

"I always wanted to know when you considered returning to Paul." Sam says. ""You made the understandable choice, but did you have any misgivings about going back?"

"That decision might have been closer than you think. Not that I wanted to put my life in your hands; of course I hardly knew you. But I was tempted—to pursue the relationship. But if you're asking me was I afraid of him? No. I thought I had time to consider things. It all went downhill faster than I could have imagined."

Sam shakes his head. "I wish I'd had the wherewithal to push those questions then. There was so little time."

"Unbelievable as it sounds now, Paul meant security to me—a father figure. Dad was going off in impulsive directions. Mom was dead. And here was this very attractive college professor that seemed like he adored me and wanted to marry me. He had money, stability, a hot car, and a great job. But there were things I should have seen; our sex life was troubled, he had no past, no close friends. And there was my old impulse to beat a dead horse, to believe if I tried hard enough I could fix our problems. In contrast to you—you definitely have never been a father figure...."

We're quiet together, thinking.

"I have to ask. What happened? Why were you so—so ill when you got off the train?"

"Maybe that's the worst—that I didn't take care of myself. When I got away, I should have immediately called Dad, Susan, Leslie—but I didn't. Somewhere during that whole mess I lost myself. All I could think of was coming out here and putting the problem off on you. It was terrible. I've been trying to come to terms with that. I'm never going to do that to myself again."

"We're going to make it," he says. "Together we ought to be able to fight off the dragons."

I can see him smiling in the darkness.

"Cora, do you feel better now, safer?"

"I feel like I have you and two big brothers looking after me. Despite all that's happened, I feel safe here. And we're all looking after you, too."

"I know," Sam says, a bit sheepishly. "I need it every bit as much as you do. And I have one more question. I did all those horrible things to you, and tormented you for two days. Why did you trust me enough to come here? I can't figure it out."

"Your evolution over those two days was breathtaking. I traced all your decisions over and over in my mind. Every time you could have taken a darker path you fought off the impulse. And you know what else?" She looks over at me.

"What?"

"You moved away from hatred. I saw it. It was one of the most inspiring things that I've ever encountered."

He pulls me inside to the couch and starts caressing me. I love every inch of him. It's very dark inside, just a soft glow of the few remaining embers in the wood stove. The dark enhances the sense of feeling, skin against skin. Our fingers become more demanding as we pull and unbutton each other's clothes.

He whispers his desire.

I give him what he wants. I'm shoved down against the cushions of the couch, primitive need, almost violent. We both want the fierceness. Maybe it's the fear we both feel, the need to up the emotional connection. But on the edge of consciousness, there's a gnawing voice I can't still. *The forces are gathering on the horizon. Stay focused. Pay attention.*

CHAPTER 20: SAM

WE SLEEP IN ON SUNDAY MORNING. I look at the clock—9:30. Cora's still sleeping with a small smile on her face and I hope she's dreaming of me. I slip out of bed and down the ladder to start coffee. It's the time of morning I love best. The sun is just starting to peek over the trees behind the cabin and warm the porch. I settle down and listen to the birds and the sound of the river.

I love to count sounds. I can get to seven or eight if I'm patient. Usually there are two or three different birds, and the creek of course. There are forest sounds, a tree creaking in the wind or leaves fluttering in a light breeze, even a small animal walking in the leaves. We're a mile from the Highway 49 and I can still hear car noise or, if it's very still, the air brakes of a semi, way out on distant Highway 89. Then there's a faint bark of a dog or a cow bawling and occasionally the howl of a coyote or even a wolf. The most special is a distant train whistle. I love that sound. It speaks of far-off lands and adventures around the next bend.

I'm at seven when I hear another soft sound behind me. It's Cora with two coffee cups as she sits down beside me on the deck. She gives me a contented sexy smile and I smile back at her. "Beautiful morning," she says. "What number are you up to?"

"You're eight," I grin. "Looks like you slept well."

"I was dreaming of you," she says. "I'll save the details for later."

"You look relaxed."

"Sam, I feel much better. I'd been holding all that in for a long time. It wasn't that I didn't trust you. I knew you'd be upset and I've loved for you to be so happy. It's been a lovely three weeks here, like a vacation in Never-Never Land."

"I've been happy, too. It's nice to feel so contented. It's like the world was grey and white for the past 10 years and now it's all in Technicolor, like stepping into Oz. I owe it all to you, Cora."

"You silly guy," she says. "You ain't seen nothin' yet." And she attacks me.

"Hey, you guys, get a room," booms Willie, coming up the path from the creek. "Dave's behind me with goodies."

"Hellooo," echoes Dave. "I've been trying to keep Willie out of the donuts for the past eight miles. So far I've only lost one apple fritter."

"I'll put on the sausage and eggs," Cora scrambles up.

Minutes later we're eating like fiends off paper plates on the porch. I'm starved. We all are. "Well, what are your thoughts after last night?" Dave asks.

"For whatever it's worth," I say, "I think this is where we should stay. We're protected here from unexpected things. And we have friends to help and keep watch."

"We need to do everything we can think of just in case," Willie says. "I suppose monitoring the road is overkill, and besides, there's a lot of summer hiking traffic. What do you think, Dave?"

"Well, a deadbolt on both cabin doors is the place to start. A simple monitoring device with a motion sensor when you get the driveway plowed, and you could see the whole length up the hill if someone parks down below. When are you going to get that done?"

"I'll talk to Stanley tomorrow. He's got that big dozer and has offered to do it for a steak dinner. And I'll look for a camera on-line. What else?"

"How about a dog?" Dave asks. "You can't beat a dog as an early warning system."

I glance at Cora and know immediately that's a great idea.

"Vinnie and I'll get on that," she says eagerly. "I love dogs."

"Okay," I say, "just no Pekinese or miniature poodles,"

"Trust me," she smiles. "I promise. A real man's dog."

"What else?" I ask.

"I think we need to get the grapevine network going now." Willie says. "Exactly what do we want to put out and to whom?"

"Everyone in town already knows about Cora and how she was when she first got here," Dave says. "Let it be known that a male stranger might want to do Cora harm. If anyone starts asking about either Cora or Sam, they should let me or Les know ASAP by cell phone or 911. We'll all do a diligent job staying in contact. I think we should talk at least once a day plus each evening. Let us know you're locked up for the night, Sam."

We all think quietly for a few minutes.

"Any distinguishing features," asks Dave. "What does he look like?"

"He looks like me with longer darker hair. People were starting to confuse us before. We look like—brothers."

Cora gives me a look. Even the word produces pain.

Can anyone think of anything else? Dave asks.

"I think that about covers it," I say. "If we make this too complicated, it will only confuse people. Anything else?"

"Just keep a watch out for anything," Dave says, "Anything unusual. Let us know if Paul surfaces anywhere. And try to relax. Most of these kinds of things defuse as time passes and things calm down."

"What about guns?" Willie asks. "Come on, Dave. We need to discuss that."

Dave turns to us both. "How familiar are you both with guns?"

"I don't have one," I say, "but I'm fine with them. I've used both small caliber rifles and target pistols and I know how to take care of them. What about you, Cora?"

"I've shot a rifle several times, but I'm not trained, even in gun safety. I'd need some instruction to be any help. I might panic; I don't know. Do you think we need to do this?"

Dave continues, "Well, forgetting all that's going on, with you living isolated out here, a gun would be a good idea. You may never need it, but it would be a good insurance policy. We have bears and mountain lions here; shooting a gun usually scares them away. You'd want to keep any gun secure, of course. The worst thing would be to have someone steal it."

I turn to Cora. "What do you think? Would having a gun cause you more worry than not having one?"

"No," she replies. "I'd rather have one and be trained to use it."

We look at each other gravely.

"You know him better than any of us, Cora. Could Paul plan to hurt anyone?" asks Dave. "From what you've told us, he never has before that you know of."

After a minute she nods, "It's possible."

"Okay," Dave says. "I have an old 12-gauge pump shotgun I can loan you. It would be hard for you to shoot with any accuracy, Cora, and it has quite a kick. But it would sure as hell scare anyone. And a nice little .38 revolver would cover anything close in. We can have Bill look for a good used one or you could get a new one for $350 or so."

"I'll get on that," I say. "As soon as I have a handgun, we can go out to the gun range and one of you can give us a lesson."

"Okay, Sam. You're going to check with Bill about a handgun. You're also responsible for an outside monitor, and talk to Stanley soon about the dozer for the driveway. Cora, you and Vinnie are on the dog-finding committee. Find one that makes noise. I'll get the shotgun down and clean it and get it out to you.

"Willie, you start telling key people to spread the word on who to be on the lookout for. If it's okay with you, I'll make you officer in charge of gun training. I'll take Tuesday afternoon off and we'll meet here at two. Any questions?"

I feel like saluting. "Guys," I say, "thanks for the professional help. It's relieved our minds."

Dave smiles, "Don't tell Linda I said this. Sometimes I go crazy with the peace and quiet out here. After 20 years of professional excitement, sometimes I feel like pacing and yelling. I resort to reading Westerns with my feet up on my desk. This is more stimulating. Not that I'm hoping for drama in your life, but believe me—this is no hardship."

"Is it lunchtime yet?" Willie asks.

"Jeez, Willie. We just finished breakfast 45 minutes ago," Dave replies.

Cora goes in to make him a sandwich. Willie is always hungry.

"I've got beer in the car," Dave offers, "Linda will be back in six hours and I have to get a few brews down the old hatch."

I feel like the troops have landed.

*   *   *

The guys have left and Cora and I are relaxing on my green and yellow blanket on the riverbank. I don't call it a creek now; it's too big. There were ice crystals along the banks until a week ago, but now the flow is increasing noticeably each day. The water is changing from crystal clear to murky gray-green and if I listen carefully I can hear rocks being scraped against each other in the rising current. Willie says it will grow twice this size by late May.

"How did you make such great friends?" Cora asks, rolling over on her side to smile at me.

I shake my head. "It's amazing to me, too. I've spent the past 10 years on the outskirts of life."

"I think it has more to do with putting yourself out there," Cora says. "I think there are great people all over. We're too busy or self-absorbed to see them. But Willie and Dave are incredible. What are their stories, anyway?"

"Willie was born here. His dad, as you already know, is Vinnie's son and his family moved away when he was 18. But Willie always loved it here and, after a stretch in the navy, he came back to settle down about three years ago."

"Somehow I have trouble seeing Willie in the military," Cora says. "He's kind of an independent thinker."

"I don't think it was a good fit. He says if he never sees another ocean it'll be fine with him. He and his uncle own a tourist business and they do guided tours in Glacier Park."

"He'd be perfect. An affable outdoorsman."

"They'll be doing the first organized tour, the first of June, as the snow melts off on the lower trails. For now, he's working with the park service getting buildings ready for the summer season. Did I ever tell you he has a degree in geology?"

"You're kidding," Cora says. "I mean, I can tell he's smart, but he downplays it."

"He's passionate about the park and combines his interest in geology with his work. And he's one of the calmest people I've ever seen in an emergency. I was with him a few months ago when we came across a bad accident. He had the guy out of the car, lying on the ground with his neck supported, and dialed 911, all in a matter of seconds."

"Perfect friend...."

"He's also shrewd and insightful, but he's so laid back you could miss it."

I close my eyes, lie back, and feel the warm sun on my face. It's been a long winter. A lot has happened since I last relaxed by a river.

I crack my eyes open to glance at Cora, who grins and curls up with her head resting on my arm. Then she closes her eyes too.

"What about girls, you know...?" she asks, finally.

"From what I can tell, he likes playing the field. I think half the girls in Glacier County between 15 and 35 are flirting with him. I've never seen him seriously interested. I expect, when he falls for some girl, the sound of his tree falling will be heard for a hundred miles."

"And Dave?"

"He and Linda have been married for years and wanted kids. They had about given up when she got pregnant last November. He doesn't talk about it much, but when he does, I've never seen anybody so excited."

"What did he do before he was here?"

"He was an army helicopter medic. Some long relaxed evening we'll ask for the whole story. I'd like to know, too. He put in a full career, 20 years, got out, and found this job three or four years ago, about the same time Willie got back in the area. He's sort of a one-man militia here in town. Fits him like a glove."

I'm quiet, thinking about that for a while. Dave told me I could be an uncle, which pleases me hugely; another tie to a normal life.

"So, what kind of a dog do you want?" Cora asks.

"A great big one that licks my hand and loves me all to pieces," I reply.

Cora picks up my hand and licks across the top of my knuckles, looking up at me through her lashes.

"That, missy, can get you into a lot of trouble," I grin.

We start back up the rise toward the cabin and I take one last glance at the river. I swear that it's grown bigger in the hour we spent down here. It's almost frightening.

*   *   *

I'm looking at Cora asleep in the bed next to me. I roll my legs over the side of the bed and put my hands behind my neck. Please. Please, I say to myself. Just let me have this woman, this place, and my friends. This is all I need. I wish Paul could have some of this, too. It would solve a lot of my problems.

And, reluctantly, I'm starting to put myself in Paul's world. I'd like to see him in a warm place, too, not the glacial world he's put himself in. I shiver. It comes to me clearly for the first time that I'm arming myself to kill my brother or prevent him from doing the same to me. I desperately don't want it to come to that. My mind keeps shifting to well-buried times, caring times we shared as kids.

Shit. Where has my head been all these years that I couldn't just give a little?

I've been talking to Stan about the grading job for the driveway. We had already settled on $2,000 to get the well drilled and the trenches dug, with waterlines installed to the house, which was a great deal. And he's agreed to throw in the driveway for free. That is the last of any major expenses on the cabin and I'm pleased. I should still have $15,000 left, give or take.

The weather is supposed to be good all week and we settle on Wednesday, two days from now, to do the driveway. Stan is coming back out with the scaffolding rig to dig the well the following Monday. Fortunately, he has time to get the road in first.

Getting the scaffolding in place is the hardest part of drilling in rough country, which is why we need the driveway. Thursday, or the day after, we should start the actual drilling and it might only take up a few hours depending on underlying soil and rock formations. He's already dug the trenches with the backhoe and has waterlines partially installed, ready to be hooked up, so water is in our immediate future.

Cora and I plan on setting chairs out to supervise the well drill. My head is bursting with all that's going on, and Cora, whose education involves water issues, is looking at this project as an internship in the real world.

Stanley will be out after lunch and should take about four hours to do the job. Then we plan on sharing a few beers and that steak I promised him. I'm eager. I love big noisy machinery and digging in the dirt.

I've already ordered a security camera combined with a motion detector on-line and, as soon as the driveway is done, opening up the view to the road, Willie and I will install it.

I head over to talk to Bill at the hardware store and inquire about a gun since he's also the local gun dealer. Cora and I had breakfast with the boys at the cafe. She's now over at Vinnie's handling the dog search. As I walk into the hardware store, I hear Bill's voice.

"Hey, Sam," he smiles. "Hear you're looking for some security."

Small town, I think. "How'd you know?"

"Dave was in and gave me a head's up. I think I've got just the ticket; nice little .38 revolver that's got some punch to it, but not too much kickback if Cora's going to fire it. Less intimidating than a semi-automatic, too. Chris Stanford just brought it in. It belonged to his dad who moved in with him recently, but he's got two little kids and doesn't want to worry about having it in the house."

Bill pulls it out of a drawer and hands it to me. It feels comfortable in my hand and looks brand new.

"It's been well maintained and I understand Willie's going to give you both some target practice and safety information. Feel free to try it out and have Willie look it over. If you have any hesitation, bring it back anytime. Two hundred ought to cover it and I'll throw in two boxes of ammo."

"Perfect. Thanks Bill,"

"This will fix you up fine, Sam. Dave gave me a description of the guy that might be up to no good. Believe me, we don't want anything to happen to either of you. We're going to have a little staff meeting about this at lunch and we'll all have our eyes open. And I'll tell my wife tonight. Evelyn should have it spread all over the county by eight o'clock."

I reach over and shake his hand. "I hope we're all overreacting about this. It'll probably come to nothing, but thanks a lot."

"You bet, Sam. Besides, I can't have anything happen to my best customer, times being what they are." We both smile at each other.

I'm leaving the store with the unusual weight of a gun in a leather pouch and 50 rounds in my jacket pocket. I've also purchased a small lockable gun box that fits in my glove compartment and I can lock that, too. I plan to talk to Willie about how to store the damn thing and be safe.

I'm trying to get in a mental place of being *armed*. Despite the kidnapping event, I'm not naturally aggressive. It doesn't give me pleasure to swagger around. I don't like to drive around with a gun in my car or on a rack in a pick-up. Paul was always the wilder personality. I released that part of myself on the soccer field. I guess I need to ramp up. Our lives might depend on it.

As I walk out the door, I'm accosted by a big, yellow, flop-eared dog that rears up and puts his paws on my chest, nose to nose, panting a mile a minute. And, I swear, he's grinning at me.

"Meet Grover," Vinnie and Cora say together.

I give him sort of a wincing smile and say, "Does he always pant so loudly?"

"He's excited," says Cora.

And Vinnie adds, "He's looking forward to a move to the country."

"This is the best you could find?" I ask.

"You'll love him," Cora gushes. "Really. He'll grow on you. You said you wanted a dog that adores you."

"I had something more subtle in mind."

"He is subtle," Vinnie says. "He's really asking for dinner."

"Okay. Okay," I say. "How did we find this treasure of a dog?"

"Chris Stanford's dad just moved in with him, and Grover kept knocking him over, so they were looking for a new home for him. Grover, I mean."

Chris Stanford must be having a memorable day, I think. "What breed is he?"

"Mixed, I think," says Cora.

I think so, too.

We're all in the car, Cora, Grover, and I, in the front. He's sharing a bucket seat with Cora. We tried putting him in the back seat, but he kept trying to crawl over both of us to get in the front, so we gave up. I imagine this is what having a kid is like.

"Does he bark?" I ask.

"When you're counting sounds, I think you're going to get your first one easily," Cora says. "It's a really unusual sound."

In 15 minutes, we're at the base of our hill. "Okay, let him loose," I say. Cora opens the door and I swear that dumb dog gives us both a grin before bolting over her lap and out the door. He's up the hill and running around the cabin for the third time before we get our gear and stand up. He's sniffing every inch of ground and peeing to mark his domain. Then he flops down on the porch, puts his head on his paws, and gives us a soul-satisfied look of happiness.

"Guess he's settled in," I say.

"Cora, I've been meaning to ask you. When's your birthday?"

"June 1st," she answers. "When's yours?"

"August 15th," I answer back. "The reason I wanted to know is I've bought you a present and I'm trying to decide whether to give it to you now or wait 'til then. It's something we could use now. I've got it stored at the hardware store and can have it brought over any time." I tilt my head at her quizzically, "What do you think?"

"Now," she says.

"Okay, I'll have them bring it out Friday. I have some work to do first at the lumberyard."

We settle in for the day. Cora's going to make banana bread and I'm going to put locks on the doors. The preparations have been completed. The term *quiet before the storm* comes to mind.

*   *   *

It's Tuesday afternoon, the day before the great bulldozer arrival, and I get a text. It's Dave. "Got shotgun. Bring Friday."

Cora's cell phone rings. It's Susan Sherwood, Cora's best friend. Cora listens for a few minutes.

"Well, at least Reno's a long way from here," she says. "Yes, I did spend a few days there a while back," followed by laughter.

I grimace. Cora has told Susan more about that episode than I'm comfortable with.

"That's odd," she says when she hangs up. "Susan had an update about Paul. Seems the college got an e-mail request to forward any print correspondence to a post office box in Reno. What do you think he's doing there?"

I immediately fear that he's trying to pick up a cold trail to me. "He found me in Reno three years ago, remember. Maybe he hopes to find an old connection. I wonder if he could trace me from the rental. I had that landlord return a second set of car keys that I left there, but I sent it to a post office box in Great Falls just to be safe. I only kept it for a month then closed it, but I'd hate to think Paul followed it up. That's only a hundred-some miles from here, and someone might have heard of us."

Cora gives me a wide-eyed look.

"I'll call that guy if I can still find his number on the Internet."

It takes me a few minutes, but I'm able to get the number and dial it. The same guy I talked to before answers the phone. "Hello," I say. "I'm the guy that rented your house last September.... Yeah, that's me. I'm wondering if it might be available again this fall. I'm just starting to make vacation plans. Oh, great. I'll let you know soon. Oh, by the way, I referred a guy from my area to you and I wonder if there was anyone who mentioned me? Oh, there was.... And what did you tell him…? Okay, well, if he tries to get in touch with me, I'm back in Oregon.... Yeah, I'll let you know. Thanks...."

I turn and look at Cora, "There was a guy asking about me. He said he'd talked about the rental with me, but had lost touch, and asked the landlord if he knew where I might be. That was about two and a half weeks ago and the landlord couldn't remember where I'd had him send the keys, but he told him it was somewhere in Montana."

"What does that mean?" Cora asks.

"I'm not sure, but that was right after you came here. Maybe he's not looking any more, but I don't think we can count on it." Suddenly, I'm thinking I'd like to have that shotgun after all.

I look at Cora, "Crap. In some ways I'd like to go and confront him. I hate waiting and not knowing, but even if I wanted to, I don't know where he is."

"It would be good if you could let him know you don't want him dead or miserable," Cora says. "Maybe—if you could defuse some of the anger?"

"I'll think about that. I promise. I hardly know what I want anymore."

"All I want is for you and Paul not to hurt each other. It's spinning out of control."

I'm thinking about what led up to Paul's last desperate act. Cora says she should have left earlier, putting blame on herself. I always disagree. It's all Paul's fault—isn't it? But am I blameless? Haven't I had a part driving him to this desperation now? Am I perfect and he horrible? I'm confused and nauseated by memories: Paul and I sitting on our old rec-room couch watching Indiana Jones movies, him watching every single one of my soccer games, camping out with my idiotic friends. He loved me and I've never given him a shred of forgiveness. I told him I wanted him dead. God!

I look at her soberly. "I need to contact Paul. I'm starting to believe that I should have given him some slack, probably for years. If I could let him know that I understand his point of view, even if I don't want to see him—maybe he can let go, too. And I want to do everything I can to prevent him from coming here. Someone could get seriously hurt." I sigh. "Okay. What's his number?"

"Think what you want to say. If this goes wrong, it could make things worse."

I think a bit. "Okay. How does this sound? I'll tell him I understand that he didn't mean to hurt anyone, and can't we just live our lives."

"Sam, I don't know. You're going to have to say something about forgiving him—and mean it. And what will you do if he loses it, starts screaming at you?"

"Hell, Cora," I say. "I'd probably start screaming back."

We look soberly at each other.

"Give me a minute, okay?"

Several minutes pass. "Yes, I see your point. Yes, I think I can say something like that. I'll try very hard."

"And try very hard to keep calm."

I give her the thumbs up sign. "What's his number?"

She gives it to me. I dial it. I'm pumped. It rings once and a voice comes on to say the number's been disconnected.

Damn.

"Do you know any other numbers that I could reach him at?"

"Yes. Maybe. The college has a hotline number, an inter-administrative number, that's not given out to students. Maybe it still works."

CHAPTER 21: PAUL

I MANAGED TO GET THROUGH the last days of the winter quarter after Cora left. Classes were finished and I had to grade finals and deliver the grades to the powers-that-be.

I was a generous grader. Everyone, if their work was on the fence, was marked up, not down. People don't usually complain if they did better than they expected.

I wanted out of there. I don't think I slept for a week, nor was I completely awake. Just existed in limbo-land inside my house as I tried to think of what to do with my life, or even whether I wanted it anymore.

I know this is all Sam's doing. That first night when he brought her back, she was different. Come on. Did she think I wouldn't notice? In three days she changed from adoring playful Cora to—different.

Fuck them both. My dear brother screwed her. He admitted it that first day. "Cooperative—cooperative—cooperative." The word kept circling in my head, like wheels of a train on a train track, like *The Little Engine That Could*.

I was close. I almost pulled it off. If my brother hadn't found me, maybe I could have made it work with Cora. I tried so hard. Now I need something to leave the house for. I can't stay in here forever. I've run out of ideas.

* * *

I told John Clifford, my department head, that I had an emergency—my mother, on the East Coast with a serious illness. I'd never spoken to him about my personal life and he let me go without too many questions. He seemed concerned.

I have one goal: Find Sam. At gunpoint, he might condescend to talk to me. I need to understand his hatred.

I know I need help. All I can focus on is talking to Sam. At the very least, I want to understand his hatred. I can't seem to focus on anything else.

I tried calling Sam's friend, Castro, the one remaining link to our past. He answered on the third ring. Surprising, really. It had been over three years and the number was still good.

"Hello, Paul."

"Castro, I'm surprised you're still at this number."

"Yeah, well, I'm an old married man now, pretty stable and boring. Tell me, did you ever reach Sam that last time? It's been a few years."

"Yes. I was hoping you were still in contact. It—it didn't go well in Reno. Do you have any idea how I could get in contact with him?"

"No, man, I wish I did. We hung in there for all those years and let it go around the last time you called. He—was still hovering out in no-man's-land. I wish he could get it together. I miss him. We had some great times, Paul. You were the best soccer player I ever saw. I almost lived at your house."

"Thanks, Castro. Are you happy? Any kids?"

"One and a half. Second one's going to be a girl, too. I'm a lucky dude."

"Yeah, Castro, you are."

"Well, wish I could be more help. I know he liked Reno. Maybe you could check some listings down there. Could you let me know if you find him? I'd like to get back together."

"Sure thing."

"If you're ever near Glendale...."

"Thanks, Castro. I'd like that."

* * *

So I went on the road to Reno. Isn't that a song? R.E.M.? Spent a little time there. Even had the department at school fax a contract for the fall semester to me which I signed on the off chance that I can pull myself together in time to teach in September.

I had the Reno idea from some things Cora said before everything went south. I know Sam held her in an isolated vacation rental that he got off the Internet. I pieced together some information that Cora gave me about location and, damn if I wasn't able to find the guy. He admitted Sam had rented the house, paid cash. He also remembered that Sam had left a second set of car keys in the house and he had to mail them to him, "somewhere in Northern Montana," if he remembered correctly.

That was something. I even drove to the house, the scene of the crime. I felt driven to be there, experience what must have happened there. I kept thinking of Sam with my girl there. I can't seem to let that thought go. Somehow, I know they're together. He won—all the marbles.

* * *

So now I'm back in McMinnville. I used to think of Sam, the way it used to be. Now when I think of Sam, I see them together. My phone rings. That's odd. It never rings.

I get it on the second ring, "Paul Thomas, here."

"Paul, it's Sam."

I hesitate while I orient myself to his voice, "Well, Sam. How the hell are you?"

That stops him.

"Paul. I wanted to say—to say I'm trying to understand. I believe you didn't hurt anyone on purpose. I wanted you to know that."

"Well, well? So—you forgive me then?" There's something wrong with my voice. I'm trying unsuccessfully to control my fury. I can feel my eyes narrow. "And where are you, by the way? We could get together, like old times." I imagine his face, with a cold smile on mine.

"Paul, I'm trying here to forgive—so we can go on with our lives; trying to forgive myself, too."

A long pause and then I say, "Wonderful. I feel so much better. What's brought this on, Sam? Do you have a life now? That's just great! And do you have it with Cora?"

Silence.

"Ah," I say. "Is it possible that I might have something to forgive? What happened on your little road trip, Sam? Did you steal my girl? How did you put it? Oh, I remember – 'cooperative.' She was cooperative."

Silence.

"Cat got your tongue, brother? Well, the worm has turned, Sam. The worm has turned. Oh, and before I hang up, that was from Henry VI."

Just before I click off the phone, I hear Sam say to someone, "I don't think that helped a whole lot."

CHAPTER 22: SAM

IT'S AROUND DINNERTIME when Dave pulls up at the bottom of the hill and starts the trek up the path. "I brought out 'Old Betsy,'" he says. "I think the last time she was used in earnest was at the Battle of Bunker Hill."

"Great," I say. "I think we won that one."

At this point we all hear a mournful howl that sounds something like a dying whale.

"Grover's on duty," says Cora.

"My God!" I say. "I wouldn't exactly call that a bark."

"Not exactly what I meant when I said guard dog," Dave says, "but he'll do."

"Yeah" I say. "I think he might love an intruder to death. I'm hoping he at least might knock them over."

"Here's the shotgun," Dave says, handing it over. "I used her last fall for grouse hunting, but I don't like to. I had to keep it pumped because the noise scared everything away, but that might come in handy for you."

"I'll call Willie and tell him we have the guns and try the target range with him. What do you think, Cora?"

"I'm not sure if I can lift it, let alone shoot it. But sure; it looks like it would scare away anything."

* * *

We're awakened early the next morning by a very loud rumbling. I yank on my pants and stumble down the ladder. It's Stanley with the biggest, meanest bulldozer I've ever seen, and he's backing it off a trailer.

"Sorry, guys," he yells. "I got an emergency job this afternoon and want to get this done first. Come on down here and we'll decide where you want the driveway. And what in the hell is that?" he yells, pointing at Grover pawing on his leg.

"Guard dog," I grin.

I run back in the cabin, pull on a shirt and boots and yell at Cora, "Put on some coffee. I'll be working with Stan."

Shit. This is so much fun. I'm marking the road with tape and Stan's coming along behind me, knocking down big trees with the dozer. Thunk. Crash. Thunk. Crash. Thunk. Crash.

By noon it's done. Stan's pushed all the brush and trees off to the side and smoothed over the driveway so it's even and drivable. He's driven up and down several times to pack it down. I'm in awe of his ability. And I can see the road, and everything in between, from the house now.

"Wow!" I say.

"Double-wow!" Cora says back. "It's miraculous!"

Stan yells up, "Keep the steaks frozen." He loads that dozer in two minutes and rumbles away.

*   *   *

I'm cleaning up after an afternoon of woodcutting. I'm buff, but also sore. Even my eyebrows hurt, but I know I'll get used to it. I wince, putting on my clean shirt. "Cora, we're going to have to just hold hands for a while."

"We'll see if you can resist my charms." She gives me a wide-eyed smile.

I'm wondering where I put the Tylenol.

A truck pulls up to the bottom of the hill and Ken, Bill's son, yells up, "Where do you want this?"

It's Cora's birthday surprise. "I'll be right down," I yell. "Let's unload it right over there. See that flat place about 10 feet above the river?"

"Want to see your present?" I ask Cora, and point to the pile down by the river. I hold up a picture of a large wooden swing. "It's going to hang from a wooden frame," I say. "We can sit down by the river and count sounds on it."

I get one of those up-through-the-lashes looks. I'm really going to need that Tylenol.

Willie arrives followed by Dave, and Linda, looking very pregnant.

Dave, Willie and I go down to work on the swing. With Dave's power tools and all that muscle, the whole thing is bolted together in an hour. "Okay," I say, "let the birthday girl through. You too, Linda."

The girls sit down and push off a bit. "This is great," Cora says. "We're never getting off. You guys can start the steaks whenever you want."

The boys and I go up the hill for some beers and sit, legs dangling, on the porch.

"I need to run something new by you guys," I say. "Cora's friend Susan called, and the latest news on Paul is that he'd set up a post office address in Reno two weeks ago."

"That's great isn't it?" Willie asks.

"Not exactly," I sigh, trying to figure out how I'm going to tell them this part of the story. "Um, there's a part of Cora's and my past that you need to know. I want you to hang in with me until I can get this all out."

"Oh, God," says Willie, and rolls his eyes.

I wince back at him, "You remember I told you that Paul was involved in Mom's death. It was worse than that. He hid the bomb in the trunk of Mom's car. There was a traffic accident and it detonated, killing her, plus the driver of the other car. I was seventeen. When I figured it out, I tried to kill him with my bare hands.

"Years passed and—I sort of stole Cora to get back at Paul, and it all went haywire."

After a pause Willie asks, "Um, how do you sort of steal someone?"

"All right," I admit. "I kidnapped her."

Willie and Dave sit there with their mouths open, for a long time. It was a real Kodak moment.

"The bottom line is, I was a really nice kidnapper and we sort of became involved after she escaped." This is sounding weirder and weirder.

Willie and Dave are still sitting there with their mouths open.

"So, anyway," I try to go on, "I took her to a place near Reno to hide her and he's tracked us there and may have a lead here. What do you think?"

At least they've finally closed their mouths.

"So, guys. What do you think?" I finally say again.

"Fuck," they say in unison.

"Come on guys. Do you think he can trace us here?"

Dave takes a deep sigh, "Give me a minute."

He manages to pull himself together. "Barring a witness protection program, I think it's only a matter of time. What was the lead?"

"The guy who rented me the house, where I kept Cora for a few days, told him he sent a set of keys to me, somewhere in Northern Montana, he couldn't remember where. But I had them sent to a PO Box in Great Falls that I kept for a month last fall."

"If he knows you had a post office box in Montana," Dave says, "I think we have to assume he can find a record of that and trace you to Great Falls. And that's getting pretty damn close."

"What do you think about turning this around?" I say. "What if I get in touch with him again and suggest we meet?"

"When did you talk to Paul?" asks Dave.

"It was only a week ago. I had an old number that still worked. I tried to let him know I'd forgiven him but—let's just say it didn't help. He was livid. It was a scary conversation."

"But what if Cora's the target now?" Willie points out. "She left him and we all know he's a lit fuse at times."

We all wince, bad choice of words.

"Oh, hell! I want Cora out of this mess." I look down at her, swinging happily with Linda. "Could we inform any more authorities?" I ask Dave.

"The problem is that he hasn't broken any laws in the past 10 years. He was never charged in the fire incident and he wasn't trying to murder anyone. I suppose you could have him arrested for manslaughter, but it'd be really hard to make anything stick after all this time and you'd be implicated for not reporting it then.

"You could encourage Cora to report the bondage incident, but it would be a terrible thing to put her through, and if she's not a target now she could become one. Besides, you might have to explain kidnapping Cora in the first place."

"So there's nothing we can do?" I ask.

"About the best I can do is talk to my friends, off the record, in Great Falls and have them alerted to the situation, but there's really not much they can do unless you decide to press charges. See if you can download a picture from the college in McMinnville and I'll pass it around. What do you think, Willie?"

Willie nods his head. "I agree, Sam. Let's go out to the gun range tomorrow and get you guys trained. And let me know when the camera stuff arrives and I'll help you set it up."

"I think we've done all the right stuff," Dave says. "Is there anyone checking on him back at the college?"

"Cora has a friend in the chemistry department who has his ear on this. He's the one that found out about the Reno information. He'll let us know if anything new turns up."

"Fine," Willie says. "I'm up for another beer and I'm dying to hear more details about sort of stealing someone. Unbelievable."

"Another time," I grimace. Sometimes I hate Willie's grin. "Maybe when I've known you 50 years."

* * *

We've had our gun lesson with Willie, who's a great teacher. Even Cora feels pretty comfortable handling and shooting both guns, but I friggin' hope she never has to.

The main difficulty is how to keep them safely in the house, but also accessible in an emergency. We've settled on a solid wood cabinet in the kitchen with a coded number lock that we can get access to in about five seconds. We've even practiced that. Willie will give us another session at the gun-range in a few weeks. I think that's the best we can do.

The camera is installed overlooking the driveway with a motion-sensor alarm. It goes off occasionally, activated by deer or Grover on patrol. Grover is one happy dog. He runs around and sleeps and eats. Most of the time he can be found lying on the porch with his head on his paws. He doesn't do his dying-whale sound more than once or twice a day. For a while, we'd both snap to and look anxiously around, but like anything else you get indifferent to it. The typical response now is "Grovvverrr!"

The drilling rig was successfully set up yesterday and we're waiting impatiently for Stan who, along with Walter, is acting as assistant drilling-helper person. Actually, we're all here to watch the action. We've brought an extra chair for the helper and are settling in our seats to watch as Stan pulls in the driveway.

"Big day, huh?" yells Stan, as they walk over.

"I feel like I'm drilling for liquid gold," I reply.

"Have you warned Grover?" Walter asks.

"Nah. Gonna let it play out," I smile.

"I'm so excited I can hardly sit still," Cora says. "I feel like there might be a shower in my future."

"Well, let's get at it," says Stan with a grin. Off he goes to adjust fittings and perform other mysterious activities.

I can't stand it so I walk over to ask questions. In a minute, so does Cora, then Walter, and we totally get in Stan's way. He's good-natured about it, though.

"Everybody ready?" Stan asks.

We give a thumbs-up, a switch is flipped, and the pounding begins. It's faster than I imagined—more of a grinding noise—and dust begins to fly up out the hole. In the modern world, we spend so much time in cyberspace that it's exciting to experience noise, dirt, and vibrations shaking the ground. Even Stan just watches, mostly waiting for anything unusual to happen.

Grover runs over and starts racing around the drilling rig, howling and setting a new standard of noise pollution that makes bizarre harmonic music with the grinding. At least it would, if you were high on something.

After several hours and numerous adjustments later, the noise changes. Stan grins and says, "If you don't want to get wet, you might think about backing up a little."

We run back one hundred feet or so and there's a giant *whoooosh*, just like in the movies, and a hundred foot geyser of water gushes out of the well hole. Cora, Walter and I jump in the air and scream. It's fantastic! Stan's grin gets larger.

By dinnertime the well is capped and connections completed to the pipes leading to the house. We're eating pizza that Dave brought out from town. Willie and I are going to finish connections, and we have planned a formal water ceremony for tomorrow when we turn it on.

We've invited several of Willie's Blackfeet friends from Browning— Win Sanders and Lew Black River—to come along and sanctify the effort. From what Willie says, they're not picky about what gets sanctified, as long as there's food and beer involved. Also, according to Willie, they're good guys to know in a bad situation and you never know when a little extra security might be a good idea. He's given them a summary of what's going on and I understand he has complete trust in both of them. They were childhood friends. They've both said that they're willing to help if things go bad.

Cora and I are also planning on a small private showering ceremony, including a certain small blue bath towel that has special significance.

* * *

It was fascinating getting to know Willie's Blackfeet friends. I'm not sure what I expected, but they both were appealing, fit, and generous in their desire to help. And they had some great stories to tell about Willie growing up. The three of them obviously kept a lot of people frantic over the years.

Lew is a quiet techy with understated intelligence. He runs the computer store in Browning and, when pressed, acknowledges extensive computer savvy. He's as tall as Willie and good looking if you can get beyond his short, do-it-yourself haircut that looks like he shouldn't have. According to Willie, Lew's father died of alcoholism years ago, and an extended reservation family brought him up.

Win is responsible for the large, complex network of volunteer fire department services that protect the entire reservation. He's shockingly photogenic, with flowing black hair down his back, looking noble enough that he should be making a movie somewhere.

He usually wears his hair tied back, Blackfeet style, but lets it flow free when there are women around. Cora had a stunned grin on her face when she was introduced. Win grinned back. Willie had warned me that Win had that effect on women. I saw that he also didn't miss a thing; I sensed layers of complexity and intelligence.

Lew and Win had an overdeveloped fondness for bad quality Indian jokes, but I got the impression I could count on them if things got very bad, and that Willie was extremely proud of his friends. There were situations alluded to that indicated they had helped each other through some hard times. And I could envision all three of them, galloping around on horses, screaming war-whoops in the wind.

*   *   *

Cora's dad calls every couple weeks or so and Cora's started calling him, even making an effort to talk to her stepmother. She says she feels good about that. We've talked about what happened to my parents and it scared her to death. Between the two of us, he's our only living parent.

One bit of good news: A great aunt of Cora's died. Not that that's such good news, but she left Cora $10,000. That's more than enough to finish her degree and we're starting to talk about when and how to do that. The easiest way would be to go back to the college in McMinnville for two quarters. Of course, this situation has to get resolved first.

Cora's birthday is in a week. Susan, her best friend, has told us she'd like to come out for a four-day visit. I'm not exactly anxious, but I get the feeling I'll be checked out. But I'm hoping to get her perspective on Paul; see whether she is as concerned as we are.

There has been no news of him. It's been over two weeks since the Reno connection and I know we're getting complacent. Whenever I leave the cabin, I try to look around carefully, and always scan for Paul's black BMW in town. But I find that I'm starting to forget to do even that. I wish he'd resurface somewhere, anywhere.

The weather has been unusually good. Willie is busy getting ready to start the season's tourist treks into the park. We've hardly seen him since the steak cookout, but he's invited us all, including Susan, for an overnight backpack into the Park. It's an excuse to test his gear and check out one of the lower elevation trails, hopefully clear of snow, up to an alpine lake.

* * *

Today is Monday and Susan is coming in on the train Wednesday morning. Cora hurries in, carrying another armload of extra towels and sheets. "Vinnie is doing spring cleaning at her house by filling ours up. Susan's going to think we're a luxury hotel."

"Sort of Hobbit luxury," I reply.

"She's invited us over for brunch when Susan gets off the train at ten. She's closing down the post office for two hours; another national emergency."

"Great! I know Vinnie will talk me up like I'm God's gift to humanity, which is good because I'm still on probation."

"I've given her a script."

"I also know you told Susan some things about Paul and what he did to you. Does she know everything, how volatile he can be?"

"She knows it all, including the fact that he may be coming here. I tried to warn her away, but when you meet Susan, you'll find out that nothing stops her."

"Is she naturally brave? I'm picturing some sort of Amazonian warrior-type."

"I'll let you be surprised," Cora says.

* * *

It's Wednesday morning and Cora and I are waiting for Susan on the train platform. We hear the train and Cora's looking up at me with a *just wait* sort of smile. I smile innocently back. How bad could she be?

First off the train is a smallish teenager. Then I see she's older than she looks and two squealing females convince me that this munchkin is Susan. She's about five-foot two and lucky to weigh a hundred pounds. I was picturing a tiny pit bull and chuckling when they walk up to introduce us.

"Sorry," I say. "Cora had me convinced that I'd better practice my martial arts skills to survive meeting you."

"She's right, you know," Susan replies. "I'm a holy terror, and I'm taller in four-inch stilettos."

She has pixy cut blond hair, flashing blue eyes, and I like her right away.

We're off to Vinnie's, and are welcomed with blueberry pancakes. Vinnie gushes on and on about how I've singlehandedly saved the town from ruin.

"Come on, Vinnie," I say. "Even Cora doesn't believe that."

"Oh, yes, I do," says Cora.

"Absolutely," Vinnie says. "Besides, you should have seen this young lady when she arrived. Sam about moved heaven and earth helping her to get back in shape."

"Come on," I say. "Talk about something great I've done recently, like my dog-training skills."

"From what I hear from Cora," Vinnie says, "you've been able to train him to sleep more."

"You've heard his howling," I laugh, "so you know that's a significant achievement."

*   *   *

Soon we're drinking ice tea on my porch after an early dinner and Susan's been brought up to date on everything. We're due to meet Willie at the Moose at 7:30 for a few beers and to plan our hiking trip for tomorrow.

Susan has been a pleasant addition. She's a no-nonsense kind of girl with a funny, offbeat sense of humor and nothing fazes her. Plus she repeatedly gushes about my handiwork on the cabin.

"This is a special place, Sam," Susan sighs. "I'm sort of a minimalist and it's got everything compacted, including my fancy guest room."

"Sorry about the rollaway bed. My ex-landlord donated it."

"Are you kidding? I was expecting the floor in a sleeping bag."

"You're easy to please," Cora smiles.

"And the view from the ridge—It's spectacular. I want to watch the sunset up there every night I'm here. How did you ever stumble into this part of the world?"

"I happened by the area years ago as a kid when I worked a summer at the lodge. This time I met one fantastic person after another—my ex-landlord Jack the first day, Charlie the realtor, and Vinnie, who's a national treasure. And it goes on from there."

"It's incredible—your entire story."

"I've been accepted and cared about." I pause. "You're aware of my empty life before Cora fell into it—I'm adjusting to the richness...."

Cora gives me that special look she has.

"Changing the subject," I say. "Cora, have you heard about the new bartender at the Moose; one of Carson's lady-cousins from Missoula. Willie was his usual joking self her first night, and she almost took his head off. He won't even order drinks from her. I can't imagine an intimidated Willie. I can hardly wait to meet her."

"I can't wait to meet Willie," Susan says. "I know he's your best friend, Sam. Cora goes on and on about him. He can't be that great."

"He's been my general contractor on the cabin. But yeah, he's a pretty special guy."

"I'm feeling good about you two," Susan says. "On paper you look a little, well—iffy. And some of Cora's choices in the past have been...."

"Yeah," Cora interrupts and rolls her eyes. "You should talk."

"But the fact that you have all these people helping and supporting you. I'm impressed."

She gives me a big sincere smile, which I return.

"What's your impression of Paul?" I ask. "You know what happened to Cora before she came out here. Just how dangerous could he be? What do you think he's capable of?"

"Give me a minute," she says, frowning and looking off into space.

Cora stares intently into her face, waiting....

Finally she says, "There's nothing simple about Paul. Cora told me in strictest confidence what happened to your mother. It doesn't completely surprise me. Not because he's mean or bad, but because he's so closed off. I've always thought, if he could only talk things over with people, he'd be a lot happier, maybe a lot more normal. I tried, early on, when Cora tried to get us to be friends, but he was so distant. Every time I'd try to get personal he'd close down. It was like he couldn't risk letting me in. I don't think he ever let Cora in either."

I nod. Apparently none of us know the man he is now.

Susan continues, "Now that I understand something about what made him so isolated, I get a better picture. I never saw him be unkind or even normally upset. He was careful not to let anything spontaneous come out. I think I could have liked him a lot if he hadn't hurt Cora. But he needs help—professional help."

"Do you think he could hurt us on purpose?"

"I don't know, Sam. Before this last incident, no. I definitely didn't see that coming. And now he's so isolated. He has nothing. I guess if you're asking me if he could completely lose it and hurt someone, well, I'd have to say yes. He frightens me."

"I guess it was too much to hope for that you would say I was the crazy guy," I say.

"Let me reserve judgment until I've know you more than eight hours," Susan says.

* * *

We pull into the Moose and I see Willie's truck, which has a newly installed canoe rack mounted on top and a newly repainted "Long's Adventures" sign painted on the doors. As we walk in, Willie waves from a back table, far away from the stage, and a very long way from the bartender. We walk over and Willie stands and holds out his hand to Susan.

"Hello. I'm the notorious friend, Willie. And you must be Susan."

Susan reaches up to grasp Willie's hand and smiles. He's close to 6'3"; she's tiny in comparison. We all sit down and I wave at Cheryl for three beers. Willie subtly points a finger at the bartender, rolls his eyes, then cringes. We all gape, including Susan. God. Willie's right.

She's formidable, about 6'4" in cowboy boots, rolled up sleeves, and looks like she spends a lot of time at the gym.

"Not only that," he mutters, "her name is Willamina and they call her 'Willie.'"

Now I'm laughing and Cora and Susan are trying not to. We all sit there enjoying the moment.

"So," Willie says, trying to change the subject, "the weather looks perfect all through the weekend. I know Cora likes to hike, but what about you, Susan?" He looks at her like he'd be surprised if she could hike around the table.

"Well, the last hike I was on was 32 miles along the Cascade Crest Trail last fall. We took it easy and made it a four-day hike. I love backpacking!"

"Well, good," he says, obviously surprised. "Then I'm thinking about the Snyder Lake trail. It's low level enough that the snow should be about gone and we can pack in, hang out at the lake four or five hours, and have a cookout in the evening. I have tents, sleeping bags, and cooking stuff. I got the food tonight. All you have to do is bring clothes and a toothbrush; it's only for one night. I'll handle the 10 essentials, but do you have any rain gear? It's supposed to be beautiful, but sometimes the mountains make their own weather."

I'm impressed with Willie, but this is what he does, after all. We all have good rain jackets and Willie says that'll be enough for a two-day trip.

It will be nice to get away from the cabin, even for an overnight. Thinking about Paul lurking behind every tree has been tiring.

We share a few more beers and become comfortable together. We're spending a fair amount of time describing town characters and intrigue, Willamina's attraction—or lack thereof—for Willie and other world-shattering issues.

Susan starts talking about the cabin and she mentions that she wants to see the sunset from the ridge. The sun doesn't set for another half hour this time of year so we make an instant decision to go for it. Cora goes with me and we head out toward our place. Willie's trailing us in his truck with Susan, and in 15 minutes we're driving up my new driveway.

"Willie and Susan seem to be getting along well," I say to Cora.

"He's such a nice guy, how could you not like him?" Cora says.

"Willie's acting a bit funny, though," I say. "Quieter than usual and more serious. Not his usual joking self, but I don't think it's a problem. I can tell he likes Susan. It's a mystery."

"Maybe he's nervous?" Cora says.

"Willie?"

They pull up behind us and get out. We hightail it together up the back trail, making it to the ridge 10 minutes before sunset. It's crystal clear in the mountain air and the Rockies shimmer in the evening light 10 miles away. I put my arm around Cora's shoulders and the four of us stand there enjoying the moment. You can follow the movement of the shadows of the top ridges, sliding across the flat land toward the river below, from the uplift of the mountains.

The sun sets dramatically, bathing the land in sudden darkness. I see Susan slip her hand into Willie's. He puts his arm around her, bends down and kisses her quickly as she stands up on her tiptoes to reach his lips.

Whoa, Willie.

I look over at Cora who's watching them, too.

She's grinning. "Mystery solved," she whispers.

We're walking back to the cabin slowly in the rapidly dimming light. Cora and I are arm-in-arm and Willie still has Susan's hand in his. I look down at Cora and give her an amazed look; she gives one back at me. They're dawdling so we go into the house as Susan walks out to the truck with Willie. A very long time later, she comes in the front door, giving Cora a perplexed look, and disappears into the bedroom.

* * *

We get an early morning start. No other cars are parked at the trailhead when we get there, around nine in the morning, and start sorting out our packs. I hear another car coming up the road behind us from a long distance, but it pulls up before reaching us, somewhere further down the road. It surprises Willie because we had to let ourselves in through a closed barrier to get up here. It's early in the hiking season and not many people know this trail is clear this early. He'd told us we probably wouldn't see any other hikers.

"Probably another local," Willie says. "Someone who knows the Park."

We've packed two small tents plus the cook stove we guys are carrying but everything else, including sleeping bags and foam pads, is divided up evenly. Willie has the food too, and an all-purpose safety kit including insect repellent, with everything sorted into Ziploc bags. It's an easy pack because we're going in for such a short time.

The cloudless morning is still chilly, but we won't be wearing our jackets long as the sun has begun to hit us. The trail is dry now as we start up the four and a half mile trail with its 2,000 foot elevation gain. I keep looking around to see if any other hikers appear, but almost nothing. One time I see a solitary man, a long way back, carrying something long and narrow. I only have him in view a few seconds before he disappears into the trees.

Before I can mention the lone hiker, Willie interrupts. "Do you want part of the guided tour or the quiet friend tour?"

"The guided tour!" the girls say, and I decide to try to let my concerns go.

Willie smiles, "I can get a little carried away. I love this park. Just let me know if I'm overdoing it, and feel free to ask questions."

We start hiking and Willie starts talking. "I'll do most of the travelogue at viewpoints, but start noticing the type of trees and ground cover and I'll point out how it changes with altitude." We continue along a fern-lined trail with new leaves on the aspen and vine maple. After 20 minutes or so we step out on a rocky overlook with a good view of the layered and tilted rock walls.

"The park has been formed over the past 170 million years," Willie says. "The multiple glaciers advancing and retreating have carved these sheer deep valleys through uplifted ancient sedimentary rock. The rock on some of the highest elevations is some of the oldest in the park, up to 1.6 billion years old. The oldest rock overlays much younger cretaceous rock less than 200 million years old." He smiles at us with obvious pride.

Cora and Susan look at Willie with evident surprise. They didn't know my friend was a passionate scientist.

He continues, "The glaciers have been retreating steadily for the past 160 years or so. There was a brief period where there was a reversal and the glaciers increased in size in the mid-1900s, but the melting of the glaciers has been increasing steadily since then. In the mid-1800s, there were over 150 glaciers in the park. Now we're down to 25, give or take.

"Global warming?" I ask.

"It's not disputed that global warming currently exists. What people argue about is how much of it was caused by human activity. Scientists predict if global warming continues at this pace that Glacier Park will have almost no glaciers by 2030 at the latest. I'll let you hike in peace, but we'll stop up ahead. There's something I want to point out."

Once again, I turn around and scan the trail we just came up.

Willie notices. "Sam? You okay?"

"Just nervous, I guess. I wish we'd get a clear look at that other man. I keep seeing raging brothers following us."

"He probably split off on the side trail across the low divide to Fish Lake. There are plenty of places ahead we can scan for intruders. Relax, Sam. I'll keep a watch out. I promise."

I smile at Willie, nod, and feel better.

We're all acclimated to the base elevation except Susan, but she doesn't seem to have any trouble keeping up. Willie asks her occasionally if the altitude is bothering her and she just smiles at him. He keeps giving her these big smiles back. I'm starting to think the big lug is beginning to topple.

With altitude, the trees begin to change from mixed deciduous and pine to more spruce and firs. We've come out on a view spot, looking down on a fairly large, shimmering, aqua blue lake, settled in the low point between two vertical walls forming the valley.

Willie becomes the tour guide again. "This is a fairly typical mountain lake in the park. It was formed during the retreat of the last glacier in this valley. As the ice melted, it deposited all the gravel and boulders you see at the south end and made a dam forming this lake." He points out a huge gravel bar partially covered with trees and some underbrush. "The aqua color is the result of suspended glacial silt reflecting the light."

He gives Susan a quick hidden look.

She gives him the biggest smile imaginable.

I swear he blushes.

After another hour, the trees start to thin and vistas open up, allowing panoramic views of the entire valley walls. By 11 o'clock we're really high up and start traversing Baldy Ridge at about a 7,000 foot elevation. Steep slopes descend on both sides of the ridge trail. There are still trees this high, but stunted and thinning fast.

We stop to take a break and enjoy the view. I take a moment to make a mental picture of my friends and the magic of it all. We drink some water and pass around some trail mix. I can't believe it's this warm so high up. We've taken off jackets long ago and are wearing t-shirts and jeans with hiking boots.

Suddenly, I hear a loud crack and jump several inches off the log I've been sitting on, feeling my hands clench. I don't think anyone notices this time as all our heads turn toward the noise. It's a huge bull elk, traversing the ridge behind us. I let out a slow breath and feel the blood return to my hands. *Just relax, idiot*, I think to myself.

Willie continues his narration. "Look over at that steep valley wall. There are places in the park that have over 7,000 feet of elevation difference from valley floor to ridgeline. You'll notice that the trees have changed again and now we're seeing only stunted trees, almost entirely alpine fir. It's very early in the year to be able to get to this elevation without much snow, but this ridge trail is unique, facing south the whole way, and it's melted early."

"What's your favorite place here?" asks Susan.

"It's something that's been recently identified. The Appekunny Formation is strata of alternating mudstone and siltstone on the slope of Slingshot Mountain. Sometime, when we go into the park by the St. Mary's entrance, I'll point it out. It provided evidence of animal life on this planet going back more than a billion years. It's the oldest animal life documented on this entire planet—a one-celled Metazoan." He stops for effect.

I'm sitting on a fallen log with Cora sitting on the ground between my legs. I have my arms around her shoulders and kiss her hair from time to time. I'm gloriously happy. We keep watching Susan and Willie together. They are both shy with each other, but joking and touching each other almost accidentally. This is a Willie I haven't seen before, but I recognize the symptoms.

We're really alone up here. Willie's told us this trail section of the park won't be officially open for two more weeks. Against my will, the thought crosses my mind again that we could have been followed from the trailhead at a distance. I won't be totally relaxed until this situation with Paul is resolved, but even as I push the thought under the best I can, I keep catching myself sighing.

Back on the trail, we have another 45 minutes to the lake.

*   *   *

Finally, there it is. The water is free of ice, except a small section on the north shore. It's deep blue and surrounded by sparse alpine firs, most of which are less than 20 feet high. The peaks forming the surrounding basin slope steeply up on three sides. There's a slight breeze that feels good in the unfiltered sunlight, fluttering the lake surface, and we find a flat place to camp on the east side of the water so we can watch the sunset behind the mountains across the lake to the west.

"Jeez, Willie," I say. "Couldn't you have found a place with cold beer? This is perfect except for that."

He puts his pack down and out of the top pulls out four beers and puts them in the cold lake water.

I shake my head. "Are you trying to impress someone, or what?"

We all look at Susan and laugh.

We're sitting around the small campfire after sunset watching the last of the light fade off the peaks on the east side of the basin. We're risking a fine having a campfire in the park, but we're alone up here and Willie has an in with local authorities.

It's getting cold fast. Willie has told us that it'll probably get down near freezing tonight, so those sleeping bags will feel great. I've got on every piece of clothing I brought, and the fire is holding off the cold for now. We've finished our rehydrated spaghetti and garlic French bread that we warmed up near the fire, and washed everything down with a bottle of red wine that I slipped into my pack.

Willie puts the remaining food in a bag and leaves to throw a rope over the highest tree limb in the area. When he comes back I ask, "Any problems this year?"

"Not yet," he says. "It's early and the bears are just coming out of hibernation in the high country. They'll be hungry and irritable. I have a loud gun just in case. Never had to even come close to using it, but this is grizzly country. We don't have the close bear interaction they have in Yellowstone, but every year we have a few incidents. Don't worry," he says to Susan, and puts his arm around her shoulders.

It's become apparent we won't have to have separate boys' and girls' tents. Willie's having a hard time keeping his hands off Susan and she's not discouraging him in any way. I'm glad we put the tents some distance from each other. We're tired and decide to turn in early; or maybe we want to turn to other things. We all say good night. Susan says this has been one of the most special nights she can ever remember. I know I feel that way.

We crawl into our tent and strip off all the outer layers of clothing. We've zipped our bags together. I remember when I thought I couldn't love anyone. I want to make this last and I want to give pleasure to Cora. I take her in my arms and start kissing her neck. She runs her hands up and down my chest, lowers her head and starts biting my nipples through my t-shirt. "Slow down, Cora," I plead.

"Why?" she murmurs. "I'll go slow next time."

I can't stay rational any longer, the wine, the place, the company. I pull her to me. I feel her breasts against my bare chest as I pull off my shirt. She's ripping her clothes off, too, but I don't think the cold is going to be a problem.

Afterward we're lying in each other's arms. I can hear my heartbeat return to normal in the silence of the night. Cora is stroking my arm with her hand as she lies on her side cuddled up to me. I'm wondering what's going on in the other tent. I'm hoping they're as happy as we are.

*   *   *

I wake up in the pre-dawn darkness; too early to get up. I do my drifting thing, neither awake nor asleep, just drifting. I started this when Cora arrived. It's a feeling of well-being, not thinking. I become vaguely aware of a faint noise in the direction of the lake. I listen for it again. Nothing. Just when I decide it was my imagination, I hear it again; footsteps not far away, muffled and careful. My well-being evaporates. I'm thinking about grizzlies or even worse. I freeze and wait. I'm sure Willie is sound asleep, the gun in some undisclosed place.

My leg muscles tighten and I very slowly turn into a position that I could leap upward. I wait. There's an occasional gust of wind that conceals other noises. My mouth has gone dry and I try to swallow. Several minutes pass.

I take a chance and inch my way out of my sleeping bag. I wait several more minutes—then I hear more quiet steps, closer now. If only I had the gun. My heart's pounding like a drum. Should I yell for Willie? I hear the sound again, maybe a little further off, in the direction of Willie's tent. I cautiously crawl to the tent flap and wait. I risk pulling up a corner and look out.

Stepping around from behind Willie's tent, I spot a solitary mountain sheep ram moving away. I take several deep breaths and thank my lucky stars that I didn't panic and scream for Willie to get his gun. *Crap!* I collapse back on my sleeping bag. It's several minutes until my heart rate returns to normal and I lie wide awake, staring into the darkness.

*   *   *

As the sun finally hits the tent I think about coffee, pull on my jeans and sweatshirt, and find my boots. Willie already has a fire going and coffee perking in a pot on a small camp stove. He turns to look at me and I know that our Willie has made a leap of faith.

"Sleep well?" I ask.

"Not really," he grins back. "Night was kind of short."

I nod my head and hunker down next to him. We pour some coffee and share some silent guy time.

The girls get up eventually and decide to walk around the lake. I figure they need a little girl time. They're gone about an hour and we hear soft laughter from across the water.

When they get back, we have eggs and warm rolls with butter and blackberry jam waiting, and lots of coffee. Susan gives me a wry smile and goes and sits down close to Willie, who wraps his arm around her.

Susan tells us that her friend, Jeff, has encouraged one of the secretaries to keep an eye on Paul's file. If he changes addresses, or if there's any other new information, he'll let us know. Susan also mentions that whenever she's in McMinnville she drives by Paul's house to see if he's returned.

"Susan," Cora pleads, "please don't do that. Everyone in town, including Paul, knows your VW Karmann Ghia. And for God's sake, don't drive in his driveway. You're out of sight of the road, in 25 feet."

Susan subtly rolls her eyes.

"Look," Cora continues. "You know he can be dangerous. If he cornered you, there's no telling what he might do to get information."

Willie looks like he's been struck. "Susan," he says, holding her shoulders and looking directly in her eyes. "this guy could be crazy. He could have killed Cora, accident or not. You don't want to be anywhere near him."

"Okay. Okay. I promise, all of you. I won't go near him."

I don't know Susan well, but I have a feeling she'll do what she wants. I look at Cora who is obviously worrying, too.

We all keep looking at Susan, waiting for her to say something more.

"Really," she says. "I promise. He scares me, too. I'll let Jeff check. He's there all the time."

I relax, most of the way. After a while, I decide to go fishing with Willie, and the girls sit up on the bank watching us. We catch and release some nice mountain trout and have some lunch. About two, we think about starting down.

Arriving at Willie's truck, we throw our gear in the back and start down the dirt road. Around the first turn, we pass an old pickup with a Browning, Montana license plate. "That's Jim Spotted Wolf's truck," Willie says. "Probably poaching trout before the season starts. He won't eat them himself, but he sells 'em to feed his kids, so we give him a bye. Besides, this was Blackfeet land only a few generations ago and he wouldn't have had to ask anyone."

I, goddamn, wish I'd known that. I spent all that energy tying myself in knots. I resolve to stop being an idiot and relax. Paul's probably only normally crazy—like his brother. I grimace to myself. If I don't watch it, my anxiety is going to cause problems. All we need is for me to go ape-shit and cause an accident. Okay. I'll relax. Then I shake my head—as if wishing it can make it so.

* * *

Willie needs to put some finishing touches on his gear for a tour leaving tomorrow. He's taking a small group from Portland on a three-day pack, leaving Saturday morning, so he won't be there to see Susan off on the train on Sunday. He's planning to stop by the cabin tonight after finishing all his work.

Cora and Susan are talking on one end of the porch after dinner. I'm sitting on the other end scratching Grover's ears and half-listening to their conversation. It's been a nice three days; Susan will be here tomorrow and then gone. Tomorrow I plan to hang around here. I'm going to cut wood and the girls are going to go back to town and see Vinnie.

I overhear Cora kidding Susan about Willie, but things get serious when Susan asks Cora if she's frightened of Paul. I strain and hear her admit, "Yes. I try not to think about him at all. It brings back the nightmares."

It's late when Willie turns up. Cora and I talk a bit, then give them some privacy. I see Susan grab the yellow and green blanket off the couch and they head up the trail toward the ridge top. It's a very long time before I hear the truck on the driveway in the dark. It's going to be another short night for Willie.

* * *

We're having a late breakfast. It's a relaxed day and the sun is just hitting the river. It's still building in volume and I now know why the long bridge seemed so out of proportion last fall. I have a huge mug of hot coffee in hand and Grover's getting in his first stretch for the day.

"How'd you sleep?" I ask Susan as she walks out on the porch.

She gives me a look and replies, "Actually, I'm a little tired. Must have been the hike yesterday," she smiles. "And the stars were unbelievable last night."

"Willie's a pretty special guy. Best friend a guy could have."

"You don't need to talk him up to me," Susan smiles. "You may have noticed I'm a little smitten here."

"I haven't seen Willie like this before. I'd say he's smitten, too. It's a pleasure to see."

"Thanks, Sam. Thanks for being encouraging. That feels like a vote of confidence."

"Are you two having a love fest out here?" Cora joins us on the porch.

"Pretty much," I smile.

"Is the river always like this?" Susan asks. "It's roaring."

"Just started building with this warm weather. According to Willie, it's going to grow for another month or so and stay high until late June. I hope Grover's smart enough not to fall in."

"Oh, he's plenty smart," Cora interjects, "but I'm worried that he might jump in to save something. He has heroic tendencies.

"Takes one to know one," I say. "You took me on, after all."

*   *   *

It's long after dinner and we're up on the ridge getting a last sunset in for Susan. We have about 30 minutes to go and the light is luminous up here. We're sipping cold beers and feeling good. I'm sore after cutting wood, but not like the last time. I'm adjusting and feeling, well, macho. I haven't had shoulder muscles like this, ever.

"I want to thank you guys, for everything. It's been unbelievable," Susan says.

"You're welcome." Cora answers. "I'm glad you got to know Sam. I know you were worried."

I look sideways at Susan as she answers, "Yes, Sam. I've been very worried. It's hard to believe you could be so—so normal after all you've been through and who you were. After all, you were holding my best friend hostage a few months ago. But you do seem normal. I'm encouraged for you both."

"I'm trying to be ordinary for Cora, and myself. I worry I'm pretending to be normal, and wonder if I'll go crazy again. But you know who gives me the most hope; that this is the real me? It's Vinnie. She seems to see who I am and has confidence in me. I can't tell you what that means."

"I trust her, too," Susan says. "And you needed a family."

"It's been nine months since I went off the deep end. I can't see that I'm being deceptive. I hope I'm not kidding myself."

Susan nods, "I think that you're willing to think about it, and can talk about it—that's the best sign, Sam."

"There hasn't been a real test. I'm tied in knots about that. I don't completely know myself, and I haven't the slightest idea what's in Paul's head. I have no idea how dangerous he might be. You know about that horrible event with Cora. I don't know if it pushed Paul over some cliff."

"If only he had someone...." Cora says.

"There's another reason I'm happy about this," Susan says. "I may see quite a bit of you guys. I'm coming back in about three weeks. I have a lot of vacation time saved up, so 'Colby and Colby' will have to cut back on legal assistant help. That is, if I can wait that long."

"Fantastic," I grin. "I knew I'd made an impression. I'm sure Cora will share."

Two women pound on me as the sun descends behind the Rockies.

* * *

We're back on the platform at the railroad station saying goodbye to Susan. "See you in a few weeks," I say. "The guest room is yours."

"Stay away from Paul," Cora says. "Jeff can monitor him better than you can, okay?"

"Have you been worried about that all this time?" Susan frowns. "I'm not foolish."

"Yes, you are. That's the point. Just behave, okay?"

"I promise," she says, and they share one last hug before she gets on the train.

As the train pulls out, Cora says, "She is going to do it anyway. I know her."

* * *

Willie is over for a late dinner Tuesday evening. He's due to pack out with another larger group Friday and be away for a week. We've been mercilessly teasing him about Susan and he's handling it with as good grace as he can. Cora's going over to his apartment tomorrow to spiff up the place and I'm going to help by taking old stuff to the dump.

"What do you hear from Susan?" I ask.

"She's back in Portland working hard to get ahead to take some time off," he smiles. I'm happy because it keeps her away from McMinnville. I don't trust her to stay away from Paul's house."

Cora is coming out with chocolate cupcakes and coffee. "I'm excited about decorating," she says. "What kind of decor do you like?"

"Leather and handcuffs," Willie laughs, then winces, "Oh, God! I'm sorry Cora. I didn't think." He actually blushes.

Cora smiles and shakes her head. "Don't worry. Besides, I'm sure Dave wants to contribute something."

* * *

Cora is in seventh heaven. She loves to throw things out. The truck bed is full of old scarred furniture, dusty old bamboo blinds, old sheets and towels, and the oldest rug fragment on the planet. Poor

Willie. He makes weak little comments like "No frilly curtains, okay?" or "I really liked that coffee table." But it's no use.

Willie and I are on the way to the dump. I've got my iPod hooked into the truck speakers and we're tooling along singing old Willie Nelson songs.

"I feel like I've sort of lost control of this renovation project," Willie mutters.

"Yep," I say.

*   *   *

We're back from Great Falls with a truckload of stuff. Willie got an amazingly decent brown leather couch from a used furniture store, plus a dresser, and Cora let him buy a picture of the mountains at a tourist shop. She was able to talk him out of the mounted moose head, but we bought it for Carson anyway. It'll look great at the Dead Moose Tavern.

Dave stops by with a used desk chair. "I was going to bring the designer handcuffs, but I couldn't find them," he says, and gets a really strange look from Vinnie who's helping sort through stuff.

"Inside joke," I tell her.

"Susan's going to be pleased," Vinnie says. "A real den of iniquity, if I do say so myself."

Willie sighs, "If I can get her back out here in one piece."

I give him a look.

"Yeah," he says, "I've been worried."

CHAPTER 23: PAUL

I'VE BEEN A GHOST in McMinnville. No one knows when I come home or leave.

Home is a strange term for my house. Homes are where people live with other people who care about them. I don't have a home. I have walls and a roof and a yard full of huge trees and no one knows if I'm here, or probably cares. I've left my job, that institution which, for the past three years, I've gotten out of bed to go to.

I got some satisfaction from teaching well, relating to the students; felt some pride when they did well. I knew many of the women students were infatuated.

Cora was different. She was so genuine, quietly interesting. Somewhere in the middle of the spring session, I knew I'd make an exception and try to get to know her. It was so risky. That old expression of being comfortable in one's own skin, well, I wasn't. I thought I could fake it and maybe it could become true. I thought that if I tried to be a good person, cared about someone, was totally unselfish....

But it didn't work. Looking back, I see I was kidding myself.

My old fears and self-hatred were clawing to get free. That last little talk with Sam confirmed all my darkest fears. He did seduce her and he won. They're together now, a constant knife in my gut. For the first time, I hate him. Of all the girls on the planet, he had to go for her; take away the only chance I had to be happy, normal. I realize, in my most rational moments, that I'm the problem. If I were a mentally normal guy, I could let this go—but I'm not, am I? Desperation, that's the word. One chance—now lost.

If only he would allow me to breathe, enough to think of myself as gray, not the darkest black. He's a sadist not to have given me that—a little space to expand my lungs—not the tiny box in which I've wedged myself. I can't forgive him for that, and now Cora.

It's too late. I can't go on with my shadow existence. I can't. Cora showed me how far away from a real life I've descended. I can't go back to that—get up, go to work, go home, eat to stay alive, go to bed. Screaming is better than that.

I'm here to clean up bills, repack clean clothes and try again to find Sam. I will find him. I have to end this.

It's almost dark out and beginning to rain hard, the wind gusting against the front windows, rattling them. I have no TV or music on. I can't bear the noise.

Just before I switch on a lamp, I glance out the side window through the slats in the blinds and see movement in the trees. Someone small is sneaking around, headed for the back of the house. Coldness comes over me. I throw on my parka and slip out the front door. In several seconds the trees hide me. I work my way back to the front of my driveway, the only way out.

It's Susan, Cora's friend; Susan's car, anyway. The small black Karmann Ghia identifies her. I know instantly that she knows where they are and smile grimly to myself. Maybe the waiting is over. She'll have to come back this way.

I look inside. The keys are in the ignition and her purse is on the seat. Guess she didn't come for a social call.

It's raining even harder now. I lean back against the hood of her car to wait. The rain soaks my hair. I don't care.

Suddenly she comes around the last stand of trees, her head down in her hood, looking at the ground. Her jacket is muddy. She looks up and screeches to a halt. Her eyes widen in fear. I see her look from side to side, looking for an escape route. The heavy bushes on either side block that.

I'm barely controlling my anger. I push away from the hood of her car, walk up to her and take her by the upper arms. My voice is dead, a dead man talking. "Where is he, Susan?" I say. I can see her cringe.

"I can't tell you," she says. She's tiny next to me.

I tighten my hold on her small arms and shake her. "I disagree," I say. "The truth is, you won't tell me."

"No," she says, in a frightened but firm voice. "I won't tell you."
I crush her against my chest. "I could make you tell me," I say.

She straightens her small shoulders. "You know me. You know what it would take. Are you willing to go there?"

My eyes are glaring into hers, trying to fight down the final loss of control. Neither of us moves. There is no sound besides the drumming of the rain and the rising wind. Several minutes pass.

"Paul?" she finally says. "Have I been so wrong about you? Would you hurt me that much?"

I gradually increase the pressure on her arms. I can see the fear and pain I'm causing. Her eyes begin to water.

"I don't know what I'm capable of," I say. "Tell me, now."

I'm frozen in place. We stand there—tears start spilling down her cheeks and mingle with the rain. Am I willing to go farther? My hands start to shake. I see myself hitting her, even worse. *No. No. I couldn't. Please, God. Get me out of this wretchedness.* But my hands are locked.

I see her swallow. "Paul," she says. "Let me go. I know you don't want to hurt me. I know you won't hurt me. People know I came here."

At that, finally, I loosen my hands. My heart is breaking. I look into her eyes one final time, searching for a reflection of my soul—and step aside.

She squeezes past me, manages to get in the car, and pushes down the door lock. She sits there looking out at me, standing alone in the driving rain.

I can hear it hammering on her car roof. I scream at her. I know she can hear me through the car window. I am screaming "He should have forgiven me. He should have forgiven me when I could forgive him."

The rain pours on, a deluge, harder and harder. At last I turn and stumble back toward the house. Vaguely, I hear her car cough and start, the tires whining, spinning in the mud. She ricochets down the curved driveway, and disappears.

CHAPTER 24: SAM

IT'S FRIDAY NIGHT in the middle of June. Susan's due out on the train on Sunday morning, which means she'll be getting on the train in Portland tomorrow night. She's staying tonight with Leslie. Willie won't be done with his backpacking tour group until late afternoon Sunday, so Susan will come home with us. Willie will meet us for dinner Sunday, as soon as he can get free.

No further word of Paul. He hasn't returned to the college in McMinnville. He's still scheduled to teach fall quarter, but administration is getting antsy and wants to hear from him to confirm this. That's based on information from Susan's friend in the chemistry department.

We're having a glass of wine on the swing when Cora's cell rings.

"Hello, Susan," she says, reading her name off the phone. Her face gets a look of horror. "What—Oh my God! You're crazy!—Why? You promised!—Stop crying, and breathe—tell me." Cora puts it on speaker.

I can't even imagine Susan crying. It sounds wretched through the speaker.

"Are you hurt? Did he hurt you?" Cora asks. "Shit! Shit! Shit! Is he following you?"

"No. No."

"Are you sure? Why would you go there? Why?"

"Jeff called me this morning. The school—they've been talking about hiring another professor. Paul's number doesn't work anymore. He changed his contact address to Helena. The department head told Jeff that they need some personal assurance by July first."

She stops to take a breath.

"Jeff volunteered to drive over to see if his house was closed up, but he couldn't do it until Monday and I thought—I thought it would be good to know that before I came out—you know, to see if it looked like he was gone for good or if he'd been there recently. I thought it would help." She starts crying again.

"When did you decide this?" Cora asks.

"I talked to Jeff at lunch. It's only 40 minutes or so from my apartment, but the traffic was horrible. The weather is terrible, high wind, power lines down. I was late."

"Was he home?"

"Let me tell you everything. It was raining buckets and the light was bad. I drove around the block three times and didn't see anything. I thought it was safe for a quick look around. I pulled in the drive only a few feet so my car was right by the road. It wasn't completely dark yet, but the wind was whipping the trees and dripping with rain. I had my heavy parka with the hood pulled up and started out to walk around the house. I had a flashlight, but didn't want to use it in case.... Well anyway, I almost turned around, but you know me."

"Oh, Susan. Crap!"

"When I got to the back of his house there was his car and muddy foot prints leading to the back door. That's when I got totally freaked and ran back toward the car. I even slipped and fell I was so startled."

Cora and I grimace at each other.

"When I came back around that last turn of the driveway, I almost ran into Paul. He was standing there in the pouring rain, leaning against the front end of my car."

I lean closer to the phone to talk. "I can hear your voice shaking, Susan. Where are you? Are you in a safe place?"

"Yes. Yes. I'm at a gas station getting frightened looks from the attendant."

We're all silent for a few moments.

"Did he hurt you, Susan?" I ask.

No response.

"Susan?"

"No, not exactly, but he—he threatened me." And she starts crying again.

I take the phone from Cora, "Does he know where we are?"

"No. No. I wouldn't tell him and he finally let me go."

"I'm so sorry, Susan," I say. "I'm so glad you aren't hurt. This can't go on. I can't have people I care about hurt."

"No. No. Sam. I shouldn't have gone. I promised. I'm so sorry."

"It's all right. You're a good friend trying to help—but we've got to think this through. Take a deep breath. We need to get you on that train without Paul following you."

Cora starts to say something, but I shake my head and hold up one finger. "Now that we know he's coming, we can take precautions. It's better. Listen—Let me think a minute."

"Sam? Sam?" There's a worried tone in Susan's voice.

"Okay. I have an idea. Do you have a large mall near Leslie's apartment?"

"Yes. Yes."

"Okay, park your car at one end of the mall and go quickly inside with your suitcase. Go as fast as you can so he can't park and follow you. Walk right into the mall, right through the crowd as fast as you can, and out the other end. Have Leslie pick you up there in her car. Just leave your locked car there and give Leslie the keys. In a couple of days, she can go and pick it up and drive it to her apartment. It would be nice if you aren't followed back to Portland, but we have to assume he'll follow you at a distance."

I exhale sharply as I hand the phone back to Cora.

While Cora finishes up her conversation, I go over in my mind what I've just arranged. I suppose the safest thing would be to tell Susan not to come, but avoiding the whole thing is somehow much more difficult. I hate hiding and waiting.

We might as well try to live our lives, but I hope I'm not jeopardizing us all. What Willie said about being worried—that was upsetting. I wave my hand to tell Cora I have something to tell Susan.

"Tell Susan to call us tomorrow before she goes to the train. You and I should talk this over when we've had more time to think. I don't want to make a mistake on this. I need to talk to Willie or Dave."

"Did you hear that?" asks Cora of Susan. Then, "She promises on her word of honor to call tomorrow," she says to me.

"Love you, too," Cora says to Susan and hangs up. Now she starts to cry and I hold her 'til she's cried out. "I'm scared," she says.

"I'm scared, too," I say. After a few minutes, I call Dave, catching him just before he leaves on a short trip.

After listening to my somewhat disjointed rendition of current events, Dave agrees that my plan should work and having Susan stay in Portland isn't any safer. Time is on Paul's side and she can't hide forever. So she might as well come.

Besides, Willie would go bonkers worrying about her in Portland, and he has to be told. Trouble is, we can't get hold of Willie; he's mostly out of cell phone range in the park valleys. He'll be back day after tomorrow and there's nothing he can do, anyway.

I talk it over with Cora and she agrees. She gives Susan a call and tells her to come ahead. I think about what Paul was screaming at her through the window. He did something terrible long ago and needs to be forgiven. *But maybe so do I.*

Cora walks up the hill to finish dinner preparation, leaving me alone on the swing. I'm freaked. Totally freaked. Until now I was able to convince myself that this was going to turn out all right; that this couldn't possibly be as bad as my fantasies. Now I know it could. I remember what a bad place I was in when I decided to take Cora. And I started out being the normal brother. Paul was always closer to the edge, even before the shit hit....

For the first time, I realize someone could die. I need to face this. Cora is hanging in there, which is remarkable because she's seen his other side. Oh, holy hell. I hear myself groan out loud. I figure I can handle myself, unless he ambushes me out of the blue—but Cora. He just might be crazy enough to kill her for the betrayal. And now she's here—with me. If he knows that, he could blame her. He's not rational. He could do anything. I have to face that. I picture him hurting Cora and it's everything I can do to not go crazy. I feel the hatred resurfacing. *Damn him.*

* * *

We're back on the platform waiting for Susan. The train is stopping and there she is. I can't help but take a good look at everyone else getting off, but it's only a mother and two little kids and two old ladies with field hats and binoculars. If they're disguises, they're damn good ones.

Susan acts sad and embarrassed, "I'm so sorry, you guys. I know I promised."

"I'm glad for Paul's sake he didn't take you on," I say. "I sure wouldn't want to mess with you."

Susan gives us both a sad smile. "I've been doing a lot of thinking about taking risks. Paul was so close to losing it. If I hadn't told him that people knew where I was...?"

She looks at both of us, "Does Willie know?"

"No, we haven't been able to get a hold of him in the park," Cora says. "Besides, we thought you'd want to tell him yourself."

Susan winces.

Cora's got her arm around Susan's small shoulders and I've got her suitcase, which we load in my old Toyota.

When we get to the cabin Susan exclaims, "It's so changed in three weeks. The trees are all out and the river is huge! Is it going to get any bigger? It's frightening."

"Seriously, don't get too close to the edge. The bank's unstable in a few places and you'd wash away before we could get you. You don't sleepwalk do you?" I ask, half-seriously. "We might have to tie you to a bedpost. I have a rope on the porch in case Grover falls in and I have to rescue him."

"Wow," she says, "it's so loud. I bet you can hear it roar in the cabin."

"You can," Cora answers. "It's a lovely sound to fall asleep to. But it diminishes Grover's ability as a watchdog. I'm always scaring him because he can't hear me walk up to him."

We're waiting for Willie who is still uninformed about what has happened. Finally we hear his truck on the bridge, and then he guns it up the driveway. Jumping out, he bounds up to Susan and gives her a big hug. He looks closely at her, then all of us. "What?" he says. "What's going on?"

* * *

The whole story has been told and Willie's sitting on the porch with Susan curled up in his lap. He's been a rock in this. He seems very concerned, but levelheaded. *We'll figure out a way to handle this* is his attitude.

"From what Susan says," I say, "Paul appears to be less in control of himself, more angry and despondent, although that's hard to tell for sure. And he still seems motivated to find where we're holed up. Since it is me he's after, maybe I could meet him and talk to him."

That provokes three loud protests. "There's no way in hell I'm letting you go alone on this," Willie says, "No way at all. I know Dave feels the same way. Paul could blow your head off before you could get a word out. We just don't know how dangerous he is."

"He terrified me," Susan admits. "He's on the brink of losing it completely."

"Then what can we do?" I ask.

"He's found out that Susan knows something," Willie says. "If I were him, I'd focus on her, phone records, travel plans. He didn't try to use force with her." He swallows, then continues. "But we can't count on that to last—not if he's really desperate. He could pick her up at any time. I hate to send her back to Portland with him prowling around. She could stay with someone, but she has to work—I think...."

"Do you?" he asks her.

"I do," Susan says. "I'm not letting that jerk define my life."

An idea has been floating around in my head. "How about this?" I suggest. "Susan lives her life and, if Paul confronts or threatens her, she tells Paul the truth about where we are. If he's that motivated, he's going to find out anyway. She can give us a head's up and we'll be ready. What about that? He didn't want to hurt her. He wanted information. Besides," I say, "I'm furious he's threatening my friends. We're all affected."

Silence.

"Well?" I ask.

"Could you live with that, Willie?" Cora asks, biting her lip.

He suddenly scoots Susan off his lap, stands and starts pacing. "No. Damn it. I don't want Susan within a million miles of this freakin' guy. I want you safe, Susan. Can't you go somewhere and lay low for a while? There's no guarantee he won't go off the deep end."

I'm shocked. Willie has been so calm throughout this whole mess. Having him this upset increases my anxiety.

"But, Willie," I ask. "What other choice do we have?"

We all look to Willie for some answer.

He finally stops pacing and clears his throat, "We need Dave. He's been involved with these kinds of situations. And I'm not rational where Susan's concerned."

I see him visibly trying to calm himself.

"Dave's in Billings," he says, "but he'll be back late tonight. We need him involved. I admit I'm upset. And I know I'm not making much sense. Come on, Susan. I want you away from here." Willie takes Susan's arm and starts pulling her away.

Then he stops after a couple of steps and returns. He looks at us, anguished, then says to us, "Come to my place for the night." he says. "We can't just run off and leave you."

As he's talking, I'm wondering whether we should leave too. Maybe we should somehow—tonight. *No, that's just crazy.*

I smile weakly. "He couldn't get here yet, Willie. He doesn't know where we are. We'll be okay tonight and we'll talk to Dave tomorrow."

Willie thinks it over for several minutes. Then he turns and, without further comment, hustles Susan away.

*   *   *

Cora and I are lying in each other's arms later that night, listening to the roar of the river. "This is critical," I murmur to Cora. "Do you think I suggested the right thing?"

"Yes, I do. But I also think it's you, Sam, who has the most to fear."

"I wish I knew what's going on inside his scrambled head."

"He must be so lonely, Sam. Who has he had to love or care about all these years? When I was with him those first few months, he never talked about friends. We went to a few university social functions, but there was no personal connection with anyone. I thought that he was so into me that he let other friendships slide. I was kidding myself. There weren't any other friendships. I think he had his feelings walled off, like you did, and our relationship cracked the foundation."

"Your friends noticed something was wrong."

She nods unhappily. "We rarely hung out with my friends, and when we did, they started pointing out how careful he was with everything—with what he said, what he did. And how he was isolating me. I kept lying to myself that it was because he was older, or a professor, but they were right all along."

"How did he seem to you, honestly?"

"Truthfully? During those first few months, Paul was the perfect boyfriend. Cheerful, intelligent, absolutely absorbed with me. Looking back now, I can see I was his whole world. Then he ruined that, too. I feel so sad for him."

I roll over on my side and look at her in the moonlight. "How can you say that? How can you feel that way after all he did to you?"

Cora sighs, "You didn't see who he could have been, Sam, if the tragedy had never happened. It was all set in motion when your dad died in that pointless war, and 20 years later the ground is still moving. At his best, he was so caring; concerned to a fault about my welfare, encouraging. He should have had a happy life, been a wonderful brother to you."

My throat closes up. For all that could have been, for the love I once had for him....

When I was very young, he was my world, my protector, and my father. I've hated him for the choices he made, but for the first time, I see him tossed on the winds of circumstance, another casualty of war. This has been troubling me for a long time, at least since I dropped Cora off with him. *I'm so tired of hate.* There's something else on the edge of my understanding. Why can't I pull it into focus?

Cora rolls onto her side and falls asleep.

I lie there, listening to the sound of the river, long into the night. I miss the safety I once felt with him. I remember him standing in front of me on the playground, staring down the bullies.

I roll over on my stomach and cry.

* * *

I'm sitting at the kitchen table the next morning, drinking my second cup of coffee and watching Cora take cinnamon rolls out of the oven to take to Willie's.

"What are you thinking about?" Cora asks. "You're quiet this morning."

"I'm going over our conversation last night," I answer, "especially about you forgiving Paul. I was trying to imagine what it would have been like if we had had a normal childhood, growing up without all the sadness and anger. Most of all, I wonder what Paul and I might have meant to each other if all this had never happened.

"Why do people join the military—put themselves at such risk? What about their families?"

"No one knows what will happen, Sam. Why do we drive around in cars? They're dangerous. Some people try to play it safe. Some people want to feel alive in ways that scare the rest of us."

"It's frightening. The smallest decisions we make can influence the rest of our lives."

"What I was trying to say last night was that Paul has so much inside that could be amazing," Cora says. "That's what attracted me to him in the first place. He seemed so sensitive and understanding, more than most guys are. When he was at his best, he was so caring and grateful. Now I know how much he's suffered, and that gives me a window into what made him that way. It's made you who you are, too."

I'm trying so hard to understand. I've only felt my pain all these years. Never once did I ever care or try to comprehend what Paul must have been going through. I've been stuck as a childish tormentor. I want to tell him that I understand some of it. He had all the loss I had, multiplied by being the cause of most of it. Willie saw that right away. He tried to tell me. I know I couldn't live with that....

God! Oh my God! For the first time, I'm terrified for Paul and I want to tell him—I can't forgive him but—I should. I should. All of a sudden I get it. *It's me, not him, who needs forgiving. I've been evil. I'm the one.*

Paul made a horribly wrong decision, but it wasn't intentional. He didn't set out to hurt anyone, just scare them.

I made a choice. I sent out venomous words to decimate him. I withdrew myself, the only family he had left, for years. I did everything that I could to keep him out of my life. Have I pushed him over that final edge? Have I pushed him to want to kill? If he manages to kill Cora, I'll be responsible for that, too.

Is he alive? I have no idea how to get in touch with him. The other phone line was disconnected too, right after our last phone call.

My skin turns clammy and I start to shake. "Cora," I say, "it's me. I should have forgiven him long ago. I'm killing him. Maybe I already have. I need to find him. Now."

"Let me think," Cora says. "How do we start? We still don't know whether he wants to kill us."

"Cora, I need to get a hold of Paul. I need to talk to Dave, right now. Right this minute. I can't wait." My stomach is churning. "Let's stop at Dave's on the way to Willie's."

*   *   *

It's around 11 and we're on Willie's doorstep with cinnamon rolls. Dave is right behind us, parking his patrol car. Willie answers the door with a happy grin and sleepy eyes.

"Hello you two," yells Susan from the kitchen. "I thought you said Willie's place was a war zone. It's a palace! Willie says he's just a domestic at heart."

"I even dusted," Willie admits self-consciously.

"Isn't he about the most darling thing on the planet?" Susan gushes.

"Sorry you guys aren't getting along," I manage. I try to smile, but I botch it.

Willie looks at me closely. "Something's wrong. What's going on here?"

"Just me, Willie. I'm horribly wrong."

He gives me an alarmed look.

"Willie, I've been a fucking bastard about Paul all this time. I'm the bad guy." I grab his arms in despair. "You nailed it before."

"I see," he says earnestly. "No one is all bad or all good. We all have a past, a dark side that we don't talk about, or think about much. Sam, we'll find him. We'll find a way to work this out."

I take a deep breath, "Even you, Willie? Do you have a dark place you don't want to go?"

"Sometime I'll tell you why I joined the Navy. Not now."

"I've been torturing him all these years. Maybe I've killed him. Maybe he's dead already. Willie?" My voice is nearing hysteria. "Or maybe he wants to kill Cora," I despair. Willie grabs my upper arms as Dave hurries up the walk.

"Sam filled me in," Dave says. "We don't have a lot of options here. Susan has become the lynchpin for Paul. Either she needs to go into hiding, or we have to go with Sam's idea." He pauses. "Willie, listen to me. Susan isn't going to be safe until she passes the information on to Paul. He may do anything to find them and Susan could get hurt, even if that's not his intention. You understand that, don't you?"

Willie's eyes bore into Dave's. "Yes. You're right."

Dave goes on, "If we know he's coming we can be ready and defend ourselves. Otherwise, Paul can keep us on tenterhooks for months and we'll inevitably let our guard down. We want to deal with this on our ground and at our time."

I can see Willie's anguish. Finally, he nods.

"Then we'll go with Sam's idea," Dave says. "If we knew how to contact him, I'd tell him myself. But we'll have to wait 'til he surfaces."

"Willie," I say, "I'm so sorry."

He smiles grimly. "You're just trying to take care of your lady; same as I am. And I think Dave's right." He takes a breath. "Obviously, I'm not thrilled, but there's a simple logic to it. If Susan sees him trailing her, she should go up and say she'll tell him where you are. It doesn't seem too risky. Running around scared all the time is risky, too. You tend to make stupid mistakes and hurt yourself. Okay. I can live with this."

"Boy," Susan says. "I'm glad I didn't let him torture me for nothing."

We all look at her and smile ruefully.

* * *

It's later that evening and we're sitting around the stone-lined campfire pit that I dug by the swing.

Dave brought us up to speed while the girls were in the house fixing dinner. He didn't have anything major to add. He's got a private detective looking for Paul. We're all confused about what Paul's thinking, but thankful he was able to stop himself before seriously hurting Susan. We don't want to talk about it in front of Linda. She doesn't know much about the whole situation and Dave wants it that way.

"Besides," he says louder than he has to, "she's getting a little grumpy."

"I am not friggin' grumpy," yells Linda, from the swing. "I'm friggin' very pregnant."

We all smile. The swing stops and Linda starts to step off it when Dave bounds up to take her hand. "Thanks so much, all of you," Linda says. "It's been wonderful to meet you, Susan. I'm sorry to leave so early, but I want to get home and put my feet up."

"Thanks, guys," says Dave. "Keep me posted, okay?" he adds with a nod to me.

"He's waited a long time for this; they've been married over fifteen years," says Willie. "He's worried and I'm beginning to know what that feels like." He looks over at Susan.

I put my arm around Cora's shoulders and sigh quietly. For the first time in days, I'm calm; calmer, anyway. We have a plan, the best we all have been able to come up with. The waiting begins.

CHAPTER 25: PAUL

I'VE BEEN SITTING in my living room with the shades down. The TV is on, but it's been stuck on CNN for days. It's background noise. I haven't shopped for food. I've been eating canned soup, stale cereal from countless boxes, and emptying the freezer of frozen pizza. I can't seem to get motivated to do anything. I sit and sit, occasionally watching some stupid sports star on trial for murder, and wonder how low I can go.

I've actually been waiting for the police to come arrest me for threatening Susan but it seems that's not going to happen. I guess she never told anyone. I wonder why. I'm no friend of hers.

I'm stiff from sitting. At last, I get up from the couch and lift the blinds. It's a beautiful summer day. That finally decides it for me. I know what I'm going to do. I'm actually calm about it. I'm going to get in my car, drive to Susan's apartment, and wait for her to come home. She has to come home eventually, right? I'll sit there 'til she tells me where they are, or they haul me away. It's not in me to threaten her again. Maybe Sam will feel sorry for her and come and meet me. Then what, I wonder?

I haven't gotten that far in my thinking. Maybe he'll bring a gun and shoot me. I have a gun in my car. Maybe I'll kill him. I really don't care.

Sometimes I care. Not this minute. I want to get out of this fucking house. Maybe I'll burn it down when I leave. No, too much work.

I'll clean up and take a little trip. *Nice day for a drive.* The thought crosses my mind that I'm edging toward lunacy.

* * *

I know where she lives. I was here before looking for phone records, trying to find Cora. I pull in to her complex entrance and park my car around back, then walk up to her building and find unit 206. I knock on the door. Nothing. It's three in the afternoon and she's probably not home from work yet. Easy. If I climb up on the railing on the unit below her and stand on it, I can pull myself up onto her back patio.

It took 30 seconds. I try the slider. Not even locked. I start snooping around for addresses or phone records. I find nothing. I check the fridge. I'm sure she'd offer me something to drink, so I pour myself a glass of wine and settle in to wait.

Several hours tick by. I think about another glass of wine. No. That kind of behavior got me into a lot of trouble before. I put my feet up on her coffee table and drift. I'm patient. I finally hear footsteps on her stairs and hear the key turn in the lock. She walks in and sets something down on a table. She hasn't seen me yet; another few steps and a gasp. I look out and around the corner of the stuffed chair. "Why don't you sit down, Susan?" I say with a flat smile.

She stands there unmoving for a minute or two then, apparently resigned, walks over to her couch and sits down.

We look at each other for a while.

"I'm here to have you tell me where they are," I say. "I'll wait."

I watch her carefully. She swallows and sighs a time or two. She sits there quietly, not moving a muscle, seeming to consider what to say.

At last I say, "I'm not here to hurt you, Susan, but I'm here 'til you tell me." I uncross my feet and put them on the floor. I lean toward her, put my hands together, interlocking my fingers, and wait.

"I'm allowed to tell you where they are."

I say nothing.

"They're living near East Glacier, Montana, in a cabin outside of town."

"Sounds pleasant," I say.

We sit assessing each other. Minutes drag on. "Do they ever talk about me?" I ask.

"Yes," she says. "They think you're going to hurt them. Sam wants to talk to you."

"Does he now?"

We sit quietly. She seems less pale.

"Susan? What do you think of me? You probably know it all; what I did to Sam, what I did to Cora. I'd be interested. Do you think I deserve to live?"

She doesn't answer quickly. I suppose she has to decide. Maybe I'll do what she says.

"Yes, Paul, I think you deserve to live and Sam and Cora deserve that, too."

I look deep in her eyes, "I wanted to be forgiven for so long. I waited and hoped. He refused. Now I only want him to feel pain, too."

I wait for her to respond. Nothing.

"I want to hurt him, Susan. My life is over. If he had forgiven me, I would have had a chance."

Susan's normally a chatterbox. Why doesn't she say anything?

"And now I've hurt Cora. She'll never forgive me; just another person who hates me. I can't fight it anymore. I'm so tired. But you're a fair person. You should agree. Can't you see that he should feel pain, too? You'll see him. Talk to him. Tell him for me. I'm having a tough time controlling my rage—at him and at myself." I realize I'm rambling. "It's caused a lot of trouble before."

I stop. She still doesn't say anything. I take a long breath and let it all out. I wish we could have been friends. *I could have used a friend.* I stand up and walk over to where she's sitting. She holds her ground, doesn't flinch.

I stand in front of her and say quietly, "Susan, you were always a good friend to Cora." I lean over, kiss her softly on the cheek, and walk to the door. At the last I turn and say, "Tell him I'm on my way."

CHAPTER 26: SAM

GROVER AND I ARE TAKING A BREAK from stacking wood when I see Cora make an unusually sharp turn and gun it up the driveway. I feel that ache I get in my shoulders when I'm anxious, and I jump up to meet her.

"Paul's just surfaced," she says.

We walk to the porch and sit on the front steps.

"Susan came home from work and he was sitting in her living room."

"God. What did she do?"

"She sat down, shocked into silence. She thought of all kinds of things to say later, but she couldn't think fast enough, things you told Willie. She's sick she didn't do a better job. But she told him where we are."

I'm shaking my head. My poor friends are feeling guilty they can't fix this. It's been 10 years and I couldn't fix it myself. *Stupid. Stupid.*

"She said he kept talking about wanting forgiveness and how it was too late. At the end he said 'Susan, you were always a good friend to Cora.' He walked over to where she was sitting and kissed her. She believed he was saying goodbye. He's on his way, Sam."

"I guess the ball is rolling," I say.

God, I wish I could talk to him. I wish I had taken Cora and run to Brazil. I know only two things: One, I'm responsible for a good portion of this disaster. And two, Paul may be coming to kill Cora, and I'll kill him before I let that happen. I go back and forth. I ache for resolution. I've planned my ambush. If he comes here, gun-in-hand, I'll have to kill him. He hasn't done anything to be arrested for, yet, and I can't afford to wait around until he decides to kill us. I need some warning. If not—if he appears crazy, then I'll do the best I can.

Sometimes, I look on Paul as a tortured mess, almost an innocent who is caught up in an overpowering whirlpool. But I also believe that he's coming to kill me, and maybe Cora, who gives my life hope. *Then I hate him.* My body aches with the conflict. There's no logic. It just is.

* * *

It's been a long day with no sign of Paul. Susan flew in to Great Falls and is driving herself up here alone. I've moved the revolver to a wooden box on the porch during the day. It's not locked. We know it's there, but try not to think about it.

Susan is turning in the driveway in her rental car and we'll wait together for Willie, who's coming here, just behind her, back from a tour. We all sense things are climaxing. Susan said she had to stop by—for a few minutes.

Linda could go at any time; due date is seven days away. She's pretty much sitting in the shade on her front porch in East Glacier where there's a breeze, and waiting. Dave is checking on her at least four times a day and is clearly preoccupied.

It's a beautiful Sunday afternoon and I'm trying to appreciate it. It's only two minutes before Willie drives up the driveway.

"Any word?" Willie asks, looking at me.

"Nope. No news is good news—I guess."

"I guess," Willie says.

We sit around, talking about nothing, essentially scanning cars on the road. Willie finally says, "I'm bushed and I need a shower. I'm taking my girl home, unless you have any other ideas, Susan?"

"Nope. I've stocked your fridge and I'll fix a little dinner while you clean up."

"Are you talking to Dave?" Willie asks.

"All the time."

"I'm not leaving again until this is resolved. I've told my uncle and he understands. I'll clean up and come right back after I get a quick bite to eat."

"Thanks, Willie."

"I've arranged with Dave. One of us will be out here continually for guard duty. Win Sanders and Lew Black River have volunteered for shifts. Win's on his way out here now. We need to talk about nighttime security."

I nod soberly as Willie and Susan give us a hug and head out.

As soon as Willie and Susan leave, I get agitated. "I've got to try to connect with Paul again, Cora. When he gets here, it's not going to be for a friendly discussion. Things could happen fast. If you see him, I want you to start running in the other direction, no matter what. Can you do that?"

"I don't think I could do that, Sam."

"Please understand. If I don't have to worry about you, I can function better, think better. If you're here, protecting you will be my only thought. Can you try?"

"I'll try, Sam. I can't promise. I need to tell you something. This has been bothering me for a long time and I need to say it." Her eyes fall. "Sam, you're always talking about your guilt and Paul's."

"Yes?"

"What about mine?"

"What on earth could you have to feel guilty about?"

She looks up at me. "Remember when we talked, after you had rescued me? Remember when we almost made love?"

I nod.

"Well—I wasn't afraid of you anymore. I didn't think you were going to hurt me. I would have done it. I wanted you. I was supposed to be in love with Paul and I wanted you. And on the way back, in the car, after I had made my choice, I would have made love to you again. I was trying to seduce you in the car. I think I was starting to look for a reason not to resume my relationship with Paul. I was trying to put you in a position to give me an out. Remember?"

I nod again.

"And he could tell, when I got back. I was different. I'm not sure if a lot of his anger isn't from that. If I hadn't cheated—and I was mentally cheating—if I had still been all his, I could have made him believe it."

We think a minute.

"And that's not all."

I look at her.

"Sam, I was going back to Paul. I didn't have enough strength to even think about another decision. I was going to have sex with you and go right on back to Paul. Think what it would have done to you. I knew it would hurt you. You were already messed up mentally and I was going to...."

"Cora, listen to me. You're wrong. This mess is not your fault. But even if it were true that you made a mistake, desire, wanting someone, is not a killing offense. Please. Please. Try to run, for me if not for you. Let's just try to get through this alive. No one is blameless in the world. I know this doesn't make any sense, but part of me wants to kill him, to end this. I don't need any excuse to do that."

"Sam. Do you think you could kill him, your brother, if it came to that?"

"All those years, I thought that I wanted him punished. Dead. Cold. Gone. Now I want him to live. But I don't know what I could do. I would kill him to protect you. But to protect myself—God, I don't know. How could I know something like that for sure? That's the reason I want you out of here. If you're gone, I won't be forced to kill him."

"Then I'll try to run. You're really afraid aren't you? He's going to try to kill someone."

I can't say it. *But yes.*

Cora and I walk down to the swing by the river. "Anything on the private detective Dave hired?" Cora asks.

"Nothing. Paul's dropped out. The college got the contract back, signed, but no personal contact at all. I don't know what that means. The contract was mailed from McMinnville."

We swing for a while. Cora has her head in my lap, and I run my fingers through her hair. The water in the river is starting to diminish as the summer lengthens, but it's still roaring. I had to rescue Grover a week ago when he got too close to the edge following a raccoon and fell in. I was able to run down the bank and snag his collar as he floated by. He won't even go close to it now.

Cora reaches up to pull me down for a kiss when my phone rings and I fumble to get it out of my pocket. "Yo," I answer.

"Sam, it's Dave." His voice is urgent. "Lola just called from the cafe, very upset. Twenty minutes ago a guy was in asking where the Walker Creek Road was. She gave him directions, but something nagged—He looked familiar and so did his voice. He was acting edgy. A few minutes ago it hit her. He looked a lot like you. I'm on my way out. Ten minutes. I'm calling Willie. Les is coming. Get the gun."

That same instant Grover does his howl and Paul steps out from the grove of trees.

"It's too late. Paul's here. Hurry!"

I shut the phone off, automatically, and stand up to face him.

CHAPTER 27: CORA

I WATCH AS PAUL MOVES TOWARD US, 40 feet away. A large handgun is in his right hand, pointed more or less at Sam and me. It seems so out of place. I can't wrap my head around it. Our gun is out of reach on the porch. I remember that Sam told me to run. I stand up slowly, looking at the gun in horror.

"Hello, Sam," he says flatly. "Found you at last."

"Paul," he says. His voice is trembling. "Please let Cora go into the house. This is between us." I can see him slowly maneuvering himself between Paul and me.

"No. She stays. I want her here. She's part of this now." He turns to me. "Sit down," he says, pointing the gun in my direction.

I sink slowly down on the edge of the seat. He moves the gun back toward Sam.

We're now about 20 feet apart. I can see the sweat rolling down his brow. His face is white. And I know something about guns now. This is a bad distance. If he were closer, Sam could rush him before he could get the gun up, but this is enough distance to give him a really good shot, or shots. I'm trying to calm myself. My heart is pounding.

"Paul," Sam says, "I didn't take Cora from you. She was so scared—after.... She needed to get away. She was in bad shape." His voice sounds surprisingly calm. "I know you didn't want to hurt her; we both know that."

Sam takes a small step toward Paul.

"No, Sam," I whisper. Is he trying to get close enough to rush Paul—to grab the gun or to kill him? I see Paul back up a step to keep the distance. Sam's body is like a compressed spring. I can feel the tension. He said he'd try to kill him. I desperately wish I'd been able to run.

Paul gives Sam a confused stare. "What? What are you saying?"

"I mean," he says, inching closer "don't blame Cora. Please. Please, let her go."

"I'm not blaming Cora for anything," he says. "And about not taking Cora from me, you fucking asshole—did you think I wouldn't figure out that you slept together during the kidnapping? Deny it, either of you. It was just one more way to stick it to me. Right, Sam? Like you've been doing for 10 years, twisting the knife."

"Paul. We didn't—honestly. We didn't have sex. Not then. But I've been a fucking prick, a fool, for years."

"Well, you finally got something right, little brother." He seems to spit the words. "I loved you, more than anything in this world. But not anymore. Not anymore."

"We don't want to do this," Sam says. "I don't want to try to fight you off. Please, Paul. You're my only brother. And I'm the only brother you've got."

Paul laughs, a sickening painful laugh. "Who should I kill, Sam, you—or me—or both of us? You gave me a similar choice once. You choose. It doesn't matter."

I see Paul measure with his eyes the distance between himself and the riverbank.

I think they both may die. I take a chance and plead, "Please, Paul. Please, don't. I'm begging you."

He turns his head slowly and stares at me with a look of total disdain, moving the gun in my direction. I see Sam ready himself to spring.

"Don't play with me," Paul says. "Why in the hell would you care? About me anyway?"

"I do care, Paul," I plead. "For what we shared; for who you are."

"When you left, you took all that was good; all that was possible. I'm nothing. There's nothing left. Nothing." His anger fades into cold blankness. He turns his gaze back to Sam.

"Paul," Sam pleads, "please don't take yourself away from me. You're my brother, my only family. Please! I want you in my life."

I look at these two brothers. *Stop!* I want to scream. *Stop. It can't end like this. Stop, Paul. Give him a chance.*

"I know you want me dead," Paul says venomously. "That's what you said."

"No. God. No, Paul. That's not what I want. Not anymore."

"So, what's changed?"

"I haven't been blameless in this. We're alike in so many ways. We went through the end of the world together. Dear God! Everything you said is true. I've been evil to you, horrible...."

"Now, when it's too late, you decide to forgive me; to look at your own fucking self. That's just perfect." He lifts the gun up toward Sam's head.

"No. No, Paul," Sam is pleading. "It's not too late. I'm sorry it took me so long to get it. Please, God. Please. Just throw that gun away."

"You hate me."

"I've been sick with that hatred for so long. I don't want it anymore. Listen. Please, listen. I'm worse than you. You were involved in an accident. I chose to torture you. I'm the fucked-up one. We can get better together."

Paul stands motionless for a very long time. All of our lives hang in the balance. Minutes pass. I can't think of anything I can say. I want to tell Sam I love him, but I keep quiet. I'm trying frantically to think of something else, anything to change Paul's mind. I'm pleading silently. *Please. Please. Please keep trying.*

Sam takes a few agonizingly slow steps toward Paul and holds out his hand. Paul raises the gun to point directly at Sam's head. They are now only feet apart.

The pain on Paul's face is excruciating.

I hear Sam say out loud what I'd been thinking. "Please keep trying. If you kill me, your life is over. You told me the same thing once. For God's sake."

I hold my breath.

Suddenly, Sam drops to his knees before him. "Please forgive me, Paul."

Sam's face is horrible to look at, tortured. He remains motionless, his hands at his sides, looking up at Paul.

I hear only the roar of the river. The world stops. Time is ticking away, maybe all our lives. I imagine a cylinder of light connecting their eyes, as if nothing else exists in the world.

Paul suddenly whirls around as the bank collapses under him, the gun flying in a high rolling arc into the river. He disappears into the raging torrent.

Sam leaps to his feet and starts running down the riverbank, trying to keep a glimpse of his brother. The river is thrashing and rolling, thrusting Paul up, then pulling him under.

Sam yells back at me, "Get help! Get the rope!"

Dave's squad car screeches in.

"The rope. The rope," I scream pointing to the porch.

Willie appears on the scene with Win Sanders. Dave races up to get the rope as Willie, Win and Sam run down the bank.

CHAPTER 28: SAM

THERE'S ONE CHANCE.

I know there's a deep pool right below the small falls, about 200 feet downriver. I stop there, searching frantically for a flash of blue jacket. I think I see it.

The water is horrible—deadly strong. I want to see Cora's face. I want love. I want to live. I've hated this man, my brother. There's death in that pool, Paul's and mine. Can I choose to die? Can I live with myself if I don't try? That's not enough to motivate me. *Maybe I still hate him.*

I look at Willie, the calm one, and the sensible one.

Seconds are ticking away.

Cora is standing on the shore screaming, a horrible sound.

Willie looks back at me and holds out his hands, palms up, and shakes his head. He won't do it. He won't help me. Win shakes his head, too.

It comes shrieking toward me. I love my brother. I can't let him die. Not now.

I give Willie one last look of desperation and throw myself in the pool.

The water is glacial run off, probably only a few degrees above freezing. It's overpowering.

For a few, terrible seconds, I feel like my heart has stopped. I think I'm dead. *No, I'm alive.*

I dive down once and then again.

On the third try, I manage to grab a part of Paul's jacket.

I kick with all my fury and barely get him to the surface. He's mostly unconscious from a gash on his head that's gushing blood. The river is turning red below him.

I can't move in that current, but I manage to position us against a huge rock midstream with Paul's head above water.

Waves of churning gray water roll over my head. As I try to breathe I take in water, gagging and choking.

By this time, Dave appears on the bank with the 200 feet of rope.

Willie and Dave are screaming at each other, deciding what to do. Willie ties the rope around his waist and wades into the water. Immediately, he loses his footing and Dave and Win reel him in.

Les and Susan appear on the shore. Cora has waded into the river up to her knees, about to be swept away, but Les grabs her and wrestles her back onto dry land while Susan grabs her.

Dave screams something to Win, who sprints across our driveway and over the bridge toward the opposite shore.

The water is treacherously cold. My hands are getting too numb to grip Paul well.

"Hold on!" I hear, over the roar of the water. "Hold on!"

Win has reached a point opposite us on the other side of the river, 40 feet away. Dave ties one end of the rope to a tree; then, with every ounce of strength, he tosses Win the other coiled end of the rope. Win ties it to a tree by the bank, pulling it as tight as he can, his arms straining, one leg jammed against the trunk.

Now Willie's in the water again. With the taunt rope, he's able to hold on and make progress toward us.

Dave and Win wade in from opposite sides, battling the current.

Many times the raging water covers their heads. I fear they'll be lost downriver.

Somehow they're able to maintain a grip on the lifeline.

At last Win and Willie get to us. I give Paul over to them and with Dave's help the five of us start moving back across the river.

I realize immediately that I can't help them and I can't make it alone. I'm too cold. My hands can't grip the rope.

I scream that I'll wait at the rock until they get Paul to shallow water.

Les, Cora, and Susan are standing in thigh deep water holding onto the rope and, together with Dave, are able to haul the unconscious Paul up on the bank.

Willie and Win start on their way back toward me.

The current is horrible.

Win's hands slip on the rope and he lets go with one hand. His body starts to float downstream, with him just hanging on with one hand. Willie manages to grab his flailing arm and pull it back so that Win can get a grip on the rope. He just manages to get his footing, and I can see them both stop to pant for several seconds.

I can feel shadows narrowing my vision.

The sound of the river is dimming, too.

If I can hang on just a little longer....

Blackness begins to engulf me.

I feel Willie's strong arms start to wrap around me and I know no more.

* * *

When I come to, I'm wrapped in blankets on the grass. They tell me Paul's in an ambulance on his way to the hospital, and a second one is coming for me. Cora is shaking and crying. Dave and Willie are almost as bad. *I can't believe I'm alive.*

I know it was close. Thoughts flash disjointedly through my head. I'm elated that Willie and Dave are alive. I hardly know Win and he risked his life for me. God, if anything had happened to Dave with the baby coming....

I owe them all everything there is in the world. I try to tell them this, but my mouth won't work. I hear the sound of the ambulance coming down the road with the siren on and I hear Grover chime in.

* * *

It's after midnight. Dave left to check on Linda. I'm doing better, but I guess it was touch and go. I didn't know that sometimes hypothermia goes too far and your body can't restart. I thought you give people hot chocolate and they're fine. I'm starting to make sense, too. I guess I've been muttering strange things about baseball. *Go figure. I don't even like baseball.*

They just moved me out of ICU in the Browning Medical clinic on the reservation. Paul is here somewhere. I'm in a private room with IVs and monitors, but at least I've stopped shivering. I'm exhausted from shivering. All my muscles are sore. They keep replacing my blankets with warm ones and constantly give me warm liquids to sip.

Cora's holding my hand and smiling weakly at me. Susan is sitting on Willie's lap on an aqua vinyl recliner. I look at Willie and mumble, "How'd you get through this so easy?"

"I wasn't in the water for as long as you were and I was hauling big lugs around. I admit, though, I don't want to do that again for awhile."

"I sort of blacked out there," I say.

"We were incredibly lucky," Willie says. "I reached you just as you lost consciousness. If you had let go of that rock and been swept downriver...."

"As it was," he continued, "Win and I barely got you to shore. We laid you out next to Paul in the sun and wrapped you both in blankets and sleeping bags. Les had already called 911. All we could do was wait. Dave said the first ambulance made it in six minutes. I guess they were flying when they brought you and Paul here. Like I said, you were both in bad shape and they didn't think the East Glacier clinic was up to it. This place is pretty small, too, but it's a district trauma center. They're set up to handle a wide range of emergencies from the park."

"How's Paul doing?" I asked.

"They aren't sure yet. He's got a pretty big head gash and lost a lot of blood, plus he's got a broken shoulder and multiple rib fractures, with a sliver of bone perforating one lung. They've done one surgery already. His body temperature was down to 83 degrees, about the point that heart fibrillation starts. They're well into internal warming with warm IVs and a forced warm-air pump. They're watching for any head swelling. If he doesn't look like he'll come around soon, they'll airlift him to Great Falls."

As Willie says that, we hear the sound of a chopper landing at the helipad in the grassy field outside of ICU. We look soberly at each other.

"He'll be okay, Sam," Cora says. "You'll get another chance," and she squeezes my hand.

I want my brother back.

"Do you know why I wouldn't try for Paul, Sam?" Willie asks.

"Because you thought it was a lost cause?"

"It's not as simple as that. You're right though. I didn't think it was possible to save him. I thought he was as good as dead."

"Why, then?"

"I knew, if I dove in, that I probably wouldn't be able to get myself out of that river. You or Win or Dave would have likely tried to get Paul, or me, and been killed—died with me. I couldn't let that happen. I would have tried to stop you, too, but that seemed immoral. It was your choice. I also figured that I might be able to save you, with Win's help. It seemed the best shot."

I know all that Willie is saying is true. "Dave and Win? They're okay?"

"They're fine. Dave's with Linda, still waiting, and Win's already back on fire duty in Browning."

My gratitude overwhelms me.

"Cora said he threw the gun away," Willie says, "that he decided not to kill anyone."

"I think he needed a reason to go on living."

* * *

I'm being loaded into the Toyota from a wheelchair the next morning. I'm feeling like a complete clown, but it's hospital policy. Cora's laughing at me and I join in. At least I got rid of that god-awful hospital gown with fresh air ventilating my rear.

The latest word on Paul is that he had some internal bleeding in addition to everything else. He had to have a second emergency surgery last evening, but is holding his own. He's still unconscious. The next 24 hours are critical.

Willie and Susan are trailing us in the truck and we're heading to a motel, close to the hospital in Great Falls, to wait for news about

Paul. I'm still so exhausted that I can barely sit up, and I've had my head on Cora's shoulder the whole trip down.

When we arrive, I'm helped out of the vehicle and settled into a bed. It hasn't been 24 hours since the river episode, but it feels like a lot longer. I'm dazed, but filled with anxiety about Paul.

Then I realize—I've been worried about Cora for so long I've forgotten what it's like not to worry about her. At least that's nice.

"All I can think about is going to see how Paul's doing."

"I know," Cora says. "First thing tomorrow, unless we hear a reason to hurry, okay? We're calling every hour."

"Makes sense," I murmur. "I'm not sure I can move, anyway." And I drift off to sleep.

When I wake up, Cora's sitting next to me on the bed and stroking my face. "I almost lost you," she says.

"Let's not do anything else dangerous for a few years," I say. "Willie, Dave and Win were really something, weren't they?"

"You were all heroes."

"I don't remember making any decision at all. I didn't want my brother to die."

"Don't kid yourself," she says. "Most people would have watched from the riverbank."

* * *

Cora and I walk into the ICU at Great Falls General Hospital early the next morning. Paul looks terrible. His head is wrapped up in a giant bandage about the size of a bowling ball. His eyes are black and most of his face is bluish gray and swollen. His left arm is in a splint and I have never seen so many tubes going in and out of a person in my life.

We've talked to one of Paul's doctors who thinks he's going to be all right, given some time. They're still watching his head to make sure intracranial bleeding doesn't resume. He's due for another MRI later this morning. His left shoulder fracture will be pinned in a couple of days when his overall condition has improved. The ribs are now in good position to heal on their own. He had a small bleed in his spleen. They didn't have to remove it, but they had to go in and repair it; that was the second emergency surgery.

He'll be in the hospital for about a week, then should be able to go home with some help. He's young, though, the doctor says. We will be amazed at how much better he'll be in a couple of weeks.

They are keeping Paul somewhat sedated to allow better healing and to keep him more comfortable. He's alert enough to acknowledge us when we come in. We walk up to the bed.

"Hello, Paul," I say. "You've got to start taking better care of your head."

He gives me a weak half-smile.

"Paul," says Cora. "The doctor says you're going to be fine."

He mumbles something and we have to lean down really close to hear. Finally I understand. "I'm sorry," he whispers.

Cora picks up his good hand, sits down and holds it.

"Paul," I say. "I'm sorry, too. There's plenty of blame to go around. I want to get to know my brother again."

He manages to open his eyes a bit more and nods a bit. Then he lets his eyes shut and goes back to sleep.

We stay for several hours, Paul asleep the entire time. They finally come with a stretcher to take Paul for his MRI, so Cora and I leave. We plan to stay in the city overnight and go back to the hospital in the morning.

We're ambling around the old section of Great Falls. We find a place to have lunch at a small restaurant with outdoor tables near the town center. "He looks terrible, but I'm feeling optimistic," I say to Cora.

"His head seems to be working," Cora says, "That's the main thing."

"What should we do when he gets out of the hospital?" I ask Cora.

"I'm fairly convinced he doesn't want to shoot anyone anymore," she says.

"Let's see how it goes. He can't be mentally stable. I don't want to put him under any pressure, having us together."

"You're right, of course."

"Cora. I thought we were all going to die. First you and I from the gun, and then Paul and I in the river."

"It was so close. I'm trying not to think how close it was. I keep seeing you holding onto that rock. The water was so wild. I thought you were going to be washed away every second. All I did was scream and scream."

"I never understood how it could go so wrong. One minute your life is in your control, and the next it can spin away. I kept saying over and over to myself, 'If you let go you're dead. If you let go you're dead.'"

Cora slips her hand in mine and we sit there in the warm sun. I don't think I'll ever take being warm for granted.

CHAPTER 29: PAUL

THEY'RE BEGINNING TO THAW ME OUT so I can think. I've been told my head scan looks much better. I keep fighting the desire to go back to that unconscious place, the place without guilt or worry. I almost did it again. I almost killed Sam, and even worse, part of me wanted to.

They have me hooked up to a machine that gives me pain meds on demand, but I found out that they have safety limits. Damn. I keep pushing the button, anyway.

I look up. Sam and Cora are walking through the door. I moan internally. I'm ashamed to the depths of my soul. I don't want to look at either one of them, but there's something in Sam's eyes that makes me believe he wants to see me, maybe even accepts me. I don't know what to do with that thought. It's so—different.

"Morning, Paul," he says. "If it's possible, you look worse than yesterday. Please don't ask me for a mirror."

"They showed me," I mumble.

"You look like you were run over by a herd of rhinos."

"That's what I feel like," I say. My speech is slow and slurred.

"How does your head feel?"

"Like they shrunk my skull—and fit my brains back in with a shoe horn."

"Poetic," he says. "I think you're going to live."

"I want to live," I say. "That surprises me."

"I'm going to get some coffee," Cora says, giving me a smile.

We watch her leave and sit there in silence for a while.

"I thought you were going to kill us," Sam says, finally.

"I – I'm messed up. I gave up. Giving up hope – it's the worst...."

"I wanted to talk to you, but I didn't know how to contact you. I—I've changed."

I look at Sam's face. *I think he means it.*

"Have you stopped—wanting me dead?" I can't look at him, asking such a horrible question.

"We lost everything. I blamed you for so long. I've thought about it so much in these past few weeks. I've finally realized what a fucking bloody asshole I've been. I'm the one who needs forgiveness. I wasn't just saying that at the river. I meant it. I'm so sorry."

"You really mean it?"

"You gave everything to me when I was little and we'd lost our father. I've buried that for so long. I'd given up—on both of us."

"It's enough, Sam – it's enough that you don't hate me."

"There's more. I want my brother back. I want to be your brother again."

A shattering sound comes from inside me. It's the sound of hope being created. *Sam seems to understand.* We sit in silence trying to come to terms with it all. It's not as if things are all better. I know there's still a lot of anguish and mistrust under the surface, but I feel like the heavy burden I've carried for so long is lightening.

He sighs, "How do you feel about me—and Cora?"

I pause to think. There are undetonated minefields all over that question. "I hurt her—in many ways. She was the first person I let inside—all those years. She was my lifeline. That's over, now and forever. But it will take some time...."

"I desperately wish she wasn't between us," Sam says earnestly. "We're going to have enough trouble trying to learn to trust each other."

"I won't lie, it's painful. I was a mess. I was not the man for her. I'm starting to see that."

Sam's eyes study mine.

"But it was losing you, again, Sam. I couldn't stand it. After Dad died—then Mom. You were my whole world—and I lost you. I couldn't fight any longer."

"Did you...." Sam paused, considering his question. "Did you fall in the water?"

I look at him for a long time, "I'm not sure."

He comes over and sits on the side of my bed. "Listen to me. This wouldn't have happened if Dad hadn't been killed. I was too little to get a grip on it. You were older and so smart. You seemed so together that nobody worried or paid much attention to you. You looked for vengeance and never got help. I couldn't help the way I reacted and you couldn't help what you did. We were just kids."

I sigh deeply. "It would have helped to talk it out."

"You might have tried to talk to Cora."

"I couldn't risk it. I was afraid I'd be alone again. She was all I had."

We sit in silence for many minutes.

Finally Sam says, "I isolated myself for years, too, Paul. I kept hiding. It was easier to blame you. That way all my failures were your fault. I never grew up."

"How in the hell do I forgive myself?" I bring up my good hand and cover my eyes, "For Mom—and what I did to you?"

"I've done nothing but think about this the past 24 hours," he says, "and this is what I've come up with." He takes a deep breath. "You remember the story about Teddy Kennedy running his car off that bridge in Massachusetts? He was responsible for the death of the girl in the car. Well, I figure he had three choices. One, he could go out and kill himself. Two, he could drown himself in drink and wallow in self-pity the rest of his life. Or, three, he could try his best to redeem himself, to do something worthwhile with his life. Well, the way I figure, it took him a while, but he finally took the third choice."

I nod.

"I believe, now, that everyone should have another chance. Most people never destroy lives and have to endlessly struggle with the guilt. Those people, who keep trying, are heroic in my mind. Maybe we can be heroes, too."

I turn to look at him and I see Cora standing in the doorway listening.

I reach out with my shaky right hand and he takes it and steadies it. It's been 11 years since we've touched as brothers. It feels good.

CHAPTER 30: SAM

IT'S THE FOLLOWING TUESDAY. I'm back in Great Falls, picking up Paul at the hospital.

We're not completely at ease with each other, but after some convincing he's agreed to come to the cabin tonight and then stay at Vinnie's for a few days. It will reduce the pressure of him seeing Cora and I together.

We both want some time to reconnect. At least I do. Paul needs to be waited on. He's been ordered to rest a lot and not jiggle everything that's been put together. He looks amazingly better, as the doctor had said. Most of the swelling is gone, and his skin has a lot of yellowing faded bruises. He's down to one long bandage that covers the head stitches, his arm is in a sling, plus he's walking gingerly.

Not much of his baggage to worry about. You don't pack much when you're planning suicide or murder.

It's a good two and a half hour drive to the cabin, but the scenery is dramatic. Cora is readying the guest room. She wanted to give us time to talk.

It rained yesterday for the first time in a long time, but the clouds are blowing away in increasing wind. The mountains off to the left have that clean brightness they get after a rain. I glance at Paul as I pull out on the main highway. He looks contented. "You look better," I say.

"I am better," he replies. "I don't trust it, but I am better. Never in my wildest dreams did I think I'd be sitting here with you, having a simple conversation, spending time with you."

"It's almost impossible to get my head around, too," I say. "A few days ago, I didn't think I'd still be alive, let alone getting inside your head. It's hard to explain, but you're fascinating. I want to know everything about you, how you think, what you're feeling."

"I'm having the same thoughts," Paul says. "Tell me one thing. Why do you think you held onto your hate for so long?"

I shake my head, "I'm not sure. Maybe, if I kept you dangling with guilt, I wouldn't lose you, too. If I let you off the hook, after being such an ass, maybe you'd never want to see me again. I think I needed to know that you were out there, trying to keep connected, even if only because you knew how angry I was. Does that make any sense at all?"

"Not completely, but yes, I do see where you're going. It's farther than I've been able to progress in my understanding. Sam, I promise to get counseling, for both our sakes."

"And one more thing," I say. "You've always had trouble letting things go. Well, look at me. It took 10 years for me to forgive you. We're just two sides of the same coin."

"Sam. I need to know. Who are these guys, Willie and Win and Dave? How could they do what they did? They could have died, too."

I look at Paul. "Yes, you're right. I'm proud to know them all. I try to be worthy of their friendship. Win and Willie grew up together as brothers." I look at Paul, "Maybe closer than brothers. Family and loyalty is central to their world. I've been taken into Willie's family. It's humbling. And Dave is sort of an older brother or uncle, a policeman who loves helping other people. I believe they risked their lives, not completely for you, but because they couldn't bear to see me suffer if I lost you."

"Would you have suffered?"

"Honestly? I would have been grief-stricken, but I only now am beginning to understand that. I think I would have been inconsolable and, somehow, they realized it before I did."

We drive in silence thinking about that.

"Before East Glacier, my life was a wasteland. You at least put a career together."

Paul laughs bitterly, "It looked like that to you, did it? I was doing the same thing you were doing—surviving. And then Cora came into my life."

He stops and looks at me. "I knew I was so fragile. I knew I probably wasn't going to be able to hold myself together and be normal for her, but she was so tempting. She was in my Chemistry 101 course, sitting right up front, and after her final was over I asked her out."

I give him a look, a question.

Paul smiles. "Don't worry. She's safe with me." He sees I still have a questioning look. "You mean, am I still in love with her?" I nod. He sighs. "Probably, but I'm under control."

"Is it going to be very hard with us together?"

"God, Sam. How'd you get to be such a great communicator?"

"I don't know. I've been so careful about what I say and burying what I feel for so long, I've just gone nuts in the other direction. It's like I don't have time for deception anymore. And Cora and I talked about it."

"I don't know how I'm going to feel with her. That's why I agreed so easily to stay at Mrs. Long's. I think I can be honest, though. If the pain being around her is too great, well, let's see how it goes. It's you, Sam, I want to get to know. This is an incredible opportunity—I can't let that slip by me."

We're quiet for a few miles, then Paul adds, "Cora was the first step toward this, but I don't think I was really in love with her. I just needed her so desperately. I knew it wasn't healthy, and I owe her for taking me on. I can't go back to hiding, even though it's so painful. A door has been opened. I'm getting sort of used to feeling and I'm surprised—it hasn't killed me."

After a few seconds, I add, "It was close, though." We look at each other and grimace.

"What was it that made it possible for you to start to forgive me?" Paul asks quietly. "When did it start?"

I start thinking back to something I had buried so deeply that I'd forgotten. "I know when it started. I was out in the desert, with Cora, at the hideout near Reno. She had escaped and I knew she was frantic to get away from me. She'd overheard that conversation on the phone when I was threatening to kill her. It was hot, killing hot, and she had no water. I had been looking for her for hours in the heat and had even decided to call 911 to save her. I couldn't let her die. The entire area was so isolated and desolate. I was afraid that I couldn't find her, that no one might be able to find her. It came to me, if she had died, it would have been entirely my fault; even though I had never intended that and never considered that possibility."

Paul flinches, then nods, "But those phone calls...."

"I was never going to hurt her. I wanted to torture you." Paul doesn't respond and I glance at him.

His fists are balled, teeth clenched, forehead furrowed.

"Paul?"

"Do you know—how that hurt me? I—I hated—I still...."

I pull off on the side of the road. I recognize that I'm frightened. Paul's voice is hostile.

"Paul, you should hate me for that. It was despicable, cruel."

I see him trying to control himself, taking deep breath after deep breath. His hands finally begin relaxing.

"You're still two people, Sam. One, my brother whom I love, and the other...."

"I'll try so hard, Paul, so you can forget the other one."

Finally, I see him blink his eyes. It's still several minutes before he can speak, "All I ever wanted in this life was to protect those I loved, and she was hurt because of me."

"And me."

"Yes."

We sit quietly for many minutes, thinking. Paul sighs many times as he releases the tension.

"This is going to take some time, Sam. A minute ago I wanted...."

"I know," I say. "That's my big fear. If you start understanding what a bastard I've been, maybe you'll start hating me all over again. Understanding that you weren't the only one at fault should have helped you."

"Instead hatred drove me over the edge."

"But at least we can talk about it. It should help. Don't you think?"

He nods slowly.

"One more thing, Paul. I did take Cora, eventually. I caused you terrible pain and desperation. I know you hated me. Now I need to know...?"

He's quiet for a long time. "I did hate you, Sam. It was the worst thing I've experienced in my life. I visualized killing you. You know my problem. It's hard for me to let those kinds of thoughts go. When I was at my worst, I'd think of your face, of you dying in front of me. It was like my brain exploding. I could not exist as a functioning person with that conflict of hate and love. I had to end it. It was beyond thought. That's why I had to get to you, to end my war, at the river."

We sit again in silence for some time.

"Sam. Since we're baring our souls here. What exactly were you thinking when you dropped to your knees?"

"I'd said everything I could think of. Remember when you were trying to talk me out of hurting Cora, during the kidnapping, you said I would be killing myself. I had by then realized how much at fault I was. I knew that if you killed me, your life would be over, one way or another. I thought the only chance for us both would be for you to decide not to kill me. I dropped to my knees because I believed it would have taken the most lost soul to execute his brother in cold blood."

"Sometimes, Sam, rage still overwhelms me."

Paul covers his face with his one good hand. I slide over beside him and put my arm around his shoulders. His shoulders are shaking. We sit like that for some time, until the shaking stops.

"I can breathe out here," he says, finally.

I know exactly what he means.

"I've never been able to talk about it, to anyone. If I can say to you that I wanted to hurt you then, maybe, I can start to let it go."

We sit in silence trying to absorb it all.

I put my hand on his arm and he winces. "Listen to me, Paul. I realized in the desert, on a gut level, that it was the same thing that happened to you. You were caught up with hate and vengeance and put someone's life at risk. It went terribly wrong for you. I was luckier. I stumbled on Cora at the last minute and was able to avoid a tragedy. We're the same," I say. "Exactly the same. If anyone understands all this, it's me. Let's just try to forgive each other."

Paul looks at me for what seems forever then gives a deep sigh. "Oh, why the hell not?" he says.

* * *

It's a nice thing, I'm discovering, to drive along a scenic country road in silence with a brother you want to be with, who mostly doesn't want to kill you anymore. After a while I ask, "What kind of music do you like?"

Paul gives me a look like I asked him if he likes ancient Mesopotamian coins. "I don't like any music," he says.

"Well, that's about to change. I play the guitar, and rather well, too."

"You're kidding."

"You're about to become educated in folk-rock and blues mixtures," I say, and put on a CD of Bobby Long's new album, just out. We roll the windows down and drive on toward the Rockies, letting our hair blow wild in the wind.

THE END

ABOUT THE AUTHOR

Nancy Leonard retired from a 35-year career as a Physical Therapist in 2007. She discovered the joy of writing fiction and an underlying compulsive nature. Five years and eight series manuscripts completed, it seemed appropriate to start the publishing process. In addition to Headwaters, seven additional full-length novels are being readied in various stages of professional editing. Recent other passions include playing acoustic guitar and taking flying lessons. The interest in flying was sparked by book research to better understand a pilot character. Nancy and her husband Peter have adult children and live in Port Townsend, Washington.

MORE GREAT READS FROM BOOKTROPE

Awake by **Melanie Surani** (Thriller) Five strangers wake to find themselves trapped in an abandoned art museum. They set out to free themselves – only to find that the illusion of death is sometimes worse than real thing.

Phobia by **Daniel Lance Wright** (Thriller) Heights, crowds, small spaces... How does a psychologist handle three phobia sufferers on a cruise ship in the Gulf of Mexico when the ship is overtaken by Lebanese terrorists?

Rachel's Folly by **Monica Bruno** (Thriller) Told from three unique perspectives, RACHEL'S FOLLY is a thrilling exploration of profound loss, morality, and the lengths to which we will go to keep our darkest secrets.

The Anonymous Source by **A.C. Fuller** (Thriller) One year after the 9/11 attacks, reporter Alex Vane uncovers the scoop of a lifetime. But after his editor buries the story and a source turns up dead, he finds himself caught in a violent conspiracy. Aided by a captivating professor, Alex discovers a $500-million secret that could get him killed.

The Key to Everything by **Alex Kimmell** (Thriller) When Auden discovers a curious leather-bound book, its contents will soon endanger his entire family. The pages of this book draw him into a prison that cannot be breached, a place that can only be unlocked with a very special key.

Women in Red by **Jordan Rosenfeld** (Thriller) *Women in Red* leads you by the hand and draws you into the dance; before you can protest, you're center stage.

Zed by **Jason McIntyre** (Thriller) It's the end of the summer, 1975, and nineteen-year-old Tom Mason can't wait to leave his summer job in the tiny island town of Dovetail Cove. Especially since it's conspiring to kill him.

Would you like to read more books like these?
Subscribe to **runawaygoodness.com**, get a free ebook for signing up, and never pay full price for an ebook again.

Made in the USA
Charleston, SC
23 May 2016